"What do you want?" Turcotte asked.

Aspasia's Shadow pointed down. "The mothership. With it I can leave this planet, this entire area of the universe."

"No."

Aspasia's Shadow put the Grail on the floor. "You can have that. And these." He put the stones on the cloth covering it.

"No."

"And you can keep the key and the Master Guardian. We can off-load them anywhere you would like."

"No."

"Give me the mothership. I am telling you I will leave. You'll never be bothered by me again."

"And you'll activate the interstellar drive and attract the Swarm here," Turcotte said. He felt as if he'd come full circle. He'd stopped the flight of the other mothership from Area 51 to prevent this very thing.

"Ah, the Swarm," Aspasia's Shadow said. "But you know, of course, since you seem to know everything, that it is already here."

"I know," Turcotte replied. "Why did the Swarm take Lisa Duncan?"

"To try to learn the secret of her immortality and—" Aspasia's Shadow paused.

"And?"

"Where she came from and why she came here."

Turcotte felt the hair on the back of his neck stand up. "Where?"

"What planet she came from."

Turcotte heard Yakov's sharp intake of breath.

"You really are so ignorant," Aspasia's Shadow said.

ALSO FROM ROBERT DOHERTY

The Rock
Area 51
Area 51: The Reply
Area 51: The Mission
Area 51: The Sphinx
Area 51: The Grail
Area 51: Excalibur

Psychic Warrior
Psychic Warrior: Project Aura

AVAILABLE FROM DELL

ROBERT DOHERTY

AREA 51
THE TRUTH

A DELL BOOK

Published by
Dell Publishing
a division of
Random House, Inc.
New York, New York

ISBN 0-440-23706-8

Manufactured in the United States of America

Published simultaneously in Canada

January 2003

10 9 8 7 6 5 4 3 2 1
OPM

To my father, George E. Mayer.
Thank you for everything.

AREA 51: THE TRUTH

> "Stonehenge stands as lonely in history
> as it does on the great plain."
> HENRY JAMES

STONEHENGE
A.D. *528*

The gentle breeze blowing across the Salisbury Plain carried the thick smoke produced by wood and burning flesh over the megalithic stones. It also brought the screams of the condemned and the chants of the druid priests. The sun had set two hours ago, but the stones were lit in the glow of the burning wicker man. Over fifteen meters high, the skeleton of the effigy was made of two thick logs serving as main supports up through the legs, reaching to the shoulders, from which crossbeams had been fixed with iron spikes. The skin consisted of wicker laced through the outer wooden frame.

Inside the "skin," in a jumble of torsos, limbs, and heads, were people. Crammed in so tightly that each could hardly move. Some were upright, others sideways, and others upside down, filling every square meter of the interior.

Around the wicker man's feet were bundles of straw that had just been set on fire, the flames licking up the legs, burning those who filled out the calves and thighs. Their screams of pain mixed with the pleading of those above them, all of which fell on deaf ears as the priests and priestesses who surrounded the wicker man concentrated on their chanting and dancing.

There were four distinct groups surrounding the wicker man, each one oriented on a cardinal direction. To the north they wore yellow robes, signifying air. To the west, blue for water. To the east, green for earth. And to the south, between the wicker man and the mighty stones, they wore red, signifying fire. With the great King Arthur and his foe Mordred newly dead, there was chaos in the land and the druids had come out of their hiding places to resume their ancient rites.

All those inside the wicker man had received a sentence of death over the course of the past year. Criminals and nonbelievers, and those who had served the king in the local area in suppressing the old religions and collecting taxes. The sentence was being carried out this evening through the purifying flame.

The burning of the condemned was just the beginning of the night's activities. After the flames died down, the druids would move to the south, to the standing stones. While the druids now claimed the stones as their holy place, no one gathered around the wicker man really knew who had placed the inner circles of megaliths or why.

There were legends of course. Of Gods who had ruled a land in the middle of the ocean, a place called Atlantis. Of war among Gods, and how their battles soon became man's. Of priests who came to England from over the sea. Some spoke of sorcerers and magicians moving the massive stones with the power of their minds. Merlin, the counselor of the king, was said to have had something to do with the stones when he was young, hundreds of years earlier. There were even whispers of those who were not human and the undead walking the Earth, but such talk was mixed with tales of pixies and fairies and other strange creatures. There was even a tale that the centermost massive stones had been brought up out of the Earth, sprouting like plants at the command of the Gods.

The screams grew louder as the flames rose higher on the wicker man, their volume matched each time by the druids. Away from the brutal scene, in the darkness, a slight female figure, wrapped in a black cloak with a silver fringe, led a horse pulling a litter on which another, larger cloaked figure was lashed. She stumbled and almost fell, only the support of the horse's bridle keeping her upright. Her cloak was dirty and tattered, her step weary, yet there was no doubt of her determination as she regained her step and pressed forward into the megalithic arrangement, passing the outer ring of stones.

The fiery light of the wicker man fell on the man on the litter. His robe was also worn and bloodstained though he wore armor beneath the cloth. The metal was battered and pierced. His face was lined with age, his hair white. His lifeless eyes were staring straight up at the stars above.

The complex they passed through had been built in stages. In the center where they were headed were five pairs of stones arranged in a horseshoe. Each pair consisted of two large upright stones with a lintel stone laid horizontally on top. A slab of micaceous sandstone was placed at the midpoint of the entire complex, to act as a focal point for worship and an altar for the various local religions that had flourished briefly before being swept under by the weight of the years. Later builders had constructed a second smaller ring around this, using spotted dolemites. And even later, a third encircling ring thirty meters in diameter was built of sandstone blocks called sarsen stones.

There had even been a fourth circle of wooden stakes surrounding the entire complex. Stonehenge had reached its peak around 1100 B.C., with all stones in the three circles in place along with the wooden fourth. Shortly thereafter came the

Romans, who desecrated the site, rightly believing that it was a focal point for local shamans whose power they sought to destroy, much as Arthur had tried over fifteen hundred years later. The Romans tore down some of the lintel stones and even managed to tip over a few of the upright ones. They burned the wooden outer circle, much as the druids now burned those whom they had condemned. The original centerpieces, however, had resisted all efforts at damage over the centuries.

The woman led the horse and litter up to the oldest set of stones. Two upright covered by a lintel stone. She threw back her hood, revealing lined skin and gray hair shot through with remaining black. With arthritic hands she untied the litter from the horse.

"*We waited too long, my love, and we became too noticeable,*" she whispered to her partner in a language no one else on the face of the planet would have understood. It had not yet really sunk in to her that he could not hear her and never would hear her again.

She noted the direction of his dead gaze and she too peered upward for a moment searching among the stars. She pointed. "*There, my dear Gwalcmai.*" He had been known as Gawain at Arthur's court and had fought at the battle of Camlann, where both leaders mortally wounded each other. It was there he had received the wounds that had drained the life from his body as she'd traveled hard to bring him here.

However, it was not the wounds to his body, or even his death, that frightened her. It was the damage to an artifact he wore on a chain around his neck, underneath the armor. It was shaped in the form of two hands and arms spread upward in worship with no body.

A mighty blow from Excalibur, wielded by Arthur just prior to his final confrontation with Mordred, had smashed through the armor and severed the artifact in half. A tremor passed through her body at the sight, and tears she had held in for the week of travel burst forth. An earthquake of fear and sorrow threatened to overwhelm her. She could hear the chanting and see the flickering fire to the north and knew she did not have time to wallow in her pain before the druids came here to worship what they could not comprehend.

She ran her hands lightly over the surface of the left upright stone, searching. After a moment, she found what she was looking for and pressed her right hand against the spot she had located.

For a moment it seemed as if even the chanting of the druids and the screams of the dying halted. All was still. Then the outline of a door appeared in the stone. It slid open. She unhooked the litter from the horse and grabbed the two poles. With effort beyond the capability of her aged body, she pulled it into the darkness beyond. Freed of its burden and smelling the foul air, the horse bolted away into the darkness. The door immediately shut behind them, the outline disappeared and all was as it had been.

A week later Stonehenge was abandoned. Where the wicker man had been, there was only cold ash with a smattering of blackened bone. The druids had gone back to the hills, hiding from the brigands who now roamed the land and eking out a living from the countryside. So it had been for centuries, so it continued. The stones had seen many invaders, many worshippers. And they would see more in the future.

The sky was gray and a light rain was falling, blown about by a stiff breeze. In the middle of the megalithic arrangement, the outline of the doorway reappeared on the left standing stone of the center pair. It slid open and one person appeared garbed in black robes. Noting the rain, the figure pulled back her hood. She resembled the old woman who had first entered, but fifty years younger. Instead of age-withered flesh, her face was smooth and pink. Her hair was coal-black. She turned her face upward, allowing the rain to fall on it. The falling water mixed with the rivulet of tears on her face.

She had tried and failed as she had feared. Gwalcmai was truly dead. After all the years they had been together. She reached back into the stone and pulled the litter out with the old body tied to it.

Reluctantly she stepped out of the entryway, pulling the litter, and the door closed behind her, then disappeared. She slowly walked through the stones, onto the plain, pulling his body. She passed the site of the wicker man, sparing it not even a glance, and continued. When she reached a small ridge, just before she was out of sight of Stonehenge, she turned and looked back.

It was dusk and the rain had ceased. She could see the stones in the distance. She felt very, very alone, a slight figure in the midst of a huge plain. She went to a lone oak tree, its branches withered and worn. It was a living sentinel overlooking the stones. Using a wooden spade, the woman dug into the dirt, carving out a grave. It took her the entire night to get deep enough.

As the first rays of the sun tentatively probed above the eastern horizon, she climbed out of the hole. Her robe was dirty, her dark hair matted with mud, the fresh skin on her palms blistered from the labor.

She took her husband and slid him into the hole she had made. Her hand rested on his cheek for many long minutes before she reluctantly climbed out of the grave. She reached inside her pocket and pulled out the small broken amulet. She stared at it for a while, then reached inside her robe and retrieved a chain holding a similar object, this one undamaged. She added the damaged one to the chain around her neck and held it for a moment, tracing the lines. Then she looked down at her husband and spoke in their native tongue.

"Ten thousand years. I loved you every day of those many years. And I will remember and love you for the next ten thousand."

With tears streaming down her face, she threw the first spadeful of dirt into the grave.

PROLOGUE: FROM THE PAST TO THE PRESENT

EARTH

Area 51 is ninety miles northwest of Las Vegas, in the middle of nowhere, on the way to nowhere, established on land that held no value other than its isolation and what had been hidden there years ago. Numerous mountains surrounded the dry lake bed; land the US government had gobbled up to make the location secure.

During World War II, in a cavern inside Groom Mountain, a massive alien spaceship had been discovered; the mothership. Not only had the mothership been discovered there, but also directions to the location of nine smaller atmospheric craft, nicknamed bouncers by the test pilots who subsequently learned to fly them. Test flights of bouncers over the years after World War II had led to reports of alien sightings and fueled speculation among the general public about what was hidden at the base in the Nevada desert. The speculation was mostly right, but grossly underestimated the reality.

From the very beginning, the existence of Area 51 had been classified at a higher level than anything had ever been in the United States: A committee—Majestic-12—had been immediately established to oversee the alien artifacts and granted powers by a presidential decree that allowed it to do as it pleased. For over fifty years Majestic kept the discovery secret from foreign nations and American citizens alike as it tried to find out who had put the ship there and why.

Unfortunately, Majestic hadn't been able to discover the

truth about the mothership or the aliens: that Earth had been visited by aliens over ten thousand years ago who had head-quartered themselves on a large island in the middle of the Atlantic Ocean—the legendary Atlantis. And that when other aliens of the same species, the Airlia, had arrived thousands of years later, there was civil war among them.

The initial group of aliens had been led by Aspasia; the second wave by Artad. The battling resulted in the destruction of Atlantis and a tenuous truce. Aspasia was banished to an Airlia base underneath the surface of Mars at Cydonia where human astronomers had long been intrigued by anomalies on the surface. The two primary sites were nicknamed the Face and the Fort based on the observed shapes. Artad and his followers went to China, underneath the massive tomb of Qian-Ling, and like Aspasia and his people, went into suspended animation.

Why the aliens had fought among themselves remained a mystery. During the Third World War, both sides had issued proclamations to the United Nations. Each claimed it had been sent to Earth to protect mankind from an interstellar threat by another alien race called the Swarm. And each claimed that the other side had tried to withdraw from this task and hide on Earth, ruling mankind as Gods.

Despite the Atlantis Truce, each side had continued a subversive war throughout the millennia on Earth. Aspasia's side was represented by the Mission, led by a continually regenerated human known as Aspasia's Shadow, who passed Aspasia's memories and personality through succeeding generations via the *ka*, a memory device that could be updated much like a computer hard drive. Artad's side was represented by the Ones Who Wait, Airlia-Human clones, and Shadows of Artad, such as King Arthur and ShiHuangdi, the first emperor of China.

Throughout human history both groups fought covertly,

using humans as pawns in their battles. The tenuous truce began to unravel when a guardian computer was discovered at a dig at Temiltepec in South America by Majestic-12 and brought back to Area 51's secret sister base at Dulce, New Mexico. The guardians were small golden pyramids that had been secreted around the world by the Airlia. When a guardian came in contact with a human it initiated a direct mind-computer interface through which the guardian would take control and turn the person into a Guide, who would do as the computer programmed him or her to. The members of Majestic were corrupted in this manner, prompting Presidential Science Adviser Lisa Duncan to send a covert operative named Mike Turcotte to infiltrate Area 51 and discover what was going on.

Turcotte had learned that Majestic was preparing to fly the mothership on programmed orders from the guardian, most likely to go to Mars and pick up Aspasia and his followers. He also found information on Easter Island that indicated that initiating the mothership's interstellar engine would attract the attention of the Swarm and bring destruction to Earth. Turcotte foiled that plan and all-out civil war had once more erupted between the two Airlia sides, the human race caught between them, resulting in the Earth's Third World War.

Prior to the war, Turcotte and the others had discovered much, but they still didn't know the full extent of this alien interference in human history. What they did know were just terrifying glimpses into a perverted but true history of mankind. They'd learned about the clash between Arthur (Artad's Shadow) and Mordred (Aspasia's Shadow) in early England; the development and spread of the Black Death in the Middle Ages by Artad's followers; the rise of the SS in Nazi Germany, which was manipulated by Aspasia's Shadow; the invention of the atomic bomb by the Americans prompted by their study of a similar Airlia weapon discovered underneath the Great Pyramid of Giza in the early days of World War II; and many other events throughout history. All of these were the result of efforts by one side or the other to gain the upper hand in the Airlia civil war.

Turcotte and the others had also learned that some of the human survivors of Atlantis had formed a group to monitor the aliens. Known as Watchers, they were former priests who had once worshipped the Airlia as gods, and subsequently tried to monitor their conflict over the millennia.

Turcotte had killed Aspasia and destroyed his fleet coming from Mars, but Aspasia's Shadow had secreted himself on Easter Island with the Grail in his possession and a burgeoning military force. Aspasia's Shadow had used a nanovirus and nanotechnology to capture most of the American fleet in the Pacific, invade Hawaii and threaten the West Coast of the United States. And in China, Artad had been awoken by the Ones Who Wait. He had allied with the Chinese government and supported them in their invasions of both Taiwan and South Korea.

Both sides' efforts had fallen apart when the Area 51 team Turcotte led gained control of the Master Guardian computer and its key, Excalibur, and shut down the alien computers. Artad and Aspasia's Shadow abandoned their offensives on Earth.

The Third World War had been brief, but what it lacked in length it made up for in savagery and devastation.

Seoul, South Korea, was a ghost town, having been struck by both Chinese nerve agents and American nuclear weapons. The best estimate was at least three million dead and four times that displaced.

Half of Taiwan had been scorched by a nuclear blast in a desperate attempt to stop the invading mainland forces supported by Artad. Scattered fighting was still raging as

Taiwanese troops sought out and destroyed remnants of the invading forces. At least two million had died in fighting on that island.

Muslims in western China were rising in revolt, seeing their opportunity as Beijing's backing of the alien Artad had backfired. That battle was still raging.

In the Pacific, the US Navy's Task Force Eighty, centered on the super-carrier *Kennedy*, was linking up with Task Forces Seventy-eight and Seventy-nine. The latter two had been released from alien control and their crews once more had free will, as Aspasia's Shadow's nanovirus had been rendered inert without input from the Guardian computer. The US once again ruled supreme in that part of the world.

Iran and Iraq were still fighting, and other Middle Eastern countries continued to stand on the edge of war as diplomats desperately tried to avert disaster. Israel had its nuclear arsenal fully deployed for the first time in history and it was only that threat that kept the surrounding Arab nations from invading.

Still, the world was slowly backing away from the precipice of complete disaster and the two alien sides were fleeing.

With the aliens and their followers defeated, the Third World War was officially over, although the world was far from peace.

The toll: at least twelve million dead with twice that many wounded and countless more displaced from their homes.

If the First World War had started with the assassination of Archduke Ferdinand and the Second World War with Nazi Germany's invasion of Poland (although many would argue that the Second was actually begun with the end of the First and the Treaty of Versailles), then the Third World War had begun at a remote desert site in the United States called Area 51, with the discovery of an alien mothership by the United States government. That event started a low flame boiling underneath an uneasy truce that had spanned millennia. It took over fifty years for the lid to blow off, but in terms of millennia, that was a relatively short period of time.

Unfortunately, while the Third World War was over, the First Interplanetary War for Earth was looming as a very real possibility, a fact known only to a select few. And this danger was not currently known by the man who had retrieved Excalibur, the key to the Master Guardian, from its hiding place near the top of Mount Everest, and who now sat there, unconscious, slowly freezing to death.

CHAPTER 1: THE PRESENT

MOUNT EVEREST

Mike Turcotte muttered irritably, wanting nothing more than to be left alone. He was wrapped in a warm blanket and felt very comfortable. A Sunday morning in Maine, the one day of the week he was home from the logging camp and didn't have to get up at the crack of dawn. He was wrapped in his mother's handmade comforters. He so badly just wanted to continue sleeping. A dream kept intruding, an insistent, irritating buzz in his subconscious. A woman with dark hair, dressed in a white robe, standing on a beach. Looking at him. Her mouth was moving, saying something, but he heard nothing. There was something wrong about the place though. The shadows, the water. All wrong.

He focused on her lips and he knew he had tasted them many times. They were thin and pale, her face angular. He had known her—

"Get up."

He didn't hear as much as knew that's what she was yelling at him.

"Get up."

Turcotte didn't want to. He could never remember feeling as secure and comfortable as he did right now. He'd been so tired, he knew that, and however long he had rested, it wasn't near enough.

"I need you."

She had saved him; he knew that, although he could not recall details. Beyond that, he knew they had done much together, and been many places. And he had loved her fiercely. That emotion roared through him, shaking him out of his stupor.

Turcotte opened his eyes but all he could see was white. He blinked, feeling something wet on his face. He shook his head, slowly realizing it was snow on his skin. Panicking, he sat up abruptly, six inches of snow falling off the upper half of his body.

He looked about. Open air directly in front. Rock behind.

He was flanked by bodies. Frozen solid. One dressed in a black robe with silver fringe. Another in ancient leather armor. And a third in early-twentieth-century climbing gear—Sandy Irvine, who had disappeared in 1924 while attempting to summit with George Mallory. With a smile frozen forever on his face. That shook Turcotte. He knew he'd have died with a smile on his face also if he hadn't woken. He could feel the cold throughout his body now. It was excruciatingly painful as his nerve endings came awake.

He looked down and could just make out the sword across his knees.

Excalibur.

The key to the Master Guardian that he had freed from its scabbard, activating it.

Reality came rushing back to him. Yakov had to be in the mothership with the Master Guardian. Duncan was missing. And he was high on Mount Everest.

Next to the sword was a SATPhone, its surface frozen and covered with ice. With stiff hands he reached out and picked up the phone, shoving it inside his parka. The cold made even the slightest act extremely difficult.

Mike Turcotte forced himself to get to his feet, Excalibur gripped tightly in his right hand, an ice ax in his left. He knew he had passed the peak of power the amphetamines had given him and that the oxygen richness of the blood doping was fading. How long had he sat there, he wondered. It couldn't have been too long because he still had some feeling in his hands and feet. He checked his mask, but there was no oxygen flowing. The tank on his back had to be empty by now.

He knew, as surely as he could feel the sword in his hands, that he could not make his way along the ledge or down the mountain in the same manner he had climbed up. He glanced down once more at the three bodies frozen next to him. They had known the same thing. And they had never woken from whatever their last pleasant dreams had been.

He closed his eyes and tried to force his oxygen-starved brain to think through the overwhelming exhaustion and pain. He'd trained in high altitude and the cold many times in his Special Forces career and he tried to recall what he had learned. He was higher than he had ever been. His instructors had beaten one thing into him about working in the mountains—gravity could be your friend or your enemy, depending on which direction you were heading and how fast. He considered those words of wisdom. He needed to go down, and do it quickly. He looked below at the Kanshung Face on the north side of Everest. Gravity could be his friend, but one slip and he would fall for a very, very long time.

There was one option. In a way Turcotte was glad he couldn't really think it through and figure the odds of success, because he had no doubt they would be very low.

He hooked the ice ax onto his harness and grabbed the nylon strap attached to the front of it. He clipped the snap link on the end of the strap to the safety rope. He paused for a moment, amazed that he had succeeded against the other groups that had raced to this spot to try to claim the sword. The corrupt SEALs from Aspasia's Shadow; the Chinese and the Ones Who Wait, sent by Artad; and his climbing partner and former watcher, Professor Mualama, who had been corrupted by a Swarm tentacle—all were now dead, their bodies scattered about the mountain.

Turcotte took the end of the rope, where the one SEAL had cut it, and laboriously tried to make a knot, thick enough so that it would not fit through the snap link. It took him several attempts and almost ten minutes of work before he achieved this simple task.

Taking the ice ax in his free hand again, Turcotte put his back to the mountain and faced outward, staring out over the Himalayas below him. It was dark, dawn still hours off. The stars glittered overhead and the moon was low to the west, its beams reflecting off the snow-covered peaks. Other than the nearby bodies, there was no sign of mankind as far as he could see. The silence was overwhelming, not even the wind, which had been his constant companion on his way up the mountain, was blowing. It was the most peaceful scene Turcotte had ever witnessed. It was serene and it was deadly.

Turcotte jumped outward with all his might.

The first piece of climbing protection—a piton—already weakened by Mualama's fall, tore free of the mountain. Like stitching being ripped apart, the rope popped succeeding pieces of protection from their perch and Turcotte fell, swinging to the west as each piece held for just a moment, the effect jarring him slightly and curving his trajectory before free-falling again. His climbing harness dug into his thighs and waist, but the pain was barely noticeable.

Turcotte slammed against the side of Everest, on the sheer Kanshung Face, still falling, still being swung to the west. The impact knocked what little breath he had out of his lungs and he gasped for air. He came to a halt for a moment as a piton held for a few seconds. He twisted and looked about, mouth open, lungs straining. The northwest ridge was twenty meters away. So close, yet so out of reach.

Then Turcotte dropped abruptly as the next piton holding him pulled free. The pendulum effect swung him toward the ridge and he reached the last piece of protection, where the ridge met the face. It held for the slightest of moments. Enough for Turcotte to get his bearings—he was less than two meters from the ridge. Very close, yet still too far. He braced his feet against the Kanshung Face and as the last piton gave way, he pushed off, leaping to the side, swinging his ice ax, arm fully extended.

The tip of the ax caught for a moment in the ice at the very edge of the ridge, holding him in place as the rope hurtled by. Then the ax gave way and he slid, desperately slamming it at the ridge time and time again. It caught once more and he hung there, dangling from the ax. He twisted his body to face the rock.

Dully, he realized the rope would now be heading down and when it reached its fullest extension, the weight would pull him off the mountain and he would follow the equipment to his death.

Maintaining a one-hand grip on the ax handle, most of his weight on the strap from it stretched taut around his wrist, with the other hand he swung Excalibur. The blade severed the rope a second before it was fully extended. Turcotte followed through the swing and jabbed Excalibur at the ice and rock of the ridgeline. The sword cut through the ice and into the rock, penetrating a few inches. Using the leverage of sword and ice ax, Turcotte slowly maneuvered himself off the sheer face and onto the ridge. He pulled the sword out and held it against his chest.

He rolled onto the almost knife edge of the ridge and lay

on his back, gasping for air and staring up at the stars. Only twenty-nine thousand feet to go.

THE GULF OF MEXICO

Three hundred feet under the water, an undersea habitat was joined to the leg of an abandoned oil rig platform. Inside the habitat, strapped to a steel gurney, was Lisa Duncan, former presidential science adviser and the one who had initiated the investigation into Majestic-12 and Area 51. She'd been kidnapped from Area 51 and brought here where she met Dr. Garlin, who claimed to be a member of a new Majestic-12 committee. This had occurred after it was discovered that Lisa was not who she appeared to be. Who she really was, however, remained a mystery. While under the control of Aspasia's Shadow she had partaken of the Grail, and was now immortal, something that was doing her little good in her present predicament.

She was a slender, dark-haired woman, covered with a white robe. On her head was a crown made of three bands of metal, an ancient artifact that had been carried out of Egypt by the high priest during the Exodus. Leads from the crown went to an object on a gurney next to her, something else that had been carried across the desert millennia ago: the Ark of the Covenant.

The Ark was three feet high and wide by four feet long. Gold plating covered the surface. On the open lid were two sphinxlike objects with glowing red eyes. The wires from the crown ran into the inner lid of the Ark. A thin, previously hidden screen had been pulled down, revealing a slightly curving, black surface. Just below it was a series of two dozen small hexagonal buttons with a rune on each one.

Silver-haired Garlin stood next to the Ark, wearing a

white labcoat. He stood perfectly still, watching the black surface as colors flickered across it. His face was expressionless except for a slight twitching on the left side, a muscle out of control, but it didn't seem to bother him in the least. A thin trail of blood was seeping from his left ear, but that also was ignored.

The black shimmered, flickered, then came alive with an image. Garlin leaned forward to look at what was displayed: a scarred mothership lifting off a planet's surface. The area around the launch site was crowded with people, troops holding them back. For a moment the vision focused on a small child near the front of the crowd, then it swept back. As the mothership rose, the planet's landmasses came into focus. Garlin noted the details.

Then the view shifted to the mothership moving through the vastness of space, going from one jump point to another at faster-than-light speeds.

The screen went black and then the mothership appeared again, this time looping into the edge of a planetary system at sub–light speed, but still traveling at a tremendous velocity. A cargo bay door opened and a smaller craft edged out as the mothership passed just inside the farthest planet. The craft was saucer-shaped, with a bulge in the forward center rising up and two large pods in the rear providing power. Like the mothership, its surface had also been damaged in battle. Unlike the mothership, its surface was not black metal, but rather a grayish compound. While the mothership headed back into deep space toward a jump point, the saucer flew on, toward the inner planets.

An image of Earth appeared. The craft was heading for it. Garlin took a step closer to the screen.

Duncan moaned and twisted, fighting against the restraints and the invasion of her mind. The vision of the craft and Earth blanked out.

A man appeared on the screen. Stocky, muscular. Dressed in a one-piece black jumpsuit with some sort of insignia on his chest. He was standing on a shoreline. His shadow was diffused by two suns overhead at slightly different angles. The air was tinged with yellow mist. The water was perfectly smooth with a purplish tint. The man was reaching out toward the viewer when the screen flickered again.

The man appeared once more, this time dressed in anti-quated armor. The metal was dented and bloody. A wound across his forehead dripped blood. And he was smiling, his eyes dancing with battle lust. In this scene, he only cast one shadow. The trees in the background were bright with the fiery colors of autumn.

Garlin frowned. Duncan's connection with this man was strong, very powerful, overriding his inputs to the Ark of the Covenant. Garlin wanted the location of the craft that had just been shown—where it had landed on Earth and where it was now secreted.

He reached forward and tapped a command on the keys.

The saucer appeared once more, heading toward Earth.

Duncan's back arched, the restraint stretching slightly, then pulling her back onto the gurney. Her head twisted back and forth. She moaned, a low keening sound that a sleeping dog in the midst of a bad dream might make.

The craft disappeared and the man reappeared. This time he was dressed in camouflage fatigues. Garlin leaned forward. There was something different about the man. A brief smile crossed Duncan's face.

Garlin leaned forward and tapped on the keys once more, directing the Ark to probe for the information he needed.

The man disappeared.

CHAPTER 2: THE PAST

ATLANTIS, EARTH
10,600 B.C.

The magnificent City of the Gods, set in the center of the island in the middle of the great ocean, was surrounded by concentric rings of land and water. On the large hill in the exact center was a golden palace over a mile wide at the base and stretching over three thousand feet into the sky. As magnificent as the building was, it was dwarfed by the large black mothership now descending upon it. The ship's surface was unmarred, a flat black that seemed to absorb the sun's rays.

The land in the surrounding rings had once boasted bountiful crops and many villages, but much of the land was blackened and blistered from the ravages of war. The human population was depleted, as many men had been ordered by the Gods off to distant battles and most had never returned.

Directly outside the palace, the streets were choked with people clamoring for entrance into the temple of the Gods. Warrior-priests manned the gates on the outer wall, with strict orders regarding who was to be allowed in and who was to be denied entrance. The latter outnumbered the former by a hundred to one. Some prescient souls were already in the harbor below the palace, buying their way onto sailing ships, but most had their attention on the palace from which the Gods had ruled for so long, unwilling to accept that change was coming and that the Gods would not take care of them.

Prayers were chanted, incense burned, and rich offerings

were made to the warrior-priests, but no one was allowed entry unless they were on the list. A pattern soon emerged, as only those who had fought for the Gods and worshipped them with unwavering loyalty were allowed in.

The mothership came to a hover next to the top level of the palace, its center adjacent to the tower. Large hangar doors on the side of the craft slid apart and a narrow metal gangway extended out of the ship to the tallest steeple in the temple. Priests hurried across the gangplank and took up positions in the entrance to the hangar. Four priests carefully made their way across, two by two, on their inside shoulders a wooden pole. Supported by the poles was an object covered by a white shroud. Directly behind the four was a high priest, garbed in a white linen robe, over which he wore a sleeveless blue tunic, fringed in gold. On top of that was a coat of many colors, which glittered in the sunlight. The coat was fastened at the shoulders with two precious stones, carved with runes. On his chest was a breastplate encrusted with jewels. There were two pockets over each breast, each of which emitted a greenish glow thanks to the stones placed inside. On his head was a crown made up of three bands of metal. He was chanting in a strange singsong language as they made their way into the mothership and disappeared into its vastness.

Then the first of the chosen ones were allowed out of the palace, two by two, almost running, eager to be inside the safety of the mothership.

The people outside the walls of the temple had seen the Ark of the Covenant carried across. The Ark was said to hold the Grail, the bringer of immortality, the possibility of which the Gods had held out to man since the beginning of time. If the Ark and Grail were being taken, the people knew that everything was changing and they were being abandoned.

Fighting broke out in places along the wall as many of those not selected rebelled.

Almost immediately a small golden orb extended from the pinnacle of the palace. Bolts of gold shot from it toward the troubled areas and when they struck, the resulting explosion killed not only the troublemakers but also hundreds of bystanders. Given such a brutal response, the fighting quickly ceased and the boarding continued uninterrupted.

After four hours of nonstop loading, there were no more to cross. The gangway retracted and the doors slid shut. As smoothly and quietly as it had arrived, the mothership rose to a hover about a mile above the palace. Larger doors near the front of the mothership now slid apart, revealing a massive cargo bay. On the north side of the palace a set of doors swung open. Two golden flying disks about thirty feet in diameter at the base and sloping up to a rounded top floated out—below them, caught in an invisible field they were propagating, was a large Black Sphinx, over three hundred feet long from the tip of the paws to the rear. The smaller craft maneuvered the Black Sphinx up and into the cargo bay. They set it down, then sped back to the palace, making several more trips, transporting up several twenty-foot-high golden pyramids, and lastly, a blood-red pyramid.

When all was loaded, the cargo doors shut and the mothership began flying to the southeast. It moved across the ocean, passing high over the Straits of Gibraltar and along the barren coast of North Africa until it came to a lush land with a large river running through it. Halting above the river, the cargo bay opened and the two saucers emerged, the Black Sphinx held in their traction beams. They lowered the Black Sphinx into a hole burned in the Giza Plateau, then did the same with the red pyramid.

When that was done, the mothership slowly descended until just above the stone plateau. A gangplank was extended to the ground. First off were the four priests carrying the Ark of the Covenant, followed by the high priest. Behind them came over a thousand people, mostly priests and warriors. Also sneaking off the ship as darkness fell, wrapped in black cloaks, were six strange creatures, over seven feet tall with red hair, red catlike eyes, and six fingers on the end of each hand. They were Airlia, the builders of the mothership, and a race that was spread across many galaxies. They entered a secret doorway into the underground chambers, while the humans remained above ground.

With this off-loading, the First Age of Egypt was begun, the time of the Gods, under the command of the Airlia couple Isis and Osiris, who sneaked in under cover of darkness and would rule through the priests.

The gangplank was withdrawn and the mothership flew to the east, across the Red Sea, and halted at a high mountain peak near the southern end of a desolate peninsula of land. Here a golden pyramid was off-loaded and hidden in a place prepared for it deep inside Mount Sinai. Also placed deep in the mountain were several pieces of machinery. Several of the aliens exited the ship pushing a coffinlike object, which they maneuvered into a chamber far inside the mountain. They hooked it up and swung open the lid. Lying inside was an adult human male with baby-smooth skin and vacant eyes that betrayed no sign of intelligence. His chest slowly rose and fell with each breath.

The leader of the aliens, Aspasia, was now hooked into the machine also. It was activated by one of the Airlia. Aspasia's memories, his mind, his essence, were transferred into the machine. When that was done, Aspasia stood and walked over to the tube, looking down at the body for several moments before going to the machine. He removed a medallion in the shape of two arms extended outward, a *ka*, from the top of the machine. It now held all his memories, his personality, and his essence, up to the moment of transfer. He held it in his six-fingered hand for a moment, as if weighing it, then returned it to its slot. He pushed the lid shut on the body, then set a timer on the top of the tube before quickly departing the chamber and returning to the mothership. He was leaving behind the machinations that would produce his Shadow, long after he and his opponent had gone into deep sleep.

From Sinai, the mothership continued on its way around the world, making several more stops. One was at the island farthest removed from land in the southeastern Pacific, which would not be known as Rapa Nui or Easter Island for millennia. Here another golden pyramid was secreted in a chamber deep under an extinct volcano. A handful of humans were deposited on the surface of the island, left to fend for themselves as the mothership moved on to the east.

Another stop was high in the Andes Mountains, where both a pyramid and another thousand humans were deposited, along with one of the aliens named Virachoca, to secretly rule in this most inhospitable terrain. After a few more stops, the ship was empty except for the crew and Aspasia. It headed to the least-populated continent, North America, and to the most desolate and deserted spot in that land.

Hovering next to a barren mountain, a golden beam from the nose of the craft burned a hole large enough for it to fit through and carved out a chamber inside from the solid rock. Using bouncers and their tractor beams, the crew off-loaded struts from another cargo bay and placed them on the floor of the cavern. The large ship carefully edged inside and settled down on the struts. The crew used metal to brace the cavern and built a rock wall, covering up the entrance, leaving one of the golden saucers outside. The mothership was powered down, a low power beacon was activated, and the crew departed via a small tunnel, which they blocked with stone behind them before they got on the golden saucer and flew back to Atlantis.

Aspasia had sown the seeds that would haunt the world for the next ten thousand years.

Two days after the mothership had departed, a second mothership, identical to the first, approached the island of Atlantis. There were still thousands gathered around the temple and living in the city. While many had left via sailing ship, most chose to stay rather than venture out on the wide sea, hoping against logic that things would go back to the way they had been.

The remaining people didn't even realize the mothership was a different one, but they knew something was changed when instead of docking with the top of the palace, it slowly descended to just above a large field on the outside of the city walls. A metal gangplank was extended to the ground, but there was no sign of life on board the ship and no priests from the palace to give instructions.

A few brave souls ventured up the metal way into the ship. When they reappeared, saying it was safe, thousands poured out of the city and crowded their way into the ship. This went on for hours. There were still hundreds on the gangplank and tens of thousands more crowded about on the ground when the metal abruptly began to withdraw back into the ship and the cargo door slid shut, slicing in half several people who tried to climb in. Hundreds more fell to their death and the thousands left behind wailed in terror as the ship gained altitude.

Those screams were echoed by those who had stayed in the city as seven spacecraft lifted out of the top of the palace, lean black forms silhouetted against the rising sun. The seven ships headed straight up, Aspasia and the remainder of his Airlia on board, dwindling from sight. Now the people knew the rumors were true—the Gods were indeed abandoning them.

Those on the ground could feel the displacement of air as Artad's mothership passed by overhead, finally coming to a halt a mile above the top of the palace. In the shadow of the huge ship, people in the streets fell to their knees, hands raised in supplication. Warriors looked up, holding spears and swords, aware of the uselessness of this display. In the harbor a few ships whose captains had dawdled raced to put to sea, their decks crowded with refugees.

On one of those ships a man and a woman stood side by side. They had waited to see how this latest chapter played out. She was short and slender with pale skin. A white robe fringed with silver covered her body, the hem touching the wood deck of the ship. She had dark hair, liberally marked with premature gray. The man wore leather armor, stitched in many places where blows had hit their mark. He was of average height but broad, with well-defined muscles. In his hand was a curved sword with a notched blade, the metal tinged with dried blood. Neither spoke, nor did they pay attention to the crew desperately rowing, trying to put distance between their vessel and Atlantis. Their focus was on the mothership and palace.

The air became charged with static. A bright golden light raced along the black surface of the mothership in long lines from one end to the other. It gathered at the front end and then pulsed downward in a half-mile-wide beam, passing through everything on the surface into the ground below.

Those on their knees prayed harder. Those fleeing ran faster. The oarsmen on the ships pulled more quickly. Some warriors futilely threw their spears into the air, screaming curses at the Gods who had first abandoned them and were now destroying them. On the ship, the man and woman simply continued watching, as if this was something they'd seen before and knew what to expect next.

The light once more ran along the skin of the ship, gathered at the front, and struck downward. Ten times this happened.

There was an abnormal moment of silence, as if the planet itself recognized the end of something. Even those praying paused.

Then the Earth exploded. The core of the planet below the island surged upward in one swift and devastating blast. The shock wave killed tens of thousands instantly. More died as molten magma sprayed upward and outward, almost reaching the bottom of the mothership.

Warriors held shields up against the onslaught, only to be incinerated in a second. Fathers and mothers threw themselves over children to protect them, and died. The island had lifted in the initial explosion, but now it imploded inward and downward. The ocean absorbed the force of the explosions and a wave on an unparalleled scale was born, rushing outward.

Where Atlantis had been there was only boiling sea.

Above, the mothership was slowly moving away, gaining speed. Those humans crammed in the cargo bays had not seen what had happened, but the destruction was so vast it was as if they had picked up the raw emotion of their fellow beings killed and their homeland destroyed. They moaned, cried, and prayed, now uncertain of their fate.

On the sailing ship the man called out to the ship's captain, advising him to turn the stern directly into the oncoming wave. The man slid his sword into a worn leather scabbard and watched the towering cliff of water approaching. The captain did so and as other vessels capsized and were swept under, this ship rode up the face. So high and steep was the wall of water that all on board scrambled to grab hold to prevent being thrown overboard. The man wrapped one powerful arm around the woman's waist and with the other he grabbed hold of the wooden railing.

A screaming sailor flew by, disappearing into the churning water below. The man's grip held tight as gravity tore others from the ship. Still the ship rode up the wave front, now over half a mile high. The man twisted his head upward, seeing the crest just above them. Slowly the ship went from vertical to horizontal as it passed over onto the top of the wall of water.

"Hold on still!" the man yelled to the surviving crewmen as they slid down the less steep back side of the tsunami. It took over a minute, but finally the ship settled in relatively calm water, the wave racing away from them. Debris and bodies littered the ocean. The man let go of the woman's waist, but she kept her grip on him as both looked back. Where Atlantis had been there was nothing but ruin and waste.

The woman finally spoke in a strange language. "*A truce, Gwalcmai.*"

The man seemed to know what she meant. "*They are neutralized here. They are no longer Gods.*"

"*For the time being.*"

"*Time is a valuable commodity, Donnchadh. We didn't have it, but maybe things will be different here. We have helped accomplish the first stage of our mission. The Airlia have fought among themselves and both sides, in essence, have lost.*"

Donnchadh didn't look convinced. "*But neither side has been defeated. And you know this truce is a farce. Both will try to use Guides and Shadows to—*"

Gwalcmai held a hand up, stopping her words. "*We've done what we can. Which is more than we could have hoped for. We have gained the people here time. And we will be around to help in the final war when it does come.*"

He walked to the shaken captain and gave him orders. The bow of the ship turned to the northeast. When he returned he noted that the woman's eyes were distant, as if she were looking beyond the devastation around them.

"*He has long since passed on,*" he said, knowing she was thinking of their son.

"*I know,*" Donnchadh replied, "*but I can still mourn.*"

Gwalcmai looked at the dazed sailors and refugees on the ship. "*Mourning is all that seems to come of this.*"

She nodded sadly. "*There will be much more mourning before it is all over.*"

The mothership passed over the tsunami that the explosion had caused, the wave now over three-quarters of a mile high and moving outward at four hundred miles an hour.

The mothership crossed the coast of Europe and continued to the east. It came to a halt above a landmass centrally located between Europe, Africa, and Asia. It was above the highest peak in the area, what would be called Agri Dagi and then Mount Ararat, and it descended to just above the top, where the gangplank was extended and the cargo bay doors opened. The rescued people poured out, some crushed to death in the rush to get off the ship.

After all humans were off and well on their way down Mount Ararat, the mothership, like its counterpart in North America, carved out a cavern near the top of the mountain, in which it was then buried by its crew, who later departed to the east via several saucers. The majority of the released humans fled in all directions, but a small handful remained on the mountain, old ties to the Gods holding them in place.

In the Atlantic, the tsunami first approached land along the western tip of Africa. As the depth of the water grew shallower, the wave lost speed but rose in height, almost doubling by the time it approached land. The first sign for those living along the shore that something strange was occurring was the unusual sight of the water withdrawing away from land. Fish were left flopping on the exposed ocean floor and many rushed out to gather the bounty. Unfortunately for them, the water that had disappeared had been drawn out by the tsunami to add to its height.

A sound filled the air, the worst thunderstorm any had heard, multiplied a thousand times. Then the wall of water appeared. Moving faster than any could run, even catching birds that had been feasting on the fish. The wave roared ashore, causing devastation for over a hundred miles inland, wiping out villages, flattening forests, lifting huge stones and carrying them for miles.

Following Africa, the wave hit Europe, North America, South America, and Greenland all with the same devastating effect. Part of the wave passed through and over the Straits of Gibraltar. Diminished in power it still was immense, a quarter mile high, sweeping across the Mediterranean, crashing into shorelines.

Atlantis, the Great Flood, and the rescue of those on board the mothership would pass from truth down into legend among the humans who now spread out over the face of the planet.

CHAPTER 3: THE PRESENT

EASTER ISLAND

The bouncer raced through the tunnel, up into the water of the lake in the Rano Kau crater and into the air. Aspasia's Shadow was at the controls and once he cleared the rim of the crater he directed it to the west at maximum speed.

He left behind the most remote island on the planet, with over ten thousand former "slaves" now freed of the nanovirus with which he had infected them. Naval personnel mingled with those who had been led to the island by Guides to follow Aspasia's Shadow. With the humans gaining control of the Master Guardian, he had lost control of his guardian computer and consequently lost control of the nanovirus.

But he was immortal, having partaken of the Grail, which now rested on the floor of the bouncer next to him. No longer would he continuously have to reincarnate himself via the *ka*. He also left behind the handful of guides that had been corrupted by guardian computers and come to him when he had called. Those they had misled fell upon them with a vengeance. Every Guide on Easter Island was dead within minutes, torn to pieces by the newly freed.

Aspasia's Shadow cared nothing for those he abandoned. Being free of the *ka* he could finally be free of this planet and this island on the forsaken planet. Though the humans now controlled the Master Guardian, Aspasia's Shadow had fought the humans too long not to have emergency plans pre-

pared for every contingency he had been able to imagine over
the many years he had prepared.

QIAN-LING, CHINA

The four metal dragons carrying Artad and his Kortad exited
the mountain tomb and headed west. Millennia after entering the tomb, Artad was ready to resume his mission to Earth.
He had slept for over ten thousand years in the lowest chamber under the mountain, waiting.

The alien sat in a tall seat, his seven-foot frame melding
into the contours. Six-fingered hands manipulated the controls while his red cat eyes scanned the displays. That he was
abandoning the Chinese government with which he had allied concerned him not in the slightest. The humans, against
all odds, had recovered Excalibur and taken control of the
Master Guardian, and in turn his mothership. His plans
foiled, he knew he had only one option: Get to Mars.

He'd seen what the surviving Airlia there had been building. And he knew it was the answer to all his problems. Then
there would be time to put the humans back in their place.

CAMP ROWE, NORTH CAROLINA

The Eleventh Airborne Division had trained at Camp Rowe
during World War II. The Son Tay commandos had also conducted their preparation for the raid into North Vietnam at a
mock-up built next to the long runway. And the Delta Force
commandos who had later conducted the ill-fated hostage
rescue mission into Iran had also done their training at this
spot in the North Carolina pine forests to the west of Fort
Bragg. It was also the site of Phase I and Phase III training
for Special Forces recruits.

Now the remnants of those who had operated out of Area

51 called the remote site their headquarters. Given that Yakov was in Turkey and Turcotte was on Everest, and Che Lu and Mualama were dead, the only ones left here were Major Quinn and Larry Kincaid.

The two worked out of a pair of communications vans that had been brought here from nearby Fort Bragg by the Delta Force commander, an old army buddy of Turcotte's. The vans were linked into the military's secure MILSTAR communication system. With access to this, both men could try to stay on top of the swirl of recent events.

Larry Kincaid checked the latest imagery from Mars relayed from the Hubble Space Telescope. Kincaid had worked at JPL—the Jet Propulsion Lab—and NASA for decades. He'd been drawn into Area 51 when it was discovered that the Airlia had an ancient base at Cydonia on Mars. Since then he'd been monitoring activity on the Red Planet, specifically at Cydonia and the recent construction on the high slope of Mons Olympus.

Prior to Yakov gaining control of the Master Guardian, the construction on Mons Olympus had seemed to be progressing swiftly. A series of black struts crisscrossed the massive bowl that had been excavated in the side of the volcano near the summit. By the shadows Kincaid could tell the struts were lifted above the ground about ten meters. On top of most of the struts, latticework was completed. It reminded him of a spider's web with the spaces between filled in with shiny material. Looming over the bowl and latticework he could see three inward curving pylons, two apparently finished, twins of each other, the third slightly shorter, not yet done. Their scale was staggering, even given Mars' lower gravitational field, only three-eighths that of Earth. Each one had to be at least fifteen hundred meters high, well over three times the height of the Empire State Building in New York

City. And they curved toward the center of the bowl, coming within four hundred meters of each other.

Even given the massive size of the construction, it was still dwarfed by the extinct volcano near whose peak it was located. Mons Olympus is the tallest mountain in the solar system. The peak is over fifteen miles above the surrounding Martian landscape. The base is 340 miles in width. The volcano, along with its smaller comrades that comprised the Tarsis Bulge, was so massive that it actually affected the rotation of the planet.

The mech-machines that had been working on the construction had been forced to dig partially through a four-mile-high escarpment surrounding the mountain and build up a hundred-mile ramp to clear a path to the peak. The mechs had come from Cydonia, carrying scavenged material from the "face" that had long been noted from Earth at that location.

Something had been destroyed there at Cydonia, Kincaid had concluded. And now they were rebuilding it at a much higher location. Yakov's control of the Master Guardian had shut down the control the Cydonia guardian had exercised over the mechs and construction had been halted. So close to completion, Kincaid could tell, but completion of what?

Something was nagging at the edge of Kincaid's mind—he was certain he had seen something like this before. Where? When? And more importantly, what had it been? He cleared his mind. If he had seen something like it, then it had to have been somewhere here on Earth. He ignored the Mars angle and simply thought about the construction.

A deep dish. Towers around the edge. Latticework.

Then it suddenly came to him. Where he had seen something like this on Earth. In Puerto Rico. The Arecibo Observatory—the world's largest single-dish radio telescope.

Over a thousand feet in diameter and covering twenty acres. Kincaid had visited it several times while working for NASA. It had taken three years to build, from 1960 to '63, if he remembered rightly. The Airlia had this thing almost done in that many weeks and it was so much larger.

He grabbed the imagery for a second look and had no doubt. What was being built on Mons Olympus was very similar, yet on a scale that dwarfed what had been done in Puerto Rico. He quickly did some measurements and came up with the astounding fact that the Mons Olympus array was going to be over a hundred times larger than Arecibo.

Why would they need something that large? Kincaid wondered. Arecibo was designed to pick up radio waves from deep space. Were the Airlia at Cydonia looking to receive a message? If so, from whom? And—Kincaid stopped his runaway thoughts as something frightening occurred to him—Arecibo, while primarily a receiver, could also transmit. Of course, it had never really been used like that because who was there in the heavens to transmit to? And radio waves were relatively slow when measured against interstellar distances. Even the first radio transmissions made on Earth were still making their way to the nearest star.

Unless—he felt a chill run up his spine—unless the Airlia had a way of transmitting that was faster than radio waves. Perhaps faster than light? After all, the mothership was suspected of faster-than-light travel. And if they did have a way of communicating at a reasonable speed given the distance between star systems—

Kincaid spun in his seat toward Quinn, who was on the radio monitoring events. "I need to get ahold of Mike Turcotte ASAP."

Quinn pulled the mike away from his lips. "I'd like to hear from him, never mind get ahold of him. I don't think he's coming down off the mountain."

THE GULF OF MEXICO

Garlin walked down the corridor and stopped in front of the elevator doors. They slowly slid to the side, revealing the second set of doors. He ignored the blood coating the floor from the Israeli agents who had brought the Ark and were subsequently killed. Their bodies still littered the floor, sliced in half at the waist. He walked up to the far side, stepping over a bloodless torso. The doors slid open, revealing a smooth, black, slightly curving surface. A rectangular outline appeared, then that section opened from the top, lowering to the floor. A very short passageway was beyond the hatch, ending at a metal door. Garlin walked to the door and hit a code on a panel to the left. The door slid aside, revealing a spherical chamber about fifteen feet in width, filled with gear and lit with a dull green glow. In the exact center was a thick pedestal on which rested a bizarre creature. It consisted of a gray orb, four feet in diameter with numerous eyes spaced evenly around the body. One gray arm, six feet long, extended upward, wavering in the air like a cobra ready to strike. The tip of a second tentacle was inserted into a square black box. Out of three other knobs, smaller versions of tentacles were growing, none yet at full maturity. Several eyes turned and watched Garlin approach. It was one of the Swarm, and the last thing the Israeli agent Sherev had seen when he brought the Ark of the Covenant here, believing he was delivering it to a new Majestic-12 committee.

Garlin knelt in front of the pedestal and leaned his head back, mouth opening wide, pointing directly up. A gray tentacle appeared in his throat, slowly slithering out, until all six feet of it was free of the human's body, which remained still. An identical arm on the orb reached forward and grasped the three fingers on the end of the tentacle. It lifted it free of the human body and the tentacle bent, the thick end coming toward the orb and attaching itself to a knob on the front side. Within seconds the two were reconnected.

Data was relayed from the one-hemisphere brain at the stem of the tentacle to the four-hemisphere brain inside the Swarm scout: The Ark of the Covenant was working but slowly. The mental shield around Duncan's real memories had been pierced in places. Penetration and retrieval into Duncan's real memory was progressing but there was a long way to go, particularly with regard to her real identity, purpose, and origin, which were of utmost importance to the Swarm, as was the secret of her immortality.

The details of the planet's surface that had been displayed on the Ark's screen were sent to the black box, which was a mainframe computer. The images were analyzed for a match. The result came back within seconds. Duncan's home world was pinpointed along with the information that the Swarm had already harvested it thousands of years previously. And they knew a mothership had left there prior to the fleet arriving. The assumption had been that the Airlia had abandoned the planet on board that mothership. That assumption appeared to be in error. Not Airlia, but Duncan's people had been on board. Which raised a new issue.

The Airlia were a known enemy. Humans had been encountered, but by themselves had always been easily overwhelmed. But humans who had defeated the Airlia? Not once, but twice, as recent events on this planet indicated. This was something unknown. And the Swarm, with hundreds of thousands of years of experience in battle against other species in the universe, believed the unknown to be the most dangerous threat of all.

The Swarm considered the problem. Time would normally not be a concern. After all, it had spent decades here in isolation slowly developing and putting into effect its plan to infiltrate and study the humans and counter the Airlia presence on the planet. It had even tried to destroy the key to the Master Guardian many years ago and again just recently, but been thwarted both times, losing two tentacles in the process.

Thwarted by humans.

Most strange and unprecedented.

Which brought it back to the issue that time was now a problem.

The Swarm had battled the Airlia and other intelligent species for almost half a million years on a front that stretched over dozens of galaxies. The Airlia had superior technology, but the Swarm had countered with numbers. The time and distances involved in this interstellar war were beyond anything humans could comprehend.

However, the luxury of time here on this planet was now being denied because the Master Guardian had been reached and activated by the humans. And the few Airlia left on the planet were moving. And a human from one planet had contacted others across a great distance—and defeated the Airlia once more.

The Swarm needed a way to relay information to its fleet so this planet could be targeted for infiltration, harvesting, and destruction. The escape pod that was attached to the oil rig could move through the planet's atmosphere but could not make orbit or communicate on an interstellar scale.

If the humans had the mothership, the Swarm knew, then the surviving Airlia factions faced the same problem it did. What were they going to do now? The answer came to it almost as quickly as the question was formed. On the screen in front of the Swarm, a planet was displayed, along with data stolen from the humans watching the Red Planet. Mars. The construction on Mons Olympus was highlighted. The Swarm had seen such an array before and destroyed every one it ran into. It knew what it was. On Mars was the means to contact its fleet.

But to get to Mars a craft capable of spaceflight was needed. The humans had control of the only means of interplanetary travel on the planet—the mothership and the Talon warcraft attached to it. Even as the Swarm considered this option, it suddenly realized that those weren't the only interplanetary spacecraft on the planet—the information gained indicated that Duncan had come to Earth on a spacecraft that at the very least could get to Mars. That craft was secreted on this planet somewhere. The decision on the next course of action was not hard for the Swarm to make.

The tentacle separated from the main orb and extended across to Garlin's mouth, which was still open. It slithered into his body, wrapping itself around his spinal column while microscopic probes on the ends of the three fingers extended into his brain, taking complete mental control while other probes infiltrated his spinal column, taking command of his body. The body shivered and twitched as the connections were made, then became still.

Garlin got to his feet and left the room. He walked out of the escape pod to the room where Duncan lay on a metal table, the crown on her head and thin cable looped over to the lid of the Ark of the Covenant. He typed into the control panel once more and resumed the probing of her suppressed memories with a focus on discovering where the craft was hidden.

On the table, Lisa Duncan writhed in distress. Any pain she ever remembered feeling was nothing compared to the agony that was tearing through her mind as the Ark of the Covenant battered through the mental shield with which she had been programmed and searched out her true memories, from which even she had been blocked for this very reason.

The truth was in there, buried deep inside her brain. And the small part of her that was able consciously to think despite the pain wanted to know it as badly as the Swarm. But there was also the terrible fear that she might give up the truth to the Swarm and doom billions in the process. While her past was blocked from her inside her own brain, she knew her mission, and she knew that the fate of this planet and everyone on it hung in the balance.

Garlin's eyes watched the screen, the data traveling to his brain, the information then tapped by the Swarm tentacle. Whoever he had been before being taken by the Swarm had retreated to a small part of his essence, unable to take action with his own body, his own mind. The Swarm had perfected the art of manipulating and consuming other species over the course of its existence. It was the ultimate parasite, subsisting not just on physical replenishment from other species but mental and emotional as well. Unfortunately for the Swarm, it always eventually destroyed those it subsisted on, requiring the race constantly to search out new sources of sustenance.

The Swarm was pushing the Ark to probe in the same direction it had earlier, to track where the spacecraft let off by the mothership had gone. It had to have landed somewhere on Earth. The memory was shielded, but the Swarm knew that a shield indicated something worth protecting, so it was confident the information was somewhere inside her brain.

A new image appeared on screen. A large plain of tall grass beneath a gray and rainy sky extending in all directions as far as could be seen. A river meandered through the plain, cutting deep into the ground.

A saucer-shaped craft appeared, hovering just above the plain. The skin of the craft glowed bright red from its journey and deceleration through the Earth's atmosphere. It flew over the plane, crisscrossing. Then it moved to the north to mountainous terrain. It halted above a jumble of large boulders on the side of a mountain. A powerful beam flashed down, cutting into stone, shaping three of the boulders into large rectangular shapes. Then a tractor beam on the bottom of the craft was activated and the three stones were lifted off the ground.

The spaceship flew back to the plain, the stones in tow.

The screen went dark, the mental shield cutting off the view.

Garlin's hands touched the controls and the probe resumed where it had left off.

The craft was over the river. The stones were laid out on the plain about sixty feet away. The craft dropped altitude to just above the surface of the water. Steam hissed up from the river at the craft's proximity.

The forward edge of the craft touched the riverbank. The two pod engines whined with exertion as the narrow forward edge of the craft dug into the ground. Ever so slowly, the craft dug into the dirt and rock, angling down and burying itself until only the engine pod and the rear edge of the craft were visible. It rocked back and forth, widening the cavity it had dug in the earth. The heat from the spacecraft's surface fused the limestone, creating a cavern. The craft then backed out of the large hole it had created and landed on the plain above.

A hatch near the front protrusion opened and a man and woman dressed in black jumpsuits climbed out. They both stood on top of the ship, faces turned up to the rain, letting the fresh water stream down their bodies. The woman was the exact image of Duncan, but younger. The man was of average height and well built, the same man from the earlier images.

The woman raised her arms and twirled about, dancing, feeling the rain on her face. The man watched her dance with a slight smile for a few moments, then opened a cargo door. He pulled out a bundle, which he opened to reveal red web netting. He carried this to the rear of the ship and draped the netting over one of the engine pods. Then he went back to the cargo bay and removed a similar bundle. He put that netting over the other pod, connecting the two with wire loops along the edge.

As he retrieved a third bundle, the woman finally stopped dancing and joined him. They worked without a word, completely covering the craft in the red netting. The woman climbed down the slope of the craft and onto the plain while the man reentered the ship.

The craft lifted and went back over the plain. The stones were lifted by the traction beam and placed on the plain above the cavern that had been dug. Two were placed upright, set deep into the ground, while the third was placed across the top, forming a lintel.

Then the craft carefully edged forward into the cavern it had dug, sliding along the bottom of the opening so the netting would not be disturbed. At last, after its long journey, the craft finally came to rest.

The screen once more went blank.

And once more, Garlin pressed the Ark of the Covenant to probe.

Standing on the plain, the woman was watching the stones. Steam began to rise out of one of them. This went on for several minutes. Then the woman stepped forward toward the structure when the outline of a door appeared on the left stone. It slid open and the man exited, a large pack on his back and another in his arms. The door slid shut and the outline disappeared. The two looked at the structure for several moments, then the man gave the woman the pack he had carried. He pointed in a direction and they set off across the plain, leaving the strange marker behind.

The screen flickered and went dark.

The craft was indeed on Earth—and buried. But where exactly were these strange stones that marked the site? That was what the Swarm still had to discover.

MOUNT EVEREST

Turcotte was blindly following the furrow in the snow that the SEALs had made earlier and that he and Mualama had trudged up. He reached Morris's body and paused for a moment, looking at the frozen blood and mangled flesh of the medic. A man dedicated to saving lives, Morris had given his own so Turcotte could make it to the sword. He knelt next to the body and removed the Special Forces crest from his parka and placed it on Morris's chest.

"*De Oppresso Liber*," Turcotte said as he stood back up. To Free The Oppressed. The motto of the Special Forces. Turcotte realized it fit the war he had been fighting against the aliens perfectly. He felt a surge of guilt, standing over the dead man. He had almost given up. He stiffened to attention and saluted. He held his position for several moments, then his hand fell to his side. He spun about and faced downhill.

With some renewed vigor he made his way down the ridgeline until he arrived at the two climbers' bodies frozen in the snow. They had died years previously in a vain attempt to make the summit. Turcotte stared at them for a few seconds, wondering why people would give their lives for such a self-ish pursuit. Was it for the glory, he wondered? Over the course of the past few months, while battling the Airlia and their minions, he had never really stopped to consider how humans might be viewed by other intelligent species. Besides physical appearance, how were we different than the Airlia, he asked himself. Which brought him back to the same question he'd had from the very beginning, once he realized the Airlia had been here so long ago: Why had they come here? What did they want with the planet and with us? The Airlia had had plenty of opportunities to wipe mankind out, but had never followed through completely. Indeed, what he had learned was that it seemed as if both factions of the Airlia had gone out of their way to keep humans around.

Turcotte shook his head, his mind too tired and oxygen-starved to delve deeply into such issues and questions. He used the ice ax to tear the climbing rope from the top of one man's pack. With great effort he anchored the rope through the harnesses on both bodies, then tossed the end over the side of the ridge, down the southern slope, where the bouncer was. Since both were frozen to the mountain, he felt confident they would serve as a good anchor. He peered down. The end of the rope reached the top of the alien craft.

He looped the rope around a snap link in the front of his harness and turned his back to the open air on the south side of the ridge. He pushed off, rappelling down toward the golden craft wedged into the mountain. He barely had enough energy to pull his rope arm in and brake as he descended. He slammed into the side of Everest, his bulky clothes breaking the fall a little, his body too numb to notice the pain of the impact. He pulled his knees up to his chest while supporting his weight with the rope, then pushed out and away, pushing out his rope arm at the same time so it would slide free through the snap link.

His knees buckled as he landed on top of the bouncer and he continued through the fall, collapsing on top of the alien craft. He lay there for several moments, futilely trying to catch his breath. With great difficulty he unhooked the rope from the snap link. He crawled over to the open hatch and fell inside. He didn't have the energy to climb back up the ladder and close it. He slid into the pilot's depression and pulled back on the controls.

The bouncer shuddered and vibrated, but didn't move. Turcotte leaned on the controls, not accepting defeat now. Ice cracked and very slowly the craft began to break free of Mount Everest. Then with an abrupt snap it was airborne.

There was none of the loss of power he had experienced arriving here. He directed the craft up the mountain toward the location he had just come from.

The magnificent north face of Everest was before him. Even in his exhausted, oxygen-starved state, he couldn't help but admire the mountain. The peak was above, twenty-eight feet above twenty-nine thousand in altitude. Adjusting the controls, he directed the bouncer back up the mountain, retracing his route down.

Turcotte gasped for breath as he edged the front end in toward the narrow cave where the scabbard rested. Touching the mountain, he released the controls. He clambered up the ladder, out the hatch, and carefully made his way down the top of the bouncer. He stepped onto the ledge. Working as quickly as he could with the ice ax, out of breath and fighting the cold, he dug the scabbard out of its icy tomb, then retraced his steps into the bouncer, putting the scabbard down next to him, leaving the sword's blade exposed.

Turcotte pulled the bouncer away from the mountain. He pointed the forward edge down and to the southwest, accelerating away from Everest and the resting place of so many who had tried to conquer the mountain and failed.

With his shaking free hand he reached for the mike to the satellite radio. "This is Turcotte," he whispered.

There was no answer.

"Turcotte here."

There was a burst of static, then Quinn's excited voice. "Major! Where are you?"

"In the bouncer. Coming down."

"Thank God. You've been off the air for a while. We thought you were dead."

"What's happening?" Turcotte asked. "Easter Island? Qian-Ling?"

"The shields are down in both places. As near as we can

tell from tracking their craft, Aspasia's Shadow and Artad are fleeing."

"Fleeing to where?" Turcotte asked.

"Uh—well, we don't know. Artad is heading southwest and Aspasia's Shadow to the west across the Pacific."

"Duncan?" Turcotte asked.

"Nothing on her location."

Victory is fleeting. The thought came unbidden to Turcotte's mind and he knew he had heard it from someone. Someone important.

There was a voice in the background, yelling something. "Kincaid's here," Quinn said. "He says he has to tell you something."

The hatch on top of the bouncer was open and Turcotte could feel the level of oxygen inside rise as he descended over India. The sun streaming in through the skin of the aircraft brought welcome warmth. It was probably just around freezing inside the craft now, but to Turcotte it was beginning to feel like being in an oven. Snow that had drifted in was beginning to melt, forming puddles of water on the floor.

"Mike, this is Larry Kincaid."

"Go ahead."

"Mars. What the Airlia from Cydonia are building on Mons Olympus. I figured it out. It's a transmitter/receiver of some sort. A very, very big one. I assume it has some way of sending and receiving a message across interstellar distances. Possibly faster than the speed of light. I can't be sure of that, but who knows what technology they have in that area. We assume the mothership was capable of faster-than-light speed, so we have to assume they have some way of communicating like that. I think they had an array at Cydonia, but it was destroyed long ago. Now they're rebuilding it on Mons Olympus."

The words seemed to resound in Turcotte's mind, a jumbled,

confusing mess for several seconds before the pieces fell into place. "So." He drew the word out as the implications sank in. "We've won the battle of Earth. But if Artad gets to Mars and gets a message out to his people, we can end up losing everything."

There was no response to that.

Turcotte glanced down at the green fields flashing by below. He was feeling a bit dizzy. And much too warm. His body felt as if it were burning up. He was nauseous and he twisted his head to the side as he retched, but nothing came up. He couldn't remember the last time he'd eaten. He'd survived for too long on too little. Now he was overwhelmed by too much oxygen, too much warmth, too quickly he realized. He let go of the radio and tried to unzip his parka.

"We need to finish this once and for all," Turcotte muttered, and then passed out, his hand dropping off the controls.

CHAPTER 4: THE NEAR PAST

VICINITY GROOM LAKE, NEVADA
1942

Balancing in the open back of the jeep, both hands holding on tight to the M-2 fifty-caliber machine gun, the OSS agent imagined himself in North Africa driving across the desert in pursuit of Rommel's Afrika Corps. The fact that the gun had no rounds loaded was something he chose to ignore.

The driver, Special Agent Cavanaugh, usually tried to do his best to ignore his younger partner. But when, above the never-ending sounds of the wind, he could swear he heard him making rat-a-tat-tat noises, Cavanaugh tapped the brakes, causing his partner's chest to bang against the back of the gun painfully. Cavanaugh then slowed the jeep to a halt. He got out of the driver's seat and walked ten feet away, before pulling out his compass to make a map check. He wanted to be sure they could find their way back.

They were northwest of the newly established Nellis Air Force Base tracking a plume of dust several miles ahead of them. They'd been following the German agent from New York, via train to Salt Lake City and then by car to this area and now by jeep into the desert. Cavanaugh couldn't imagine what the hell the German was up to in this godforsaken place, but they had their orders from Wild Bill Donovan himself.

The OSS—Office of Strategic Services—was a new entity, developed in response to the war and mimicking the British SOE, Special Operation Executive, an organization designed to do the dirtier work of warfare. Donovan, the head of the OSS, had told Cavanaugh that the arrival date and time of the German agent in New York had been forwarded from the British, but there was no clue as to the agent's mission.

"Kramer," Cavanaugh called out.

His partner was rubbing his chest. "What?"

"You need to look at this."

Reluctantly, Kramer gave up the gun position and climbed out of the jeep. "What is it?"

Cavanaugh simply held out the compass.

"Yes?"

Cavanaugh held in his sigh of contempt. "The sun is there. North is that way." He pointed in the direction indicated by the compass, one hundred and eighty degrees out from north.

"There must be a large ore deposit nearby," was Kramer's best guess.

Cavanaugh looked about, then checked the map. They were on a dry lake bed, marked Groom Lake on the surveying map they'd been given. The compass was pointing at a mountain to their south.

Cavanaugh rubbed away some sand stuck to the sweat on his face. Both men were sunburned, tired, and worn. And subconsciously feeling guilty that they weren't at the front, whether it be in the Pacific or Atlantic. When he'd joined the OSS, Cavanaugh had envisioned parachuting into Europe to work behind the lines, not driving across the desert in Nevada. He checked his watch, then walked back over to the jeep and picked up the handset for the radio to make their check-in with Nellis.

When he keyed the handset a sharp burst of static came out of the speaker. Cavanaugh cursed and fiddled with the frequency knob, checking to make sure it was set correctly. When he tried again, he still found only static. He switched to the alternate frequency but the result remained the same.

Cavanaugh looked at the mountain to the south. He pulled a set of binoculars out and focused them. He couldn't see the German's car, but he could see the dust trail it was kicking up. Straight for the mountain.

"Let's go."

They hopped back in the jeep and Cavanaugh held the speed down to keep their own dust cloud from being too large. He felt exposed, but there was no other way to do this. He slowed as the plume ahead disappeared. At the base of the mountain. He stopped the jeep.

"What now?" Kramer asked.

"We wait a little bit," Cavanaugh said for lack of a better plan.

"What the hell is this guy doing out here?" Kramer asked.

Cavanaugh shrugged. Nellis was nearby and it was a large air base, but there was nothing out here as far as he knew. He pulled up the binoculars, but he was too far away to make out anything.

Kramer was swinging the fifty-caliber around, shooting at imaginary enemies. Cavanaugh wondered how the man had made it through the screening process to be allowed into the OSS. He started as the crack of an explosion rolled across the desert. Cavanaugh looked through the binoculars and could see the dust cloud coming off the lower side of the mountain.

He started the jeep's engine and threw it into gear, nearly knocking Kramer out of the rear as he hit the gas. He was trying to figure out what the German was up to, but he couldn't even come up with possibilities.

He drove between two large boulders and skidded to a halt, seeing the German's dust-covered car and thirty feet above it, on the side of the mountain, blasted rock, indicating where the explosion had gone off. A rope dangled from a ledge, but he couldn't see what was just above the ledge.

Cavanaugh reached between the canvas seats and grabbed

a Thompson submachine gun. He pulled the charging knob back, putting a round in the chamber. He noted that Kramer's normally ruddy cheeks had gone white.

"Let's go," he ordered.

Kramer grabbed his own Thompson and clumsily did the same. Cavanaugh looped the sling over his shoulder and grabbed hold of the rope. When he saw Kramer sling his own weapon, Cavanaugh paused. "How about covering me until I get to the ledge, then I'll cover you?"

Kramer nodded nervously, unslung his weapon, and backed up a few feet, putting the stock in his shoulder and squinting up. Cavanaugh had a moment of doubt, wondering if it might be better to not have Kramer below him with a gun in his hands, then decided to trust that the OSS training had had some effect. He grabbed the rope and began climbing.

Just before he got to the ledge, Cavanaugh considered his dilemma. If the German was waiting for him, he was a dead man. Of course, then the German was trapped, with Kramer waiting below near his car. He remembered something an instructor had said during his training: Too much thinking made a man fearful. Easily said in a classroom.

Cavanaugh pulled himself onto the ledge, springing to his feet and unslinging the Thompson as quickly as he could. There was no one. Directly ahead a charge had obviously been placed in a crevice and a dark hole beckoned. Cavanaugh let out a deep breath, then glanced down. Kramer was in place, submachine gun tight to his shoulder. Cavanaugh signaled for him to climb up.

As soon as his partner was with him, Cavanaugh moved forward into the crevice, the muzzle of the Thompson leading the way. He could smell something familiar, then realized it was the odor of the demolitions range during OSS training.

It grew darker as he got farther into the mountain and he briefly debated going back for the flashlight he had left in the jeep. Then he caught the shimmer of a light ahead so he pressed on.

He came out of the crevice into an open space and he immediately saw the German, ten meters away, flashlight in hand, looking at some sort of console.

"Don't move!" Cavanaugh yelled, as Kramer came up on his left.

The German spun about, shining the light directly at them, and Cavanaugh was blinded. His finger twitched on the trigger, uncertain what to do. A shot rang out and Cavanaugh pulled the trigger, the Thompson bucking in his hands as it spit out .45-caliber rounds toward the light. His firing was echoed by Kramer to the right and together they emptied their twenty-round box magazines in less than four seconds.

The beam swung upward as the German was hit and slammed back against the wall, blood spattering the rock. The sound of the guns echoed from a long distance but Cavanaugh didn't notice that at first. Kramer started to move forward but Cavanaugh stuck his arm out.

"Reload first."

Both men pulled another magazine from their packs and slammed them home, pulling back the cocking knobs.

"Cover me," Cavanaugh said. He moved forward carefully. He had little doubt that the German was dead, but caution had been pounded into him during training.

He reached the body and knelt, picking up the flashlight. The German was indeed dead, the heavy slugs having torn flesh and smashed bone to the point where the man was almost unrecognizable. A Luger was clutched in one dead hand. There was a dagger in a sheath on his belt.

He slung his Thompson and retrieved the dagger with his free hand. A small, realistically carved ivory skull was at the top of the handle. Swastikas were carved into the bone grips along with lightning bolts, which Cavanaugh knew represented the SS, the *Schutzstaffel*, run by Himmler. He turned the knife and examined the steel blade, which had intricate detailing. Something was written and he held it close to make it out: THULE.

Cavanaugh turned it over. A word was on the other side. STEINER. He assumed that was the dead man's name. Thule vaguely rang a bell, but he couldn't place the name. He tucked the dagger into his belt, then checked the body once more. A backpack, riddled with holes and soaked with blood, was on the man's back. Gingerly, Cavanaugh removed it.

Inside was a leather journal and a half dozen flares. The journal was in a style of writing that Cavanaugh couldn't read—definitely not German—so he tucked it under his arm while he took out one of the flares. He ripped the top open and ignited it.

"Geez!" Kramer's exclamation startled Cavanaugh, then he turned to look into the cavern and saw what had caused it. He took an involuntary step back as in the sputtering light of the flare he saw the mile-long black ship resting in its cradle. In the limited light he could barely see the end, but it seemed to extend forever.

"What the hell is that?" Kramer asked.

Cavanaugh swallowed, trying to find his voice, but his mouth was dry as the desert outside. "The map," he finally got out.

"What?"

"The map," Cavanaugh repeated. "What's this place? What's it listed as on the map?"

Kramer came closer and unfolded the Nellis Range map they'd been given at the base. He ran his finger across and came to a halt. "It's a training area. Only has a number. Area 51."

CHAPTER 5: THE PRESENT

MARS

In 1999 NASA launched the Mars Climate Orbiter. The stated mission was to put a satellite into orbit for one Mars rotation around the sun, the equivalent of two Earth years, to study the atmospheric conditions on the Red Planet.

That was a lie.

When the orbiter approached Mars to go into orbit, contact with it was lost and never recovered. The explanation eventually given by NASA was that a data transfer during the preparation stages of the mission between the orbiter team in Colorado and the navigation team in California was flawed. According to the after-action report, one team used English units of measure, while the other used metric units for a key spacecraft operation. This mistake caused the orbiter to plummet into the surface of the planet rather than achieve a stable orbit. A rather startling and elementary mistake by the scientists involved if true. However, this also was a lie.

In reality, the Mars Climate Orbiter project was conceived by Majestic-12. Its highly classified mission was to overfly the Cydonia region of Mars and carefully examine the area with top-of-the-line imaging equipment. Cydonia had always fascinated observers from Earth because of the several apparent anomalies that appeared to be too linear and symmetrical to have been formed naturally. The primary one was a large outcropping labeled the "Face" because of its unnatural shape mimicking that of a massive visage peering up from the planet's surface. It was over two and a half kilometers long by two wide by five hundred meters high. The second was a large pyramid not far from the Face. There was also the "Fort," four straight lines like walls, surrounding a black courtyard.

For years NASA scientists had ridiculed any who postulated that these objects were anything other than natural formations. At the same time, it seemed curious that not a single one of all the various probes launched to check out the fourth planet had ever successfully orbited over the site for a closer look. While NASA's public records indicated that no craft had ever been programmed with such an orbit, the truth was, several, like the Climate Orbiter, had secretly been given the task.

The early Viking missions had succeeded in getting two landers onto the surface of the planet but far removed from Cydonia. Pathfinder, with its Rover, also landed far away from the site. Many on the outside felt these were deliberate attempts on the part of NASA to avoid getting better information about Cydonia. They were half-right. NASA did deliberately avoid Cydonia with the Viking and Pathfinder probes. But it did so because Majestic's first attempt to get a close look at Cydonia in 1975 using the prototype of the Viking orbiter and landing had resulted in the loss of both as it came within orbiting range of Mars. Majestic did not think this was an accident but it waited almost twenty-five years before trying again with the Climate Orbiter, hoping a higher orbit might protect the craft. Again, it was stymied.

The Russians at Section IV, their equivalent of Majestic-12, had also tried to take a closer look. Stretching from the late 1960s to the present, the Russians had launched ten unmanned missions toward Mars. Two exploded on takeoff. They lost control of two and couldn't get them out of their intermediary orbits around Earth to make the journey to the

Red Planet. Two more missed Mars entirely with haywire guidance systems and for all the Russians knew were still hurtling outward from the solar system. Three made it to Mars orbit but promptly went dead, transmitting no data. They actually did get one lander into orbit and were sending it down toward Cydonia when it began sending back very strange data before also going off-line.

The Russians had speculated that the missions lost on Earth or en route had been sabotaged by the Ones Who Wait or Guides from the Mission. Because of the lack of data from Mars, they could only guess that there was some sort of defensive mechanism in Cydonia that destroyed craft that came close.

It was only after the current war with the aliens began that the true nature of what was at Cydonia was revealed, as Aspasia and his followers came out of their millennia-long sleep, powered up their Talon spacecraft hidden underneath the Fort, and headed for Earth, leaving behind only a token crew to man the base. When Turcotte destroyed this fleet by booby-trapping the Area 51 mothership, the Airlia left on Mars were stranded but not inactive.

They sent a small army of mech-machines from Cydonia across the surface of the planet toward Mons Olympus while other robots tore into the Face, pulling metal parts out of the wreckage of whatever had once been there.

At Mons Olympus, the mech-machines had begun the greatest engineering feat in the solar system as they built a ramp up to and through the four-mile-high escarpment surrounding the peak. After making a way through the escarpment, the mech-machines had continued up the long, gradual slope to a point just below the summit of the extinct volcano. There they dug out a deep, dish-shaped depression, while lining it with a latticework of black metal. At three points around the circumference, the base for a massive pylon tower was put in place and two of the pylons were now completed.

When Yakov used the Master Guardian to shut down the Cydonia guardian, which controlled the mech-machines, the dish array was already complete and two of the three towers finished. The third pylon towered over eight hundred meters high in the thin Martian atmosphere, but needed another two hundred meters of work to be completed.

Without the aid of the mech-machines, there was only one option for the surviving Airlia—to complete the last tower and emplace the transmitting array by hand. Tracked surface vehicles that had long gathered dust in an underground depot were serviced and started. Space suits and portable surface habitats were checked and tested.

Within eight hours of the guardian's shutdown, a convoy of twenty vehicles carrying sixty Airlia departed Cydonia, heading toward Mons Olympus to finish the array.

AIRSPACE IRAN

Someone was pounding on the door, very loudly.

Mike Turcotte opened his eyes to the unique vision of floating in midair, a thousand feet above a desert with a jet fighter roaring toward him at five hundred miles an hour, spraying bullets. The rounds slammed into the side of the bouncer and ricocheted off, producing the noise that had brought him back to consciousness. His eyes followed the jet as it narrowly missed his craft. Iranian markings. At least that gave him an idea of where he had been when he passed out. Other than the noise, the rounds had no apparent effect on the surface of the alien craft.

He shook his head, immediately regretting the act as his head throbbed painfully. Coming down off the blood doping and amphetamines he had taken in order to survive on Everest was proving as painful as climbing the mountain had been. At least he wasn't cold, his body drenched in sweat inside his heavy clothing. He took a moment to take off the outer garments. As he did so, he saw sunlight glinting off metal close by.

He turned, reaching out for the sword that lay next to the slight depression in the center of the bouncer, wrapping his fingers around the handle. Reality and the immediate past came back to him in fragments. Excalibur. Sword of legend, made by aliens. The key to the Master Guardian hidden for generations on the nearly inaccessible north face of Mount Everest.

That told him why he was where he was and where he had been heading. The Master Guardian. Yakov—the Russian must have made it into the second mothership, known as Noah's Ark in legend, and located the alien computer. Turcotte briefly closed his eyes and brought up a mental image of this part of the world. Turkey was west and slightly north of Iran. And Ararat was in eastern Turkey.

The jet was coming in for another gun run, this time from the opposite direction. Turcotte pressed forward on the control stick. The bouncer accelerated and easily outdistanced the jet as it reached two thousand miles an hour. The ground was zipping by below. The Iranian jet faded in the distance behind.

Turcotte grabbed the mike and keyed it. "Quinn, this is Turcotte. Over."

An excited and concerned voice answered. "Geez, Major, we thought we lost you again. You just dropped off the air."

"Have you heard from Yakov?"

"Negative. We haven't received communications from him or any of the Delta men who went with him. I've intercepted some National Security Agency intelligence briefs indicating a lot of military action around Ararat. I don't think we were the only ones going after the Ark and Master Guardian. Fortunately, it appears Yakov got to it first."

Which meant Ararat—and the mothership/Master Guardian—weren't secure yet, Turcotte realized.

"Do we know anything about Duncan?"

"Not much more than we did," Quinn admitted. "I've been checking and there is no indication there is another Majestic-12. No one knows who took Duncan but I don't think it was any government agency."

"I'm heading for Mount Ararat," Turcotte said. "I want to see what kind of mess Yakov's gotten himself into. Keep looking for Duncan. I want to find out what the hell her story is. There's another layer to all this that we don't know yet."

MOUNT ARARAT, TURKEY

Yakov stepped back from the Master Guardian and staggered, almost falling off the narrow platform on which the red pyramid sat. He blinked, reorienting himself from the world the guardian had shown him to the real world.

The large Russian smiled broadly in victory. He'd shut down the Easter Island, Qian-Ling, and Cydonia guardians. The damn aliens—both sides—were minus their base of power now.

Yakov had spent most of his adult life serving in Section IV, the secret Soviet organization that had tried to keep track of the aliens and their minions just as the American's Majestic-12 had. It had been a mission fraught with danger. Yakov vividly remembered going into the wreckage of Section IV's base on the remote island of Novata Zemlaya, seeing the bodies of his comrades, killed by the Ones Who Wait, Airlia-Human clones who had waited millennia for Artad to be reborn. They'd done that to recover something from the

Section IV archives. Today he had paid them back for that deadly deed.

The room he was in was deep inside the mothership, a perfectly round chamber encompassing the Master Guardian. He had sealed himself off from the rest of the ship as Artad's troops were on board and had almost caught him before the Master Guardian was activated. The mothership was buried in a cavern deep inside Mount Ararat, hidden from sight for over ten thousand years.

Yakov heard a buzzing noise and reached into his pocket, pulling out his SATPhone. "Yes?"

"This is Quinn. Turcotte's coming to your location."

"And how will he get to me?"

"I don't know. Can you move—" Quinn's next words were lost since Yakov turned his head to the right as a loud thud echoed through the mothership. The sound was repeated a few seconds later. Yakov put the phone away and placed both hands on the side of the Master Guardian, making contact with the computer. He sorted through the rush of images that assaulted him, searching for some information on the current status of the mothership. He zoomed through several internal views until he received one relayed from a monitor in the cavern, looking down on the mothership just as a third thud reverberated through the ship.

At first he saw nothing, then, near the nose, he spotted a clamp to one of the Talons withdrawing, slamming back into the hull of the ship, just as a fourth thud announced the action. The rapierlike ship floated free of the mothership and rose a few meters. Yakov tried to access a connection with the Talon via the guardian but he reached a dead end. He realized the Kortad must have cut any control the Master Guardian could have over the warship.

But they were still trapped in the chamber, Yakov knew, as he turned his attention to any controls for an exit from the

large cavern. At that moment, a golden beam lashed out of
the nose of the Talon and struck the side of the cavern.

Turcotte looked down on Mount Ararat, noting the still-
smoldering ruins of armored vehicles on the lower slopes. He
could see other tanks and armored personnel carriers on the
roads approaching the mountain. Several helicopters with
Turkish markings flitted about, but he ignored them.

He'd gotten the coordinates for the mothership cavern
from Quinn and he edged the bouncer up the Ahora Gorge
toward the spot. As he got close to a half-mile-high rock wall,
he abruptly pulled back on the controls as the rock exploded
outward with a thunderous roar.

A car-sized boulder hit the left side of the bouncer and the
craft flipped from the impact. Turcotte had both hands on the
controls and he stopped the rotation and leveled out, just as
the nose of a Talon appeared in the large hole that had just
been blasted.

He held the bouncer still as the entire two hundred meters
of alien craft carefully exited. It had the same black metal
skin as the mothership and was thirty meters wide at the base,
tapering forward with a slight bend to a needle point at the
front. Once clear of the mountain, the Talon turned to the east
and accelerated away.

Turcotte keyed the radio. "Quinn, this is Turcotte. A Talon
just exited Ararat and is heading east. I need you to get Space
Command to track it. Over."

"I'm on it," Quinn responded.

Turcotte pushed forward on the controls and entered the cavern, seeing the mothership below, partly covered with debris
near the front. He saw the other Talons parked on the outside and
the empty space where the one that had just left had been stored.

·   ·   ·

Yakov "saw" the bouncer enter through the hole the Talon had just exited. He accessed controls for the mothership and opened a hatch to a cargo bay not far from the room he was in. Then he headed for the exit to the Master Guardian room.

Turcotte saw the hatch opening on the side of the mothership and guided the bouncer to it. He entered the mothership, the hatch closing behind him. He set the bouncer down and unbuckled from the pilot's spot. He held Excalibur in one hand and the MP-5 in the other as he climbed the ladder and exited the bouncer.

The cargo bay was practically empty except for some debris littered across the floor. Turcotte walked over to the nearest pile. Broken clay pots and a leather sandal. Very old. He frowned, wondering how that had gotten in here. A door slid open and he smiled as he saw Yakov's massive form filling the opening.

"Old friend," Yakov called out. He walked forward, arms spread wide, and Turcotte allowed himself to be caught in the Russian's embrace.

Yakov let go and stepped back. He saw the sword. "Excalibur?"

Turcotte nodded. "Yes."

"Stupid question," Yakov said. "If you did not have it, I would not have been able to accomplish what I did." His smile grew broader. "We have defeated the bastards finally."

"Who was in the Talon?" Turcotte asked.

Yakov spit. "Airlia. I would assume from Qian-Ling as there were Chinese forces with them. They came here to get the Master but we beat them to it."

"Where are the others?"

Yakov's smile disappeared. "All dead. The Airlia and the Chinese almost defeated us. Many brave men gave their lives."

More casualties. Turcotte had lost count of how many had died battling over control of Airlia artifacts. He silently made a promise to those who had given their lives that once this war was finally resolved, he would make it his mission to ensure that the Airlia legacy did not interfere ever again with the human race.

"There's a problem," Turcotte said.

"There is always a problem," Yakov lamented. "It is something a Russian learns to accept as a child. What is this new problem?"

"The Airlia on Mars are building what Kincaid thinks is a communications array on Mons Olympus. He doesn't think it's quite done yet, but it's close to being finished."

Yakov considered that information. "So. If Artad gets on that Talon and makes it to Mars, and they finish the array, he can communicate with his home world and bring more Airlia here."

"Yes."

"That is a problem," Yakov acknowledged.

Turcotte felt faint and staggered, the Russian grabbing his shoulder and steadying him. "Are you all right?

Turcotte ran his hand across his forehead, feeling the perspiration. He was burning up. "Just a little woozy."

" 'Woozy'?"

"Too much altitude and temperature change, too quickly," Turcotte said. "Where's the Master Guardian?"

Yakov indicated for Turcotte to follow him as he turned and headed down the corridor, staying close by his side. "What about Aspasia's Shadow and the Grail?"

"The nanovirus is nonfunctional," Turcotte said.

"I know. I shut down his guardian, which controlled it. All the subordinate guardians are shut down, including the one on Mars. That should delay their efforts there."

"My navy has regained control of the two lost task forces.

The combined fleet is heading toward Easter Island. Without the guardian, Aspasia's Shadow has no shield and little power. Quinn says he's fled the island on a bouncer, but they are tracking him. We ought to be able to deal with him and recover the Grail. The fleet can rescue Kelly Reynolds."

Yakov frowned as he reached the door to the Master Guardian chamber. "You should not underestimate Aspasia's Shadow. He has been around for a very long time and faced adversity before. Plus, we must assume he has partaken of the Grail and is now immortal. Also, what about the Guides? Even with the Easter Island guardian shut down, they still have the mental programming they received. And I am sure there are more scattered around the world."

"The Guides are few in number," Turcotte said as he paused in the entrance, looking at the glowing red pyramid. "Without the nanovirus, their power is limited." His thoughts went to Lisa Duncan, who had also partaken of the Grail and then been kidnapped, by who, he had yet to find out. "Have you picked up anything on Duncan's whereabouts from that thing?" he asked.

"I have not tried," Yakov said. "I have been busy with other matters. I will also check to see if there is any information on this array." He walked across the gangway to the pyramid and placed his hands on one side.

Turcotte had no desire to meld with the Master Guardian. He'd touched a regular guardian once before, in the secret base at Dulce where Majestic had been conducting bio-experiments on people they abducted. The direct contact between his mind and the alien machine had repelled him on a visceral level.

"Nothing," Yakov said after about ten seconds. "The only thing"—he frowned, his eyes closed—"strange. Very strange. I'm getting some images that were relayed from the other guardians once the Master activated before I shut them down."

"Images of what?" Turcotte asked.

"Something in the sky. Moving. Black. Spherical main body with six extensions. Some kind of spacecraft." Yakov paused, then continued, "It's exploding. High over endless forest. Ah, I have seen forest like that before. I know what this is." He let go of the Master Guardian and stepped back, turning toward Turcotte. "Remember General Hemstadt on Devil's Island?"

It seemed to Turcotte that the destruction of the Mission's base of operations had happened long ago, though it was actually relatively recent. They had narrowly stopped the Mission's attempt to wipe out mankind with a deadly virus. "Yes."

"His last words before he killed himself were about Tunguska. In 1908. I just saw the explosion that occurred there. It was caused by the craft I described getting hit by some sort of energy weapon."

"An Airlia weapon?"

"No. It appears to be a human weapon."

Turcotte felt a stir of excitement. "What kind of weapon? Who made it?"

"I can see if the guardian has stored that information," Yakov said, "but more importantly at the moment, there was an escape pod from that alien craft. Survivors."

"What does that have to do with Lisa Duncan?"

"The Master Guardian confirms that neither Artad nor Aspasia's Shadow have her—at least their guardians had no information on that and they were interfacing with their computers up until I shut them down. Its best estimate based on the available data is that she has been taken by the survivors in that pod."

"Who?"

"The Swarm."

Turcotte felt his skin tighten as he recalled the gray orb inside the tank that he and Yakov had seen at Section IV. That had been even more repellent than the contact with the guardian at Dulce. "Where are they?"

"I don't know. Let me see what else it has."

Yakov leaned against the Master Guardian, searching for more information. Turcotte radioed Quinn, telling him to get every bit of information he could on Tunguska and what had happened there in 1908. And what had managed to destroy the Swarm craft.

Yakov kept his hands on the Master but turned his head and called out to Turcotte. "The array they're building on Mars is indeed for communications. It's a little confusing, but the impression I've picked up is that with this array they can reach the Airlia Empire relatively quickly."

"That's all we need," Turcotte muttered.

Yakov frowned. "Something's happening."

"You could be a little more specific."

"Another bouncer just entered the cavern," Yakov said. "A hatch is opening near the front in another hangar."

"Can you override?"

Yakov shook his head. "The Kortad damaged the mothership's control room before they left, cutting off the Master Guardian from complete mothership control so they could take the Talon. The only way to control the ship is from the control room."

"Who's in the bouncer?" Turcotte asked as he checked his MP-5 submachine gun, making sure a round was in the chamber and he had a full magazine.

"The only person I know who has one is Aspasia's Shadow," Yakov said. "Unless some have been removed from Area 51."

Turcotte realized that his asking a question with such an

obvious answer indicated that he wasn't functioning at a very
high level. "Can you get us to the hangar that just opened?"

Yakov removed his hands from the Master. "Yes." He ran
for the exit to the room and turned right in the central corridor, Turcotte on his heels.

"Remember, my friend, if it is Aspasia's Shadow, he has
partaken of the Grail," Yakov said over his shoulder, as they
raced down the passageway.

"We'll see how immortal he is after I blow his head off,"
Turcotte muttered, one hand tight on the MP-5, the other
holding Excalibur. He felt a line of sweat soaking the middle
of his back. His vision went blank for a second and he staggered, but his sight returned as suddenly as it had gone and he
continued behind the Russian.

After six hundred meters, Yakov skidded to a halt in front
of a door. He hit a panel on the side and a door slid open.

"Here." Turcotte tossed Excalibur to the Russian, who
caught it by the handle and looked at it with less than enthu-
siasm. "I'll take point," Turcotte said.

"How nice of you. And I am supposed to back you up with
this?" Yakov held the sword in front of him.

"Better than nothing," Turcotte said, remembering Mount
Sinai, which was the last time he'd entered a place with
Yakov holding a gun. That had ended with Yakov "killing"
Lisa Duncan while trying to stop Aspasia's Shadow from
stealing the Grail. Neither man had known at the time that
she had partaken of the Grail and was immortal. Of course,
Turcotte realized, they hadn't really known at the time that
Duncan wasn't who she had appeared to be either.

Turcotte edged inside the doorway, taking in his surroundings. The cargo bay was about a hundred meters wide by fifty
deep. And empty except for a bouncer that was settling down
on the floor about twenty meters directly in front of him.
Turcotte put the stock of the MP-5 tight into his shoulder and

aimed at the top hatch. He could sense Yakov's hulking presence right behind him.

The hatch was flung open and a figure climbed out. Turcotte recognized Aspasia's Shadow from Mount Sinai, except he had an intact hand where Turcotte had shot one off. And in that hand was a cloth-covered object.

"Hold it right there," Turcotte yelled.

Aspasia's Shadow laughed without humor, as if he had just been spoken to by a cockroach he planned to crush under his boot. "You humans certainly are persistent. Very irritating to say the least." He slid down the side of the bouncer to the hangar floor and he lifted his arms wide, the object in one hand, stretching his body. "I have fought among you stinking people for millennia. It grows tiring after so long."

"And you've finally lost," Turcotte said.

"No. Not lost. Just a setback. And Artad is running, isn't he? So the old civil war is finally over. Congratulations." He glanced at Yakov, noting the sword in his hand, and recoiled a half step back before stopping himself. "I will trade you." He held up the shroud-covered object. "The Grail for Excalibur." He grimaced as if remembering something unpleasant. "I made an offer like that once before. Many years ago. To Artad's Shadow masquerading as Arthur."

"And he obviously didn't accept the offer," Turcotte said.

"Ah, that is true," Aspasia's Shadow said. "And Artad's Shadow—Arthur—like me, was smarter and more aware than the original. We were so close to—" He paused, as if suddenly aware to whom he was talking. "Ah, but it ended in blood and death as always. Merlin. The supposed Watcher. He was very troublesome. Another human interfering in things beyond his scope and awareness. As you are now.

"But back then I didn't have these," he added as he used his free hand to pull out two stones. "The thummin and urim.

You need them for the Grail to work." He took a step closer. "Think about it, gentlemen. I am offering you immortality."

"If we give you the sword," Turcotte said, "you will control the Master Guardian and the other guardians. So you're offering us immortality in order to live in a world you dominate? You want us to give up so easily everything we've just won?"

"I am tired of you humans," Aspasia's Shadow said. "And this planet." He abruptly changed the subject. "As I entered the cavern I saw that one of the Talons is missing. I would assume that Artad's Kortad took one and are rendezvousing with him. Do you know where he will go with it?"

"Mars. Mons Olympus," Turcotte said.

Aspasia's Shadow was surprised. "Very good. Do you know why he is going there?"

"The Airlia at Cydonia whom you've abandoned are building a transmitter."

"Impressive," Aspasia's Shadow acknowledged. "For a human, that is."

Turcotte's finger caressed the trigger. He was tired of being treated like an ignorant child. "Artad is going there so he can make contact with the Airlia home world and get rescued."

"Which will bring this planet back under the thrall of the Airlia," Aspasia's Shadow said. "And put it back on the front lines in the war against the Swarm."

"What happened to the original transmitter at Cydonia?" Turcotte asked.

"Destroyed. And it wasn't very powerful, just enough power to reach the nearest fleet base, which I assume no longer exists. I would further assume if the Airlia are going to the trouble of putting it on the volcano, they are building one powerful enough to reach back to the Airlia home system."

"If the Airlia still exist," Turcotte said.

Aspasia's Shadow laughed. "They've been around much longer than humans will be. I'm sure at least their home system still exists."

"So you were the traitor, not him," Turcotte said. Aspasia's Shadow had just confirmed Kincaid's suspicions. There had been a small part of him that hoped Kincaid was wrong.

Aspasia's Shadow shook his head. "Aspasia was the traitor. I am just a Shadow. Why should I be blamed for what he did? I have only the memories of it. I care nothing for the Airlia or their war or their civil war any longer. Or humans. Of course, neither does Artad or any of the Airlia. The Kortad are Airlia police, sent here to find out why he stopped communicating with the home world."

"And why did he?"

"It is not important."

"What do you care about?" Turcotte demanded.

"Me." Aspasia's Shadow put the stones back in his pocket. "I am now immortal. Do you know how many times I died and was reincarnated over the millennia? Now is my time for"—he smiled once more—"my heaven, so to speak; my afterlife of reward for all my suffering." His eyes lost their focus slightly. "I have Aspasia's memories of the stars and the numerous worlds that circle them. There are wonders out there beyond your imaginings that I wish to see, places in the universe where I want to go. Much nicer places than this rock you call your home."

Turcotte wondered why Aspasia's Shadow had tried negotiating if he was confident in his immortality. Of course, from his experience with what had happened to Duncan, Turcotte also knew if he shot the creature it would kill him only for a little while. Immortality did not make Aspasia's Shadow immune to damage or give him super strength as far as Turcotte knew.

"You can keep your sword," Aspasia's Shadow finally said, as if he knew exactly what Turcotte was thinking. "And the Master Guardian. For as much good as they will do you."

"What do you want?" Turcotte asked. He wondered why Aspasia's Shadow had been so concerned about the sword initially but now didn't appear to care. Was the sword more important than just as the key to the Master Guardian? Was he trying to distract attention from it?

Aspasia's Shadow pointed down. "The mothership. With it I can leave this planet, this entire area of the universe."

"No."

Aspasia's Shadow put the Grail on the floor. "You can have that. And these." He put the stones on the cloth covering it.

"No," Turcotte repeated.

"And you can keep the key and the Master Guardian. We can off-load them anywhere you would like."

"No."

"Give me the mothership. I am telling you I will leave. You'll never be bothered by me again."

"And you'll activate the interstellar drive and attract the Swarm here," Turcotte said. He felt as if he had come full circle. He'd stopped the flight of the other mothership from Area 51 to prevent this very thing. He remembered Professor Nabinger decoding the rune writing on the Roro-roro tablets from Easter Island. It seemed so long ago. And Nabinger had died also, killed in China. Everything involving the Airlia stunk of death and deceit.

"Ah, the Swarm," Aspasia's Shadow said. "The Ancient Enemy. But you know, of course, since you seem to know everything, that it is already here."

"I know," Turcotte said. "I saw one of the bodies recovered from Tunguska inside the Section IV archives. And I killed a tentacle that was inside one of my people on Mount Everest."

For the second time Aspasia's Shadow appeared surprised. "Interesting. So it stirs again."

"Again?" Turcotte asked.

"It tried to destroy Excalibur before," Aspasia's Shadow said.

"Why?"

"To strip the Airlia of their power here, just as you did by getting the sword and taking over the Master Guardian. It can be rather single-minded when it comes to pursuing its goals."

"It almost succeeded," Turcotte said. "It appears something survived the Tunguska explosion in 1908. A long time ago. And you, and Artad, the great defenders of mankind, did nothing."

There was no longer any trace of a smile on Aspasia's Shadow's face. He regarded Turcotte with his dark eyes. "Yes. Something survived. An escape pod. With no means to communicate back to its fleet. Thus not a threat and no potential to be a threat. So we did nothing. In fact, doing something held more potential for disaster than doing nothing. The Swarm is a very patient species and I saw no reason to push it to action as recent events most likely have. This happened before—a Swarm escape pod making it to the surface. Long, long ago. In ancient Egypt, when the Airlia did do something and destroyed the scout ship. And nothing happened there and then either."

"I think it has become a threat," Turcotte said. He didn't even realize he had lowered the MP-5. After all the battles, the desperate searching for information, he was beginning to find it strangely refreshing to be able to talk to someone who knew the truth. Even if it was a person who was responsible for millions of deaths and would easily lie if it suited his needs. Turcotte swung the gun back up as anger surged through him. "I think it took my friend. Dr. Duncan. And it has the Ark of the Covenant."

A frown crossed Aspasia's Shadow's face, the first sign of concern, but it was gone as quickly as it had come. He saw that the look had been noted. "An old memory. Not mine. It is strange being me. I was born with a complete set of memories from someone who wasn't me but was the formation of me. Who wasn't even the same species." He stared at Turcotte. "But perhaps you understand more of that than most?"

Turcotte didn't reply, waiting.

"But I am not Aspasia," Aspasia's Shadow finally said. "Nor am I a man. I am human in body, but have lived hundreds of lifetimes. And now I am immortal."

"As is Lisa Duncan," Turcotte replied. "Why did the Swarm take her?"

"To try to learn the secret of her immortality and—" Aspasia's Shadow paused.

"And?"

"Where she came from and why she came here."

Turcotte felt the hair on the back of his neck stand up. " 'Where'?"

"What planet she came from."

Turcotte heard Yakov's sharp intake of breath.

"You really are so ignorant," Aspasia's Shadow said.

"I will give you the mothership for the truth," Turcotte said.

"Truth?" Aspasia's Shadow cocked his head slightly as if bemused. "What is truth? Human truth? Airlia truth? My truth? The truth of things among the cosmos? Even the Swarm has its truth. And do you know, that none of them quite line up? None of them agree. Truth is all about perception, which differs from person to person, and from species to species. You would not like the Swarm's version of truth and they would care nothing for yours or any other species' for that matter."

Aspasia's Shadow took a step closer. "We have battled before, you and I. Many times. Do you know that truth?"

"You lie," Turcotte said, but even as the words left his mouth, he knew that they were wrong in some way. Aspasia's Shadow's words resonated in his head and he knew he had met the "man" before as he said. How could that be? There was too much he didn't know. If Duncan's past was a lie, was his own? Why did he have this strong connection to her if he had never met her before her ordering him to Area 51? Were his memories of Maine, of his mother and his military career all a lie, just as Duncan's memories of her family and past were? He now understood her shock when he had confronted her at Area 51 with her false history. There was a pounding in his head, as if a spike were being driven into the rear part of his brain.

"The mothership for the truth," Turcotte repeated. He felt a surge of irritation. Too many games. And he had a feeling now that he was more of a pawn than he'd ever imagined. Aspasia's Shadow could be lying to him just to unsettle things. It wouldn't be the first time the creature had tried such tactics.

"Now it is you who are lying," Aspasia's Shadow said, obviously thinking along the same lines. "You would not make such a trade. My comments got your mind working and you thought to manipulate me with a lie, but you are so unused to doing so, it is almost laughable." Aspasia's Shadow took a step closer. "You don't even know your own truth, soldier," he said.

"What are you talking about?" Turcotte demanded.

"You've learned Duncan isn't who she appears to be, correct?"

"Yes."

"Neither are you."

"You've said that already. Then tell me who I am."

Aspasia's Shadow shook his head. "That is not my place. You've done well, you and your Russian friend. You've saved your world. For the moment. In fact, you would be lucky if Artad does get to Mars and sends his message and brings the Airlia back here in force. They would rule once more, but they would also protect you from the Swarm and other enemies among the stars. The lesser of two evils."

Turcotte was holding at bay the swirl of questions and thoughts he had regarding what Aspasia's Shadow had just said, trying to focus on the larger issue. "You said the Swarm wasn't a threat because they couldn't communicate."

"Not yet. But think. Think hard. Artad is going to Mars. Where do you think the Swarm trapped here will want to go also? If it gets a message out to one of its fleets, your planet is doomed. A most terrible fate. I have memories from Aspasia of worlds that the Swarm harvested. Another reason I would really like to leave."

Yakov finally spoke. "We should not be listening to him, my friend. He fills our heads with lies to confuse us. It is a tactic as old as any."

Turcotte was uncertain what to do. He knew he could not allow Aspasia's Shadow to have the mothership. He also knew they had to get after Artad. He had to assume the missing Talon was going to rendezvous with the alien, and then head toward Mars—the clock was ticking.

"Perhaps we can make an alliance," Aspasia's Shadow suggested.

Yakov stepped up next to Turcotte. "We should not be listening to him."

"A paranoid Russian," Aspasia's Shadow said. "How refreshing."

"What kind of alliance?" Turcotte asked.

"I will help you stop Artad and destroy the array on Mars."

"How?" Turcotte demanded.

Aspasia's Shadow pointed down. "With the mothership. We will destroy him and those on Mars. Destroy the array. This planetary system will be isolated once more. Then I will depart on the mothership. I will not activate the interstellar drive for one hundred Earth years. By then I will be far enough away from your solar system that if the Swarm picks it up, they will not be able to track it back here."

Yakov's voice indicated he believed none of what Aspasia's Shadow said. "You'd wait a hundred years?"

"I have waited thousands of years to partake of the Grail," Aspasia's Shadow said. "And now I am immortal. A hundred years is nothing. Also there are deep sleep pods in this ship. For me it will be as if no time has passed at all."

"We should not do this," Yakov said.

"The array is not complete," Aspasia's Shadow said. "Nearly, but not quite done. Do you think you can stop Artad by yourself? You think you can outfly his Talon, outfight him, when it is his technology?"

"Someone destroyed the Swarm craft in 1908," Turcotte said.

"Luck," Aspasia's Shadow said.

"I doubt it," Turcotte shot back. "Who did it?"

"It is not important."

"I think it is very important," Turcotte disagreed, "because I think it was a human, using a weapon he or she invented. Something we achieved on our own, without interference from aliens."

"I will give you the Grail and the stone," Aspasia's Shadow said, ignoring Turcotte. "You can be immortal."

Turcotte shook his head. "Why do you think immortality would be such a blessing? The planet is already overpopulated. If we extend the gift of immortality to everyone, it would be an ecological disaster. We would destroy ourselves with overpopulation. There are more humans alive now than have lived throughout history—it's the worst possible time for immortality to rear its head. We'd deplete the world of natural resources within twenty years. And if we don't extend it to everyone, there would be war unlike anything this world has ever seen between those who have it and those who don't."

Aspasia's Shadow spread his arms wide. "That is not my problem. You can keep the Grail and its gift a secret. Share it with a select few. You are very good at secrets. It will give you tremendous power. You will be like a god—immortal and with the power to grant the same to others. I've seen all the major religions on this planet flourish and many have that at the core. The promise of eternal life."

"And how many of them were the Airlia or their minions like you involved in forming?" Turcotte demanded.

Aspasia's Shadow smiled slyly. "A few perhaps. Humans are very gullible. Especially when you offer them a way around that which they fear. And you do fear death, don't you?"

Turcotte ignored the last comment. "Which makes me wonder why the Airlia brought the Grail here in the first place. Was it just to be a symbol? Or was it to be used sometime? And if so, when? And who would be given the gift?"

"All very good questions," Aspasia's Shadow said.

"And the answers?"

"Not my province," Aspasia's Shadow answered.

"Wrong answer," Turcotte said as he pulled the trigger.

The round hit Aspasia's Shadow in the right leg, knocking him off his feet.

"What are you doing?" Aspasia's Shadow shouted, his hands trying to stem the flow of blood.

"It hurts, doesn't it?" Turcotte advanced, weapon aimed. "Immortality might not be all it's cracked up to be."

Aspasia's Shadow staggered to his feet. "You are making a huge mistake."

"Bye," Turcotte said as he pulled the trigger again. The round hit Aspasia's Shadow right between the eyes, flipping him backward, a pool of blood spreading beneath his head.

CHAPTER 6: THE PRESENT

QIAN-LING, CHINA

Tanks led the way along the dirt road, passing between the rows of destroyed statues that had once marked the ceremonial path to Qian-Ling. Each statue represented one of the foreign ambassadors who had attended the funeral procession of the first emperor, ShiHuangdi, who had ruled from nearby Xian.

The stone was scorched and all the statues were missing their heads. The former had happened when the current Chinese government had detonated a nuclear bomb in an attempt to destroy the mountain-tomb and what it held, prior to joining sides with Artad. The latter had occurred when vandals had desecrated and stolen what they could reach in ancient times.

Beyond the statues, as the road wound its way higher, lay the mountain that was called Qian-Ling. It rose three thousand feet above the countryside and even the most casual observer could tell from the evenly rounded sides that it was not a natural formation. It had been known as the largest tomb in the world, even bigger than the Great Pyramid of Giza.

The squeal of tank treads echoed off the side of the mountain, superseded by the supersonic roar of a jet fighter racing by overhead, providing cover. The shield wall that had guarded Qian-Ling and Artad had disappeared, an ominous sign to those Chinese soldiers who had watched the site.

Beijing's desperate messages to Artad had gone unan-

swered, and with the United States claiming victory over
both Artad and Aspasia's Shadow, those in power who had
decided to side with Artad were panicking. Their forces in
South Korea had been forced to a standstill by American nuclear weapons and those who had landed in Taiwan were being hunted down and exterminated.

Disaster loomed and Beijing wanted answers from Artad.
The word from the United Nations was not encouraging, as
the United States was now reporting that it had not only regained control of its fleets in the Pacific but additional submarines and ships that the nanovirus had constructed.

The lead tank went around a bend in the wide road and
stopped just in front of an entrance set between two large
boulders. A statue of a crouching tiger was perched on each
boulder, overlooking the entry. The main gun on the tank
was aimed directly between the boulder at two massive
bronze doors covered with rune writing, the metal blackened
and bent, but still blocking the way. There was a small
hole about chest high where an early entry had been accomplished by Che Lu, but since then the doors had been shut and
sealed.

The cannon roared and a SABOT round hit direct center,
punching through the doors. The tank followed that with several high explosive rounds until the doors were shattered and
dangling from their hinges.

Several armored personnel carriers came up and stopped
just behind the tank. Back ramps swung down and two com-
panies of infantry emerged and moved toward the opening.
Every second man carried a large flashlight that he turned on
as the troops entered the tomb.

Directly inside was a large anteroom, the walls covered
with ornate paintings. A wide tunnel was beyond, leading

down into the depths of the mountain-tomb. The tunnel was ten meters wide and straight as an arrow.

The lead soldiers moved cautiously, not sure what to expect. They came to a crossroads where two tunnels split off at ninety-degree angles. The officer in charge detailed smaller elements to go down each of these.

As he moved forward to lead the way down the main tunnel a dim red glow appeared twenty meters ahead. He signaled for his men to halt as the glow changed from a circle to a seven-foot-high line touching the floor. It widened, coalescing into a figure. The officer had seen the video Artad had sent the Chinese Parliament, so he was not surprised to see the alien form that took shape. The bright red eyes of the image stared at him, the elongated catlike pupils giving no hint of emotion.

The figure raised its right hand, fingers clenched tight in a fist. It raised the other hand, fingers wide open. Then it brought the fist smashing into the open palm of the other hand.

At that moment, deep inside the main cavern, where Artad's supplies and guardian computer were stored, an Airlia weapon exploded. Similar to a nuclear weapon, but smaller and more compact, the effect was devastating. The blast incinerated the men in the tunnels, then blew apart the mountain-tomb itself, spraying the country for fifty miles all around with debris, leaving nothing but a gaping hole in the ground where a three-thousand-foot-high mountain had once stood.

Beijing had its answer from Artad.

EASTER ISLAND

Four F-14s approached Easter Island at high altitude. The first thing they noted as they came close was that the opaque shield that had guarded the island was gone. While two of the fighter jets remained at altitude providing cover, the other two swept down to do a flyby of the international airport.

Thousands of sailors and Marines lined the runway, waving their arms like mad and jumping up and down in joy as the planes roared overhead. The pilot of the lead plane radioed in an all clear to the approaching American fleet and the following planes, then resumed a medium-altitude circling.

Easter Island covers only 171 square miles, a lonely spot in the middle of the vast South Pacific. The land was dominated by the three volcanoes that had formed its triangular shape. Surrounding the long-dormant volcanoes were the artifacts the island was best known for prior to the discovery that a guardian computer was secreted there: the eight hundred *moai* (statues). Why the islanders had gone to such great lengths not only to carve the statues out of the soft volcanic tuff of Rano Raraku crater, but then to transport them to locations along the island's shorelines, the stone faces glaring out to sea, remained a mystery until now. Now it was clear that this magnificent achievement was meant to serve as a warning for any who might happen by to stay away.

The warnings had not been heeded.

Less than five minutes after the flyby, eight C-2A Greyhound transport planes, from the carriers *Kennedy*, *Stennis*, and *Washington* approached. One by one they touched down on the runway and taxied over to the main terminal. Upon arrival, the medics and other disembarking personnel were mobbed by the thousands who'd once been held under the thrall of the nanovirus and guardian.

A special detail headed for the tunnel that had been dug by UNAOC—the United Nations Alien Oversight Committee—into Rano Kau, one of the three volcanoes on the island. The tunnel led to the chambers where Aspasia's Shadow had briefly ruled from and a guardian computer had been secreted millennia ago.

The detail found the chamber empty except for a withered figure lying on the floor near the dark pyramid. At first they thought they were recovering a corpse, but one of the doctors checked more closely with a stethoscope and was astounded to hear a very faint heartbeat. He quickly assigned a stretcher crew to carry her to the surface and radioed ahead for one of the C-2As to be ready to take off ASAP to take the body to the fleet for medical attention.

Only then did someone notice the flashing light on the control console.

GULF OF MEXICO

Lines of sweat dripped down Duncan's face onto the cold steel surface of the gurney. She moaned through clenched teeth as her body writhed against the restraints. There was a slight humming noise in the air, indicative of the high level of power surging from the Ark of the Covenant through the crown and into her mind.

A kaleidoscope of colors flashed on the small screen. Garlin watched it impassively, completely ignoring her. His hand was on the controls, just the tips of his fingers caressing them as he directed the probing. A scene appeared for a split second, a cluster of upright stones arranged in a semicircle, with lintel stones across the top, in the middle of a large field. It quickly disappeared, but Garlin's hand was already moving, directing the probe to bring it back in more detail.

The stones reappeared—but now there were six upright, and three lintels across the top. Around the base was a cluster of white-robed figures holding torches. The stones were over four times their height. The Swarm tentacle inside Garlin recognized the center two stones as those that been placed there in the previous scene by Duncan and her partner when they had buried their craft.

And there she was in the image, standing near the rear of the group, a hood covering most of her face. The man was to her right. There was the glint of armor underneath his robe.

The scene faded.

Garlin manipulated the controls. The humming noise grew louder. Duncan's back arched, then she slammed back down on the steel surface.

The image reappeared, except the chanting crowd was gone. Just Duncan and the man. A full moon hung overhead, casting long shadows from the standing stones. The man had a sword in his hand and was looking about anxiously. Duncan moved forward to the center stones.

Duncan cried out, a mixture of pain and denial. Her body vibrated against the table and restraints. Then suddenly she stopped.

The image disappeared.

Garlin shifted his gaze from the screen to the table. Duncan was still, not moving for the first time since he'd placed the crown on her head. He reached down, fingers around her neck, feeling for the carotid artery.

No pulse.

She was dead.

Garlin was still as the Swarm tentacle pondered this development for a few moments. Then he was directed to check the Ark, retracing the probe. The cause of death was uncovered almost immediately: an aneurysm in her brain, the cells of the blood vessel set to burst if activity exceeded a certain level in a specific portion of her mind.

The Swarm had seen such extreme conditioning before among Airlia captives, programmed to die before giving up the final secret. They had never discovered the Airlia's home world because of this. The captives all died before giving up that information, and captured guardian computers shut down when that data was attempted to be accessed.

And now Duncan wasn't revealing where her ship was hidden. She was conditioned to die before giving that up.

Except Duncan was now immortal. Garlin stepped back and waited. The artery repaired itself. After slightly over a minute her heart began beating again.

Garlin's fingers caressed the controls, the Ark's probe shooting for that memory. To press beyond and find the location.

The Ark's electronic probe followed the same path and smashed through the blockage.

The screen flickered. Duncan and the man were inside the ship, standing in front of some equipment. The Swarm recognized the scene and gear—two regeneration/sleep tubes. Duncan was older, her hair almost completely white, her back bent with age, her face lined.

How had they gotten in? Where was the ship?

The artery gave way, blood poured into Duncan's brain, and the screen went black. As the virus inside the body rebuilt the artery, the blood in the brain was forced through the brain lining and trickled out Duncan's ears, forming a pool under her head, staining her hair. The virus she had been given by the Grail not only worked on repairing the blood vessel, but produced additional blood cells as needed.

Garlin waited, the Swarm tentacle freezing him in place. Waiting was something the Swarm was very good at. Scouts, such as this one, sometimes spent thousands of years on target planets, observing and preparing. Occasionally acting. This Swarm had followed a previous scout's path into this star system. A scout that had simply disappeared.

That happened. The universe was a large place, and many

dangers accompanied traveling through it. But such a disappearance had to be investigated, even if it was thousands of Earth years later. The weapon that had destroyed this Swarm's scout ship was something that had not been encountered before. Because of that—and the way these humans had thrown off the shackle of the Airlia—the Swarm knew it was important that information about this world be sent back so that this world be targeted for priority harvesting.

The Swarm had encountered other potentially dangerous life-forms in the past, most of them at such a primitive level that harvesting quickly prevented them from developing sufficient technology to become a true threat.

Duncan was alive once more, the pool of blood underneath her head now so large, some of it dripped over the edge onto the floor. Garlin's fingers manipulated the controls, pushing the probe toward the same spot.

The image of the resurrection tubes reappeared. However, this time the screen showed a newly cloned Duncan inside one of the tubes while the man watched. He pulled a *ka* out of a slot on the console in front of him and placed it in a case. Then he went over to the tube and helped Duncan out. A young Duncan.

The screen went black again as Duncan's brain once more shut down.

The Swarm tentacle inside of Garlin waited.

KYZUL-KUM DESERT, KAZAKHSTAN

Four glittering dragons waited on the desert floor, one in the lead, the other three flanking it slightly to the rear. Each was ten meters long and five wide. Long arced necks stretched up from the short-winged bodies to end in serpent faces with large jaws that held black teeth. Dark red, unblinking eyes peered out over the sands.

Inside the lead dragon, Artad was watching the display screens showing the outer world. When he saw the Talon come toward his location, flying just above the desert floor, he hit a control and the back ramp to his dragon-machine slowly opened, lowering to the sand. He got up and walked out of the aircraft, followed by his Kortad.

The Talon slowed and the point rose toward the sky as the bottom settled on the ground. Five meters up a hatch opened and a long gangplank extended to the sand. The Kortad exited the flying dragons and followed as Artad walked to the plank.

The alien commander paused. He looked about, red cat eyes taking in the surrounding terrain. His troops waited patiently. They had slept for thousands of years; a few moments did not concern them. He turned to one of the Kortad, his deputy commander, speaking in the language of the Airlia.

"*This is a poor planet.*"

"*It is habitable, Lord,*" the deputy said.

"*Barely. We should leave it for the Swarm to harvest. It has caused considerable trouble.*"

The deputy remained silent.

Artad finally turned back to the gangplank. "*I will do my duty. We will bring these creatures back into the coalition. And then we will make them pay dearly for their impudence.*" He walked up the metal into the Talon.

When the last Airlia was on board, the plank retracted, the hatch closed, and the Talon rose to an altitude of one thousand meters where it paused.

A golden bolt shot from the tip of the Talon, striking in the center of the four dragons. When the dust and smoke from the explosion cleared, the desert floor was scattered with debris for miles.

The Talon then began gaining altitude, accelerating toward space.

SPACE COMMAND, CHEYENNE MOUNTAIN, COLORADO

In 1961 slightly over $8.5 million was appropriated for excavation work in Cheyenne Mountain. One year and two days later, over seven hundred thousand tons of rock had been removed from the interior of the mountain and construction on a power plant, steel building, fuel and water storage and other supporting systems was begun.

The fifteen buildings were made of three-eighths-inch continuous welded steel and set on top of huge springs. The theory was that the entire facility had a 70 percent probability of withstanding a five-megaton blast within three miles. A tunnel led into the mountain one-third of a mile to the twenty-five-ton blast doors, behind which lay the main cavern.

Initially the center was designed to link with the DEW line to counter the threat of Soviet bombers. It was updated then to track intercontinental ballistic missiles. As technology advanced, the mission of the center also evolved to the extent where it tracked SCUD missile launches during the Gulf War.

After the end of the Cold War, more and more attention was paid to space and peacetime missions, such as coordinating space shuttle flights and tracking drug smugglers. Upon receipt of a warning order from Major Quinn, the facility had shifted its capabilities to tracking the Talon from Ararat to Kazakhstan. The link-up with the four dragon-craft was captured by a KH-14 spy satellite to the degree that Artad and his followers were clearly visible walking across the desert and boarding the Talon. The destruction of the dragon-craft was also captured.

As the Talon accelerated into the atmosphere, tracking

was shifted from space down-looks to ground up-shots. The Air Force operators kept the Talon firmly on their tracking screens, monitoring it as carefully as they would the space shuttle.

MARS

While the rest of the Airlia vehicles headed toward Mons Olympus, a lone tracked vehicle rolled over to the site of the Face. Each track pad was over a meter long, the entire length of the tread over eighty meters. The two tracks supported a thirty-meter-long bullet-shaped pod with dual manipulating arms at the front. In the crew compartment, three Airlia manned the controls.

The Face had already been largely excavated by the mech-machines before the Cydonia guardian went off-line. The original array there had been specially designed using equipment brought from the Airlia home world. After it was destroyed, the resulting face figure had emerged from the rubble piled up at the spot. It no longer held that shape. The center had been dug through by mech-machines scavenging material. The vehicle slowly made its way up the rubble, treads crushing boulders beneath them.

It navigated over the top and down into the center, where the digging had gone the deepest. Carefully the Airlia edged their vehicle into the hole. At the bottom there was a dim green glow, and they headed in that direction. Just before the bottom was reached even the huge treads began to lose their traction and the vehicle lurched.

On the rear top a panel slid open and a tube extended outward. It fired a harpoon back the way they had come and the four-foot-wide barbed head slammed into the rubble, digging deep. A cable extended from it to the craft. Using the harpoon

as an anchor, the Airlia slowly spun out cable, getting closer
to the glow.

One of the Airlia in the control compartment slid his
hands into articulated gloves and took control of the arms.
Gingerly the large metal claws at the end dug through.
Finally, one of them gently cradled the source of the green
glow: a multifaceted crystal, eight feet in diameter. The arm
lifted the glowing green crystal out of the debris, then carefully brought it over the top of the vehicle and halted.

From a hatch near the front, an Airlia in black armor exited the craft, a pack on its back supplying air. Special boots
kept it attached to the skin of the craft as it made its way to
the wide middle part just below the crystal. The Airlia knelt,
sliding open an access panel and tapping in a code on the
hexagonal display revealed. A large cargo door slid open, revealing an open bay.

The Airlia was speaking to the one controlling the arm.
Slowly the crystal came down. The Airlia on the outside anxiously made sure it didn't touch the sides of the hatch, guid-
ing it with delicate touches. As soon as it was clear, the Airlia
ordered the controller to halt movement. The Airlia then slid
between the crystal and the sides of the hatch into the cargo
bay. It checked the cradle that had been specially built to accept the crystal, then ordered the controller to continue.

Gingerly, the crystal was placed in the cradle. The Airlia
in the bay waited until all its weight was supported, then gave
the all clear. The metal fingers released the crystal and the
arm retracted from the bay. The Airlia touched a control
panel and the cradle locked down on the crystal securing it.

The bay pressurized. A door in the front slid open, revealing a corridor, but the Airlia didn't leave right away. It pulled
off its black helmet, revealing pale skin and red cat eyes. It
regarded the crystal for almost a minute, then slowly, almost

reluctantly, turned and headed back toward the crew compartment.

Reeling in the cable and with the treads tearing in reverse, the vehicles slowly backed up out of the hole. As it crested the top, the crew turned it around. It moved downslope toward the line gouged in the red sand by the other vehicles, heading toward Mons Olympus.

CHAPTER 7: THE PRESENT

CAMP ROWE, NORTH CAROLINA

Major Quinn had been the operations officer for Area 51 when Majestic-12 ran it. When Majestic's corruption was uncovered by Mike Turcotte and Lisa Duncan and subsequently purged, Quinn's ignorance of the illegal activities of the organization and his expertise at running the facility had kept him in that position.

Here at Camp Rowe, thirty miles west of the Fort Bragg main post, he was the linchpin for the survivors of Area 51, coordinating their message traffic, doing whatever research they required of him, and forwarding information to whoever would listen in the United States government. With the loss of Artad's and Aspasia's Shadow's guardians, he was finding the latter to be much easier. He had already passed on word of the defeat of Artad and Aspasia's Shadow. While the world was celebrating the defeat of the aliens, he was trying to keep track of the survivors in both camps.

He had a direct link to the National Security Agency at Fort Meade, which kept track of electronic traffic, and Space Command, buried deep inside Cheyenne Mountain in Colorado. From the former he was monitoring the desperate attempts of Guides around the world to contact Aspasia's Shadow and the silence from their former leader. From the latter, the news was less positive. Space Command had tracked the Talon via satellite from Mount Ararat to Kazakhstan and now had it on an upward trajectory.

He was working out of an old aircraft hangar on the edge
of a runway on which Special Forces used to train and from
which it conducted airborne operations. The location was
guarded by members of the army's elite Delta Force. The
Area 51 survivors had been forced to move here after Area 51
was attacked by government forces operating under classified orders. Exactly who had issued those orders was something Quinn was still trying to track down, as every
government agency he had contacted so far professed ignorance.

He'd even talked to the commander of the unit that had
conducted the raid, who had given Quinn little to work with
other than that the orders had the proper clearance and the
unit had crippled the base and delivered Lisa Duncan to an
airfield outside of New Orleans, where an Osprey aircraft
waited.

Quinn understood the strangeness of the situation. He'd
operated in the gray world of covert ops for a long time
and knew that with the proper security and authorization
clearance, one could do just about anything with no questions
asked. And whoever had snatched Lisa Duncan and destroyed Area 51 obviously had had the clearance and authorization.

He turned away from his computer screen as he recognized the voice in his headset.

"Quinn?"

"Yes, Major Turcotte?"

"The Swarm has Duncan."

Quinn frowned as he considered that. They had assumed
that a new Majestic-12 committee, a backup of the original,
had snatched Duncan and destroyed the original Area 51
base. Quinn had since determined there was no indication
that there was another Majestic committee, but he had

assumed that one or the other sides of the alien civil war had
been behind her kidnapping and the destruction of Area 51.

"I want to know where it's hiding," Turcotte continued.
"What do you have so far?"

Quinn relayed the information about the airfield outside of
New Orleans that he had acquired from the troops who had
been ordered to attack Area 51. "I've queried every government agency now that we're back in favor, and received negative responses about any further information."

"Get me more," Turcotte ordered. "I want to know where
she was taken from there. Track down the Osprey. Someone
had to be piloting it."

"I'll try."

"Do better than try."

There was a short silence, then Turcotte's voice came
back over the radio. "I'm sorry about that. I know you're doing your best."

"What are you going to do?" Quinn asked.

"We need to get the mothership—and the Master
Guardian—out of here. Do you have a location on the Talon
that was taken from here?"

"Already in space, on a trajectory toward Mars."

"Time to target?"

"Say again?"

"How long until it gets to Mars?" Turcotte asked, reining
in his impatience.

"Based on current speed and what we observed when
Aspasia came here from Mars on board a Talon, I estimate
a little over a day. But this one hasn't even made it into
space yet."

"And how long does Kincaid estimate it will take the
Airlia to finish the array?"

"He says it's impossible to estimate as everything has
changed now that the mech-machines aren't functioning. It

appears as if the Airlia from Cydonia are heading there to complete it by hand."

"All right," Turcotte said. "We're going to bring this mothership back to the States. Then we're going to take it to Mars. I need backup—people able to operate in that kind of environment. See what you can get us from Space Command. They must have more than the team that went up on the shuttle."

"Yes, sir—" Quinn paused as a new report flowed across his computer screen. "I think you might want to know that it appears Aspasia's Shadow booby-trapped Easter Island. They're trying to evacuate it right now. Artad apparently did the same thing to Qian-Ling—we have reports of a massive explosion in that vicinity."

"Can the fleet get all those people off?" Turcotte asked.

"They're evacuating by air right now, but it's slow. The fleet won't be offshore for another day."

MOUNT ARARAT

Turcotte watched with interest as the wound in Aspasia's Shadow's head slowly healed. The "man's" chest had begun to rise and fall within two minutes of Turcotte's fatal shot. Using climbing rope, Turcotte had securely tied Aspasia's Shadow's hands behind his back and his feet together.

As fresh skin finally closed the wound, Aspasia's Shadow's eyes flickered open, confusion reigning for a few seconds before he looked at Turcotte.

"That was foolish."

"Why?" Turcotte asked.

"I have much to offer you."

"We have the mothership, the Master Guardian, and now"—Turcotte held up a cloth-covered object—"the Grail.

So I didn't have to make a deal after all. What more can you offer?"

"Information."

"About?"

"The truth that you are so desperate to discover."

"I wouldn't believe you even if you did tell me the truth," Turcotte said. He put the Grail down and placed one hand on the pistol grip for his submachine gun. "I tell you what. There is something you can do for me right now to try to prove your sincerity. You started a destruct mechanism on Easter Island, didn't you?"

Aspasia's Shadow smiled, revealing his sharp teeth. "So you do need me."

"How long until it detonates?"

"Soon."

"Within a day?"

"Yes."

"How do we deactivate the device?"

"Let me free and I will tell you."

Turcotte shook his head. "You are not in a position to bargain."

"I am if I have information you want."

Turcotte lifted the submachine gun. "How many times do you want to die?"

A flicker of fear crossed Aspasia's Shadow's face. "You would not do that."

"I want to know how to deactivate the destruct. Tell me."

"Only for my freedom and the mothership."

"Come with me," Turcotte said. He loosened the rope tying Aspasia's Shadow's legs. Then he tugged on the rope, and Aspasia's Shadow was forced to follow him as he headed for the Master Guardian room. When they reached the doorway,

Turcotte looked in. Yakov was communing with the guardian once more.

"Tell me how to deactivate the destruct," Turcotte said.

"Only if you give me the mothership," Aspasia's Shadow said.

"No deal." Turcotte pulled the trigger, the round hitting the same spot the previous one had.

EASTER ISLAND

The plane carrying Kelly Reynolds and other refugees lifted off the runway of the international airport and clawed its way into the sky, grossly overloaded. The C2As could only hold a fraction of the thousands that had been captured and enslaved by the nanovirus. The rest waited around the edges of the runway, eyes peering into the sky, hoping for more planes to rescue them. They knew, in the way a desperate crowd always knows once a rumor begins, that time was ticking away.

Some more enterprising souls went to the shore and launched outriggers, paddling away. The rest could only stand and wait.

SPACE COMMAND, COLORADO

The message was in code with an ST-6 clearance. Captain Manning began decrypting it and began nodding before he got halfway through. He wore a black jumpsuit with his name tag sewn above the left pocket, the Budweiser insignia of the Navy SEALs above the right pocket and a unique patch on the left shoulder. The patch had a dagger up the center with a half-moon on one side and a star on the other—the insignia of the United States Space Forces.

The unit had already deployed and lost two elements in

the war against the aliens—one on board the shuttle *Columbia* and another with Turcotte on the mission into Egypt to rescue Duncan. Manning had taken the remaining members of his fledgling force and used them to train an influx of new recruits culled from the various Special Operations forces, primarily Army Special Forces and Navy SEALs. He preferred SEALs as they were already used to working in a "weightless" environment with their water training.

Now he had orders to prepare for a third mission. Manning left the communications center with the message in his hand. They were headquartered at Peterson Air Force Base outside of Colorado Springs. The commo shack was adjacent to a large hangar that had once housed B-52 bombers, but now contained his force's primary training area.

Manning paused as he entered the hangar, noting the activity. In the center of the hangar was a large water tank, three stories high and a hundred meters in diameter. Several ramps spiraled up the side to a platform level with the top. Suspended from the ceiling, numerous metal tracks crisscrossed the space above the tank.

Manning heard one of his senior noncommissioned officers standing on the walkway yelling instructions into a radio. Manning walked over to one of the ramps and went up. The tank was full of water and inside a half dozen men in full body suits were being put through the paces by the NCO.

The men were wearing TASC suits, which stood for Tactical Articulated Space Combat suits. They were self-contained, self-breathing, and with full body armor were designed for combat operations in space. Next to actually going up into space, the tank was the best training preparation the men could get—simulated zero g and a nonbreathable medium.

The most intriguing thing about the suits was that the

outside of the helmets were solid, with no visors. Images were picked up by cameras and relayed to a screen just in front of the wearer's eyes, along with tactical information. Also the arms ended in flat black plates, attached to which were various weapons that could be used in space. On the feet were miniature rockets, used to supplement the propulsion unit on the backpack, which also contained the re-breather and a sophisticated computer.

A large part of the development of the TASC suit came out of the Air Force's Pilot 2010 Program. Realizing that their jets' capabilities were growing faster than the ability of pilots to man them, the Air Force understood that it needed to approach the entire issue in a different manner. There were fighters on the drawing board that would be able to make a twenty-g turn, but pilots would pass out at half that force. Additionally, at multiple Mach speeds, a pilot's reactions at normal speed weren't quick enough to pilot the plane accurately.

The TASC suits addressed both those problems by protecting the pilot and by allowing a faster mind-action interface via a device called a SARA—Sensory Amplified Response Activator—link. Inside the helmet was a black band with microscopic probes that went directly into the brain. The link was a two-way feed of electrical current sending input from the suit's sensors to the brain and taking orders directly from the nerve centers. The suit's miniature motors would be acting even as the nerve signal was traveling through the wearer's nervous system to his muscles.

On the previous two missions, they had not used the SARA link because of fears that the system had been built on alien technology—even Manning didn't know exactly how the skunk works had developed the damn thing. He'd had his men begin training with it again, now that it appeared the aliens had been defeated and the guardian computers were off-line. The suit itself was armored, capable of sustaining a hit from a 7.62mm round.

"Bring them up, Top," Manning ordered.

The six men surfaced, their black helmets bobbing in the water. Manning knew they could hear him, as mikes on the outsides of the helmets could amplify sound if needed.

"Men, we have a mission." He held up the decoded message. "We need to be ready to go in two hours. Area of operations—Mars. It appears the aliens are building some sort of communications facility there. We will destroy that facility. That is all."

MOUNT ARARAT

Turcotte grabbed Yakov's shoulder and pulled him away from the Master Guardian. The Russian was confused for a moment as he switched from the virtual world of the guardian to the real world.

"What is wrong?"

"Our friend there"—Turcotte pointed at Aspasia's Shadow, lying on the floor, the fresh blood behind his head contrasting with the pale skin that was already beginning to heal around the edge of the wound—"rigged Easter Island for destruction. There're about ten thousand people trapped there."

"What can we do?"

"Save them," Turcotte said.

"Don't we have other priorities?" Yakov asked.

Turcotte stared at the Russian. "You mean other than saving people?"

"Saving the planet?" Yakov countered.

Turcotte laughed, months of worry and strain seeming to fall from his face for a moment. "We've already done that several times." The smile disappeared. "First things first. Let's do this, then we'll worry about Mars and Artad and the Swarm and every other Tom, Dick, and Harry who threaten us." He headed for the main corridor. "Come on. Let's get this thing moving." As he entered the corridor, he broke into a dead sprint.

CHAPTER 8: THE PRESENT

EASTER ISLAND

For thousands of years, Airlia scientists had watched worlds being formed, carefully studying the mechanics of creation. In doing so, they'd also learned the opposite: how to use that information to damage or even destroy a planet. They'd tracked the evolution of a planet's birth at various stages and that data was stored inside the guardian computers. What Aspasia's Shadow had prepared on Easter Island as part of his revenge was based on that information.

In the beginning, Earth was merely a cluster of small rocks that came together 4.6 billion years ago as a result of the minute gravitational forces of those rocks. Six billion years later the collection was bombarded by asteroids and meteorites. That lasted millions and millions of years, producing immense amounts of energy, which in turn produced extremely high temperatures that reduced the entire planet to molten rock. It has been cooling ever since and still has not completely recovered, 4 billion years later.

Earth is currently at a stage where its interior is divided into layers depending on the extent of cooling. There are four major layers: the inner core, outer core, mantle, and crust. Inside, the rock is still molten and in flux, producing a magnetic field. The Airlia had learned that almost all planets with living creatures were at the same stage of inner flux. The Airlia had learned to tap this source of power for propulsion for their craft whenever they were within such a planet's field.

Dead planets such as Mars and the moon had no intrinsic electric and magnetic fields because they were cold and solid. On a dead planet, generators inside the Airlia ships had to produce their own fields at a great expenditure of energy.

The surface of Earth is a very thin skin representing less than .2 percent of the planet's entire mass. The skin under the continents is five times thicker than that under the oceans. However, since Easter Island is so isolated in the Pacific, it has only a very thin layer of planetary crust beneath it. Thus, the molten outer core is only six miles below the island's surface, where molten rock bubbles at four thousand degrees Celsius.

Deep under Rano Kau, the southwesternmost of the volcanoes that dotted the surface of Easter Island, a shaft had been dug by Aspasia's Shadow's mech-machines through hardened lava, extending downward until it reached molten rock. The shaft had originally been dug to tap the heat as a power source.

Aspasia's Shadow, however, after millennia of war and deception, had learned always to be prepared for disaster. One of the first things he had done after arriving on the island was prepare both an escape plan—which he had executed via the bouncer—and a destruct plan, which he had activated just prior to departure. At the bottom of the shaft, just above the glowing magma, he'd placed several five-hundred-pound bombs scavenged from the American fleet.

By themselves, the bombs weren't a threat to the island. He'd detonated them just before getting on the bouncer, and the effect had not even been felt six miles above. But the explosion had achieved what he intended, widening the energy tap beyond a controllable size. Under extreme pressure, liquid rock was now pouring upward into the vent.

Dormant for thousands of years, Rano Kau was now in the first stages of eruption.

Such an event would devastate Easter Island and kill all that lived there. However, Aspasia's Shadow had planned for something much more devastating to happen. Easter Island was merely the first domino in his scheme.

MOUNT ARARAT

Turcotte settled into the center seat in the pilot room of the mothership. Not long ago he had flown Aspasia's mothership into orbit, so he was somewhat familiar with the controls. He pressed his hand down on one console, and the curved wall in front of him gave a panoramic view of the chamber outside.

"Do you know what you're doing?" Yakov asked.

Turcotte responded by pressing his other hand down on one of the hexagons covered with rune writing. The floor beneath them shuddered as the ship's electromagnetic planetary drive was activated for the first time in over ten thousand years. The massive craft lifted off its cradle and was airborne.

"How will we get out of this place?" Yakov asked, hands grabbing on to the back of Turcotte's oversize chair, knuckles white.

Again, Turcotte answered with action, turning the prow of the mothership toward the hole the Talon had made in exiting. It was, of course, much too small to accommodate the mothership, but Turcotte had to assume that a craft designed to travel interstellar distances would not be greatly inconvenienced by a rock wall.

He was proven right as the black alien metal hit the cavern wall, knocking stone aside without slowing. Seeing clear sky ahead, Turcotte slid his palm forward and the mothership moved out of the cavern.

"Question," Turcotte said.

"Yes?"

"Which way is quicker? East or west?"

"I think they are approximately the same," Yakov guessed.

Now clear of Ararat, Turcotte accelerated while gaining altitude. "We'll go east," he announced.

A pair of Turkish jets were visible on the display, but unlike their colleagues who had intercepted the bouncer, these were racing away as quickly as possible, the pilots obviously spooked by the tremendous size of the mothership.

"Do you know how to open this thing up?" Turcotte asked Yakov. "Access all the cargo bays?"

"I got you in here," Yakov said. "I think I can figure it out. Quinn gave me the manual that Majestic assembled on the other mothership at Area 51."

"We need to get about ten thousand people in," Turcotte said.

"I'll see what the Master Guardian suggests," Yakov said.

"Do it."

Yakov left the pilot room, heading back toward the Master Guardian. Turcotte reached out and tapped another control, then suddenly frowned. He'd learned to fly the Area 51 mothership using instructions written up by scientists working for Majestic who'd studied the craft for over half a century. But he realized this felt familiar, as if he had done it more than once. But that couldn't be, he thought. He was still exhausted from his experience on Everest and he felt that his mind must be playing tricks on him.

Aspasia's Shadow's eyes slowly opened. The muscles in his arms and legs bulged as he strained against the ropes binding him. To no avail. Turning his head, he could see the large Russian once more in contact with the Master Guardian.

Even though his body was human, Aspasia's Shadow considered himself Airlia, or perhaps more accurately, beyond both species, especially now that he was immortal. He was unique, a new breed. But these humans. He had fought them for millennia and, despite his projected disdain, there was a part of him that grudgingly had to grant that they had something unique themselves. To have defeated both him and Artad in the race for the Master Guardian and mothership! And before that to have destroyed Aspasia and his fleet. Simply amazing. And years ago, to destroy the Swarm scout ship, causing it to explode over Tunguska—that had been a surprise. He realized now, too late of course, that he should have paid more attention to that warning sign, but he had been too focused on the Ones Who Wait and maintaining the status quo of their covert civil war.

Yakov stepped back from the Master Guardian and looked down at Aspasia's Shadow. "Do you wish to tell us now how long Easter Island has?"

Aspasia's Shadow shrugged. "I don't know." As Yakov's hand went toward the pistol at his waist, he was quick to add, "That's the truth. I opened a seismic fault deep underground. Rano Kau will become active. Soon. How soon, I cannot tell you."

Yakov cocked his head as he regarded the creature at his feet. "Why did you do that?"

Aspasia's Shadow blinked, as if asked why he breathed air. "It is what a commander must do in retreat. Destroy all so that the enemy gains nothing."

"A commander of what?" Yakov asked.

To that Aspasia's Shadow made no response. Yakov started to walk past him, shaking his head.

"Wait!" Aspasia's Shadow called out.

Yakov paused.

"You must deal with me now," Aspasia's Shadow said.

"Why?"

"Do you want to save those on Easter Island?"

"We'll do that without your help."

"Perhaps you will," Aspasia's Shadow acknowledged. "But can you save all who live along the Ring of Fire?"

"The what?"

"The Pacific Rim," Aspasia's Shadow clarified. "Easter Island will be just the beginning. It will start a chain reaction of volcanic eruptions and earthquakes along fault lines around the entire Pacific. The western United States"—he smiled—"say good-bye to Los Angeles and San Francisco and Seattle. Japan—devastated. Your own Russia—Kamchatka smashed.

"Tens of millions dead," Aspasia's Shadow continued. "If you think the death and destruction from the Third World War was grievous, it will be nothing compared to what is coming. Unless, of course, we make a deal, and I stop it."

Yakov's right hand snapped forward, his fist slamming into the side of Aspasia's Shadow's face. He walked out of the chamber without a word, the door sliding shut behind him.

EARTH ORBIT

Artad glanced at the tactical display. A terribly primitive space habitat was shown. Most strange—was this all these humans had managed to achieve in terms of conquering space in over ten thousand years? He was tempted to destroy it as they passed by. But it was so backward and offered so little threat that he ignored the impulse. The humans would pay a much greater price.

He reached out with a six-fingered hand and tapped the controls, bringing a view of Earth's surface into focus. He centered the screen on China and nodded as he saw the Great Wall meandering across the countryside. His Shadow, acting as ShiHuangDi, had completed the construction of the wall over twenty-three hundred years ago, shaping it to match the Airlia High Rune symbol for HELP. An indication of just how desperate Artad's followers had been. Over twenty-four hundred kilometers of wall built in just about ten years.

Looking for help from the skies that had never come.

Artad shifted the view to forward. They were moving away from Earth, picking up speed. The navigator had laid in a course for the fourth planet in the system. A dead world where they had placed their original communication array and defensive grid, both of which were destroyed during the civil war.

One of his Kortad alerted him to something the sensors had picked up. He switched to view to whatever it was that had been spotted. He sat up straighter in his command chair as the bulk of a mothership floating in orbit was identified, over a thousand kilometers away. He ordered an adjustment in the Talon's course to intercept.

Within a few minutes the Talon was alongside the much larger ship. He knew it was Aspasia's, and he'd taken in the report from the guardian describing how Aspasia's fleet had been destroyed by the humans. Still, the gaping hole in the side where the ruby sphere and nuclear weapons had been set off by the humans was startling. Artad knew the construction of the mothership and what it could sustain.

Artad noted the unusual quiet among his bridge crew as they also viewed the damage. How had all this happened, he had to wonder. It was difficult to believe that humans, acting on their own, could have accomplished such destruction.

Artad shook off these disturbing thoughts. He ordered a boarding party to be prepared to see if the ship was salvageable. High above the Earth's surface, the Talon and derelict mothership floated in orbit.

EASTER ISLAND

The lieutenant had hastily rigged the device from parts off the carrier *Stennis*. The instruments and transmitter were inside a metal case. Foam rubber had been duct-taped around the case, leaving only room for a wire antenna to poke out.

The device, and the lieutenant who had been given the task based on his academic credentials, had been flown to Easter Island on board an F-16 at max speed. The C-2As had just barely dropped off their first load of refugees on the carriers and were being refueled for a return flight. The lieutenant's job was to try to get an idea of the potential danger and how much time they might have.

"Steady," he called out as two Marines edged the device up the thermal vent that had been dug in cavern floor.

The lieutenant checked the various displays he had that received information from the instrumentation he had loaded inside the case. Everything seemed to be working.

"Drop it!" the lieutenant yelled.

The Marines tipped it over and it fell into the opening.

Even though he knew the data was being relayed via SATCOM to the fleet, the lieutenant called out what the gauges told him. "One hundred meters. One ten degrees."

He licked his lips and called out the next set of readings. "Five hundred meters. One hundred eighty degrees.

"Eight hundred. Two-ten. It must be free-falling," he added.

"One thousand. Two-forty.

"One-Five-Zero-Zero. Three hundred." He did a quick mental calculation as he watched the numbers move. "Through a mile down and no obstacles."

He stared at the displays, not quite believing how quickly the case was falling. It was indeed free-falling. He glanced over at the opening, which was only about a meter wide. How wide was this vent below? It had to widen considerably for the case not to have hit the sides.

"Two kilometers. Five hundred degrees.

"Three kilometers. Seven-fifty.

"Five kilometers. One thousand.

"Seven kilometers. Two thousand.

"Nine kilometers. Two thousand, five.

"Ten kilometers. Three thousand."

As if he felt the intense heat, beads of sweat were on the lieutenant's forehead. He blinked as all the displays went dead. He quickly hit several buttons, getting the last readings before they disappeared. "Final numbers: eleven thousand, six hundred forty-two meters down. Temperature. Three thousand eight hundred degrees. I would assume it hit molten magma." He opened up a geographic survey that had been faxed to the carrier upon request. "The crust is around twelve thousand meters thick here. Gentlemen, we've got a vent straight down to the outer core, which appears to be rising under pressure."

AIRSPACE SOUTH AMERICA

"Talk to me," Turcotte demanded.

Quinn sounded distracted, which Turcotte imagined he must be, as the officer was overwhelmed with data. "Uh, there's a report from the fleet. They sent some kind of probe down the thermal vent. Appears to go all the way to the outer core. And they think the magma is rising in the vent."

"So Aspasia's Shadow speaks the truth for once." Yakov was disappointed.

"About the vent," Turcotte said. He turned to the mike. "What about this Ring of Fire stuff?"

"That's the term," Quinn began, "for the fault lines along the various tectonic plates of the landmasses that meet with the suboceanic plates of the Pacific. It encircles the entire Pacific Ocean. Along these fault lines you have volcanoes, both active and inactive, and areas prone to earthquakes. It runs along the California coast, down along the western edge of South America—"

"Wait a second," Turcotte interrupted, looking at the screen in front of him, which showed the coastline of South America that Quinn had just mentioned. "Easter Island's a long way from South America. How can it be part of this ring?"

"There's a plate between South America and Easter Island and the Pacific Plate," Quinn responded. "It's called the Nazca Plate. Easter Island lies on the juncture of the Nazca Plate and the Pacific Plate. That fault line also extends north and links with the South American plate fault line and becomes the fault that runs along the West Coast of the US.

"This thing runs along the bottom of the Pacific, to New Zealand, through the Philippines, to Japan, up along the West Coast of Russia and along the Aleutians. Over nineteen thousand kilometers long."

"Back up," Turcotte said as he passed over the shoreline and the mothership was above the blue water of the Pacific, continuing to head west at great speed. "What the heck is this plate tectonic stuff?"

"It's a relatively new discovery," Quinn said. "The surface of the Earth, the crust, is made up of nine major plates, like the Pacific, and a dozen smaller ones, like the Nazca. It's basically a crust of hard rock floating on the molten outer core. And each plate is moving, which produces one of three effects along the boundaries. When they go away from each other they form a split where material, usually magma, comes up and forms a ridge. When they collide, one plate slides under the other, producing what's called a subduction zone. You were just at one of those zones—the Himalayas are the product of a subduction zone created by the Eurasian Plate meeting the Indian Plate. And the third is where the two plates are moving in opposite, parallel directions—the San Andreas Fault is an example of that. You've got all three types along the Ring of Fire, so you've got volcanoes and very unstable regions. When San Francisco got leveled in 1906, that was a relatively minor disturbance of the Ring— same as when Mount Hood erupted."

"Can one of the volcanoes erupting on Easter Island start a chain reaction?" Turcotte asked. "Those other events didn't."

"We have to assume the Airlia—and the guardians—know more about plate tectonics than we do," Quinn said. "I see no reason not to believe Aspasia's Shadow about this given what's at stake."

Turcotte frowned. "Except he's lied about pretty much everything else he's told us."

"Do you want to be the one to take that chance?" Quinn asked.

Looking ahead, Turcotte saw a dot on the horizon. "We're just about there. Is there anything we can do to stop this eruption?"

"I'll check," Quinn said.

"Better make that a quick check," Turcotte said, as the mothership rapidly approached the island. He brought the massive ship to a halt above the international airport, then slowly lost altitude until the belly of the spacecraft just about touched the tarmac. Thousands crowded about, staring in awe and hope at the large ship.

"Open the holds," Turcotte said.

Yakov was at another console, using the information he had gained from the Master Guardian. Cargo doors slid open and metal planks extended outward and downward. After a moment's hesitation, the people poured forward, boarding the mothership. Turcotte glanced at the display. Was it his imagination or was there already a thin tendril of smoke above Rano Kau?

Turcotte stood up and grabbed his MP-5. "When everyone's on board, let me know."

Yakov glanced over. "Where are you going?"

"To chat with our friend."

Turcotte made his way back to the Master Guardian room, where Aspasia's Shadow was tied down.

"Did the Russian pass you my message?" Aspasia's Shadow asked as soon as Turcotte entered.

"Yes."

"You know the threat?"

"If you're not lying, yes."

"I am not lying and I can stop it."

"How?"

"It is beyond your ability to understand."

Turcotte brought the muzzle of the submachine gun up.

Aspasia's Shadow shook his head. "You can kill me again, but that will cost you valuable time."

"What do you want?"

"The same thing I wanted before. The stakes on your end are higher now though."

Turcotte lowered the muzzle and didn't say anything. A few minutes passed.

"You are running out of time," Aspasia's Shadow finally said.

Turcotte still remained silent.

After a few more minutes, Aspasia's Shadow stirred, pushing against his restraints. "The process will soon be irreversible."

"You're asking me to accept two assumptions," Turcotte finally said. "First, that if that volcano erupts it will start a chain reaction all along the Pacific Rim. Second, that if that is true, that you have the power to stop what has already been started."

"They are facts."

"According to you."

"You cannot afford to disbelieve me."

"Sure I can," Turcotte said. "In your many reincarnations, did you ever play poker?"

"A game? I don't play games."

"Too bad." Turcotte lapsed into silence. Yakov's voice finally announced that all were on board from Easter Island. "We've got everyone," Turcotte told Aspasia's Shadow.

"You saved a few thousand," Aspasia's Shadow said. "What about the millions that will die shortly?"

"Your price is too high. I will never give you this mothership. I'm calling you on that."

"Then millions will die."

Turcotte felt the pressure. He felt there was a good chance Aspasia's Shadow was lying, but could he afford to take that gamble? "I'll let you go and give you a Talon if you stop it."

Aspasia's Shadow simply stared at Turcotte.

The Special Forces soldier raised the submachine gun. "Your other choice is to continue dying every time you come back to life. I think that will make you long for the *ka* and your old life. I'll partake of the Grail just so I can make your eternity hell."

Aspasia's Shadow frowned. "You have tried lying to me, but I suspect you are telling the truth now."

"Want me to confirm your suspicions?" Turcotte put his finger on the trigger.

"A Talon is not capable of interstellar jumps," Aspasia's Shadow argued.

"Not my problem. Besides, as you noted, you have all the time you'll ever need."

"I will take the deal."

Turcotte didn't lower the gun immediately. He knew the capitulation was too swift, but he also knew he didn't have much time. A fact of which he was sure Aspasia's Shadow was aware.

"What do you need to stop it?" Turcotte asked.

"Access to the control room," Aspasia's Shadow said. "You can keep your gun pointed at me if you like."

Turcotte let the submachine gun dangle from its sling as he drew his knife. He went behind Aspasia's Shadow and cut the restraints. "Let's go."

Aspasia's Shadow walked to the corridor doorway. Turcotte prodded him in the back with the muzzle of the gun. "Run."

They broke into a jog along the main corridor. As Turcotte passed doors he could hear the muted roar of thousands of people crammed into various holds. Entering the pilot room, Turcotte raised his hand as Yakov spun about, reaching for Excalibur.

"He's going to stop the destruction."

"In exchange for what?" Yakov demanded, eyeing Aspasia's Shadow as he sat down in the center control seat.

"A Talon."

"I do not think—"

Turcotte cut the Russian off. "We don't have time to think. Are all the gangways retracted and doors closed?"

Yakov nodded. "Yes."

Turcotte glanced at the screen. There was definitely smoke coming out of the top of Rano Kau now. Aspasia's Shadow grabbed the controls. The mothership slowly gained altitude. At somewhere around ten thousand feet he halted the mothership.

"What now?" Turcotte demanded.

Aspasia's Shadow ignored him as his hands moved over the glowing hexes that made up a large part of the control console. Turcotte felt his skin tingle as a charge passed over him. "What are you doing?"

"What I told you I would," Aspasia's Shadow said. "Look."

• • •

Lighter than the rock around it, the magma was getting near
the surface of the planet. About two miles below Rano Kau, it
began to melt some of the surrounding rock and had pooled,
forming a huge chamber over a mile wide. This pooling had
given Turcotte the time to get all the people off the surface of
the island.

Now, the pressure from below was intense, and there was
no place else to go but up again. The water in the crater lake
began to boil as hot gases moving ahead of the magma
reached it via the central vent. Steam poured into the air, then
gas. It was a battle between the water and gas for several minutes, then the magma chose another direction, pouring into
the guardian chamber, filling it, then heading toward a crack
in the side of the chamber.

Turcotte flinched as the seaward side of Rano Kau exploded
outward, hurling boulders the size of houses into the air. A
wave of hot gas roared outward over the sea and around the
volcano onto the surface of the island, killing every living
thing that remained. The *moai* were singed by the heat, new
paint that had been added to help make them a tourist attraction burned off.

Turcotte glanced at the other volcanoes in the other two
corners of the island. Both were emitting smoke. Bright red
magma flowed down the side of Rano Kau and met the ocean
with a hiss of steam.

The floor under Turcotte's feet shook as a pulse of power
shot down from the mothership into the island. It passed into
the ground with no apparent effect. Within five seconds a second pulse followed.

The power flowed into the planet, passing through the boiling
magma and shaking the ground. It hit the line where the crust

met the outer core, and the power dispersed, shattering rock
that sifted down into the magma, interrupting the flow. More
importantly, the amplitude and frequency of the shock wave
was the inverse of the power wave that had been initiated.
This was something only the originator of the initial wave
could have known. The dampening effect rode outward from
Easter Island, counteracting the power unleashed by the initial explosion.

Aspasia's Shadow made a few more adjustments on the controls, then turned in the chair. "I've done as you asked. Now I
will take my leave."

Turcotte could see no change on the view screens—things
didn't appear to be getting any worse, but there was still lava
flowing out of Rano Kau and smoke being emitted by the
other two volcanoes. "You have an eternity," he said. "I think
we'll wait a little before letting you go."

"You gave your word."

"And I'll honor it," Turcotte said.

"Ask your scientists with their measuring devices,"
Aspasia's Shadow said. "They will indicate the planet is
quiet once more." A smile crept across his thin lips. "I am
done as a threat. Artad and the Swarm"—he shrugged—"that
is your problem. If you would give me this ship, I would help
you with them also."

"I'd be happy right now to be done with you," Turcotte
said. "One threat at a time."

"You have no idea of the big picture," Aspasia's Shadow
said.

"And you haven't enlightened me," Turcotte replied.

Aspasia's Shadow crossed his arms and looked at Turcotte
for several long seconds. "I've done what you asked."

Turcotte nodded toward the exit. "Go."

Aspasia's Shadow stood and departed without another word.

"I do not trust him," Yakov said.

"I don't either, but at least we're rid of him now." Turcotte sat in the spot Aspasia's Shadow had just relinquished. He reached down and took the controls. He directed the nose of the mothership to the north, toward Hawaii. The sound of a clamp releasing on one of the Talons was audible throughout the ship.

Turcotte could sense the Russian's disapproval and felt compelled to defend his recent actions. "I'm just trying to make sure that when we do finally end this once and for all there are enough people around to enjoy the victory. Enough have already died."

Yakov let out a long, heavy sigh, before sitting down. "I understand. But my people have a long history of winning costly victories. And the battles and wars never seem to end. Napoleon. Hitler. And the betrayals. We were betrayed by our own government. So, I do not trust Aspasia's Shadow, but I do understand why you made the pact you just did."

Turcotte realized that was the most Yakov was going to allow him, so he picked up his SATPhone and punched in the auto-dial for Quinn. As it rang, another clamp released.

Quinn picked up his end on the third ring. He sounded distracted, and Turcotte could hear voices in the background.

"Major, what do you have on seismic activity?"

Quinn's response was immediate. "Things have settled down. Whatever you did stopped it."

"What do you have on Duncan?"

"There's a strange report. It appears that some Israelis—led by Simon Sherev—brought the Ark of the Covenant to what they thought was a new Majestic."

"Where?"

"An abandoned oil rig in the Gulf of Mexico. I've also

confirmed that an Osprey was used on a classified mission in that vicinity."

"OK, then—"

"That's not all," Quinn interrupted. "We got this report from one of Sherev's commandos who is still on the rig. He says he hasn't heard from Sherev or the others since they went inside the rig."

Another clamp released. Turcotte cursed. "We have anything near there that can investigate?"

"I'm working on it."

A fourth thud resounded through the mothership. Glancing at the screens in front of him, Turcotte could see a Talon moving away. "Good riddance," he muttered.

"I do not think we have seen the last of him," Yakov said.

Turcotte had expected the Russian to say something like that. "If we cross paths again, only one of us is walking away."

"He is immortal—" Yakov began, but Turcotte cut him off.

"If we meet again, only one of us will walk away, and it will be me."

CHAPTER 9: THE PRESENT

GULF OF MEXICO

The floor of the chamber was covered with a fine sheen of blood, but Garlin didn't appear to notice as he stared down at the body on the gurney. He had already killed Duncan two dozen times by pushing the probe farther into her brain.

The Swarm, by nature a patient creature, was becoming impatient. Intercepted messages from the human intelligence network indicated one of the surviving Airlia had a Talon and was heading toward Mars, where the communications array was being built. The cycle of probing, dying, coming back to life was growing tiresome.

The Swarm tentacle directed Garlin to take a new approach. He went to the escape pod and retrieved a flat black metal case about two feet in width and height and six inches in depth. He brought it back to the chamber and opened the front, revealing advanced surgical equipment carefully slotted in pockets inside.

He turned back to the Ark and input new commands, directing it to have the crown scan her brain and give him a map to work with. Within seconds, a display of Duncan's brain appeared. The artery that was failing was highlighted, but Garlin noticed something else. A small round object near the back of her head. Something solid and metal.

Garlin removed a drill, fitted the proper adapter to the end, and turned to Duncan. He put the tip against her skull, above the artery where the aneurysms were occurring. Just as

Duncan once more came back to life he activated the drill and pressed down.

The sickening sound of metal cutting into bone was matched by Duncan's scream.

HAWAII

Turcotte had been on Oahu several times in his military career and the only place he could think of to bring the mothership in to off-load all the people from Easter Island was the international airport. He maneuvered the mothership in low over the ocean toward the island, with Diamond Head off to his right and Pearl Harbor to the left.

There was no activity at the airport that he could see and the radio reports were very confused as the people on the island tried to recover from the aftereffects of the nanovirus. It was strange to see not a single naval vessel in the harbor.

Turcotte brought the massive ship to a halt over the main runway, got it down as low as it would go without its belly hitting the tarmac, then turned to Yakov. "Open all the cargo bays."

The doors on the side of the ship slid open and gangways extended to the ground. Thousands poured off the ship, but Turcotte didn't leave the control room.

"What now, my friend?" Yakov asked, his eyes on the monitors, watching the people. "Mars?"

"Not yet. We're not ready."

"And how can we become ready?"

Turcotte rubbed his face, feeling the stubble and the torn skin where the cold had ravaged the flesh. "Aspasia's Shadow did say some things that made sense."

"For instance?"

"Artad has a Talon. As far as we can determine Talons are warships. He knows how to use it and its weapons. We don't even know how to work the weapon on this ship that Aspasia's Shadow used on Easter Island. I watched him as he did it, but I'm not sure I could duplicate what he did and I knew he wasn't going to give us lessons. I'm pretty sure I can fly this thing to Mars, but what then?"

"Nuclear bombs?" Yakov suggested. "We drop them manually?"

"Doctor Strangelove?"

"What?"

Turcotte dropped the reference. "And if they shield the transmitter?"

Yakov shrugged. "I do not know what to tell you, my friend."

Turcotte tapped the side of his head. "Think of what we've learned, bits and pieces. Something shot down the Swarm scout ship over Tunguska. And it wasn't directed by the Airlia, the Mission, or the Ones Who Wait."

"A human?"

"Who else is left?"

"But how?"

"That's the million-dollar question," Turcotte said.

"Perhaps Major Quinn has some more information for us," Yakov said.

Turcotte glanced at the displays, checking the off-load. "We're heading there as soon as the holds are empty. After a side trip to an oil rig in the Gulf of Mexico."

GULF OF MEXICO

Garlin worked quickly, ignoring the blood that was splattering everywhere. He'd removed a section of Duncan's skull three inches in diameter, exposing the interior. He'd then made a slit through the three protective membranes surrounding the brain. He didn't even blink as he sliced through the pia mater—the innermost layer—and a spurt of cere-brospinal fluid hit him in the face.

He continued into the cerebrum so he could get to the ar-tery that was continually rupturing. He couldn't stop the con-ditioning impressed into the very cells there, so he did the next best thing. He put a shunt into the artery that bypassed that section.

Even as he did this, new flesh was regenerating, beginning to reseal the protective membrane. He got the shunt in place, then quickly exited the hole. He watched as the damage was repaired internally and bone began to grow around the open-ing in the skull. As soon as the wound was closed he picked up the drill again and turned her head so he had access to the rear. He drilled in, repeating the process of entering her brain. He found the metal sphere, less than a half inch in diameter. Using a magnifying glass, he could see that several small fil-aments ran from the sphere into Duncan's brain.

He grabbed a set of long, narrow pincers and slid them into the hole, seizing the sphere. With no concern for pain he yanked it out, the thin wires ripping free.

HAWAII

Turcotte staggered and only kept from falling by putting his hands on the large display at the front of the pilot's compart-ment.

"Are you all right?" Yakov jumped up from his seat.

Turcotte leaned over, feeling as if an arrow had been driven into the back of his head. It hurt so badly he didn't dare shake it to answer Yakov's question. It was so intense he felt physically ill, his last meal threatening to come up as he tasted bile.

"What is wrong, my friend?" Yakov hovered over Turcotte, uncertain what to do.

Turcotte removed his hand from behind his head and looked at it, expecting to see blood, but there was none. "Felt like I got shot," he said in a whisper.

The pain was receding slowly, and he straightened, touching the back of his head once more, searching for a wound. Nothing. "Damn," he muttered.

"What happened?" Yakov asked.

"I don't know," Turcotte said, "but I hope it doesn't happen again."

GULF OF MEXICO

Garlin looked at the metal sphere, turning it this way and that. Four extremely thin wires dangled from it, coated in blood. He carefully placed the sphere in a small cup, then turned back to the table. Certain Duncan was once more alive, he went back to the Ark and put his bloodstained hands on the controls. The second hole hadn't even finished healing as he began to probe once more.

Duncan didn't regain consciousness immediately, the trauma too great and overwhelming, even to her subconscious. The gift of immortality could keep her alive, but it couldn't help her deal with the pain and horror of what was being done to her. In a most primitive way, her mind was trying to protect her consciousness from what was happening.

The mental probe from the Ark of the Covenant went into Duncan's mind, traveling along the pathways of the nervous system, searching for images of her ship. The shunt kept blood flowing even as the conditioned flesh gave way once more.

The screen came to life with a new image.

The two standing stones and lintel were now part of a

circle of similar stones. Five sets of two upright, each topped
with a lintel stone. And around them a continuous circle of
lintel stones on top of smaller upright ones. It was obvious
that the site had been ravaged at some time, as some of the
stones were cast over, including one right next to the gate.
Garlin's mind recognized the structure, but the Swarm tentacle was too focused on what was being shown to pick up the
message.

Duncan was twisting on the table, pushing hard against
the straps holding her down. Her face was taut with agony,
her skin paler than usual as the alien virus strove to replace
the vast quantities of blood she had lost.

On the screen there was a paved road near the stones, indicating it was from a more recent memory. Garlin was leaning
forward. There was a sign on a post. It came into focus and he
could read the letters:

STONEHENGE

Garlin immediately shut down the Ark of the Covenant.
He removed the crown from Duncan's head. He then connected the table with Duncan to the Ark table and released
the brakes on the wheels on the bottom of both. He slowly
pushed both into the corridor and back into the escape pod.

Inside the chamber, the Swarm began preparing the pod
for launch.

The sniper had been on the derrick towering high over the
abandoned oil platform in the middle of the Gulf of Mexico
for several hours now with no sign of Simon Sherev or his
fellow Israeli commandos. He had the muzzle of the Heckler
& Koch PSG-1 resting on a railing, aimed at the elevator
where the men had gone carrying the Ark of the Covenant.

He knew something had gone wrong. Sherev and the others had been gone too long without updating him on the situ-

ation. His options, however, were limited. Entering the elevator to go after them was not a good idea. If whoever was down there had overpowered Sherev and the five commandos, the sniper knew he stood little chance of surviving. So he waited and watched. He'd made a radio call on the emergency frequency, detailing what little he knew, but he had no idea if the message had been picked up.

Three hundred feet below him, on the Gulf floor, a black sphere fifteen feet in diameter separated from the undersea habitat and began moving to the east underwater, slowly reducing depth until a mile from the platform it broke the surface and moved through the air, staying low, less than ten meters above the wave tops.

The sniper saw the black sphere but it was already out of range and moving away. He had no doubt that it was not of human origin. Cursing, he reached for the radio on his combat vest. It was FM, which meant it didn't have much range, so there was no way he could make contact with Israel. However, he felt that he had to make some sort of effort to inform someone of the location of the Ark and what he had just seen. He switched to the emergency shipping frequency for the area and began to broadcast once more, hoping someone would be close enough to pick him up.

HAWAII

The mothership was empty except for Turcotte and Yakov. They ignored entreaties from various officials to speak to them as Turcotte lifted the craft into the sky and turned to the east to head toward the mainland. His head still hurt, but nothing like it had. It was more like a strong headache now, and given all he had been through the past few weeks, not something he paid much attention to.

The adrenaline rush of saving those on Easter Island—and

the Pacific Rim—was wearing off and the exhaustion from his Everest experience was once more taking over. Turcotte felt as if he would never be rested or feel up to strength again. He knew he needed to call Quinn and see what the latest information was. Hopefully Space Command was tracking Aspasia's Shadow's Talon in addition to Artad's. At the moment, Turcotte truly could care less about either.

Where was Duncan? Was she in the Gulf of Mexico? Turcotte wondered why he cared anymore. She had lied to him, manipulated him into getting involved in the entire Area 51 fiasco in the first place. And Aspasia's Shadow's pointed references to his own past being a lie—Turcotte felt a surge of anger. All the lies, all the deaths, and there was still so much unknown, buried underneath a mountain of deception.

The West Coast of the United States appeared on the horizon. Turcotte spotted two F-16s to the south, turning in his direction. He knew the military was still jittery and the world wasn't completely at peace yet.

Turcotte keyed the mike. "Quinn, inform the Pentagon we're entering US airspace with the mothership."

"Roger that."

"Do you have anything for me?"

"A sniper on an oil rig in the Gulf of Mexico has reported a craft coming out of the water and flying away to the northeast."

"Is Space Command tracking it?"

"I've sent an alert—nothing back yet."

"What else?" Turcotte adjusted course, turning more to the east from south as he realized there was no longer any need to head to the oil rig.

"I've got some interesting stuff both on Tunguska and a man named Tesla."

" 'Tesla'?" Yakov repeated the name. "The Kurd at Ararat mentioned that name."

"He seems to be connected with the event at Tunguska," Quinn said.

"Connected how?" Turcotte asked.

"From what I've been able to find," Quinn said, "I think he may have shot down the Swarm scout ship."

CHAPTER 10: THE PRESENT

AIRSPACE ENGLISH CHANNEL

The Swarm pod was less than five meters above the wave tops and practically invisible in the darkness. Lisa Duncan was still securely strapped to the gurney, no longer connected to the Ark of the Covenant. Crammed in next to the tables was Garlin, hunched over and waiting.

The pod flew over the southern English shoreline between Weymouth and Bournemouth, the lights of both cities clearly visible on either side. It raced over eastern Dorset until it reached the Salisbury Plain, where it reduced speed. Its objective was outlined ahead by several lights, but there didn't appear to be anyone about—not unexpectedly, given the early hour.

A solitary set of headlights raced along a nearby road, then disappeared in the distance. The pod moved forward until it was directly above the lit area. It paused there, scanning the ground with penetrating radar, which revealed nothing, then moved to the northeast and slowly settled on the grassy plain, just outside a fence surrounding the compound.

SPACE COMMAND, CHEYENNE MOUNTAIN

Mary Keene had volunteered to work an extra shift so that some of her married colleagues who had been on extra duty during the recent world war could go home and see their families. What she hadn't told her supervisor was that she didn't want to go home because she was afraid of what messages she might find there. Her only daughter was in the army and had been stationed in Seoul, South Korea. She'd seen the images downloaded from the spy satellites of what had happened to that city.

As long she didn't know for sure, it wouldn't be true. Keene couldn't bear to think about it, so she focused on her screens with more attention than usual. She was inside one of the metal buildings set on heavy springs deep inside the complex. She was among a dozen operators watching their screens at a long, curved table.

Her area of observation was the North Atlantic, a region that had seen relatively little action given recent world events. She had access to three KH-14 spy satellites that observed from the East Coast of the United States to the West Coast of Europe.

She sat up straighter as she noticed activity. A very fast thermal trace, arcing from the Gulf of Mexico, across the Atlantic, across the coast of England came to an abrupt halt in southern England. Keene accessed her computer, correlated the stopping point, and discovered there was no airfield in that location. It couldn't have been a helicopter—it had moved too quickly and too far. In fact, as she entered the flight data, it had moved too quickly to be a top-of-the-line military jet.

That left the bouncers. She—and others at Space Command—had seen tracks of the alien craft prior to the truth about Area 51 being revealed, but every time they brought them to the attention of their supervisors, they were told to ignore them.

After the truth about what was at Area 51 was revealed, she had also tracked them occasionally. But this track, while similar, was somewhat different on the thermal readout. Hotter.

She also remembered that an alert had been circulated for information on any unusual flights in the Gulf of Mexico region.

She checked the alert list and noted that Area 51 was listed as the source of that alert, with contact information via MILSTAR. She hit the access code. The other end buzzed repeatedly, with no answer, and after thirty seconds she was about to cut the connection when a distracted voice came out of her speaker box.

"Major Quinn here. What?"

"Do you have a bouncer on a transatlantic flight?"

"Negative. What have you tracked?"

Keene relayed the information.

"You say it came from a location in the Gulf of Mexico?"

"Yes, sir."

"Where is it fixed now?" Quinn asked.

While she was talking, Keene had been zeroing in the nearest KH-14 for an exact location. She brought up the ground mapping for the area and mixed the two on her screen. What she saw surprised her. The spot was marked with red writing, indicating it was of national significance.

"South, middle, England. It's at Stonehenge."

STONEHENGE

Stonehenge was just off the M-43—the biggest tourist attraction in the immediate area, and one of the largest in all of England. The Swarm pod was just to the northeast, simply observing for a while before moving in. A good scout always reconnoiters before approaching a target, and the Swarm had a great deal of experience at scouting, whether on the galactic or local scale.

When the Swarm was satisfied that the area appeared to be safe and deserted, the pod moved forward. It hit the fence and tore through easily. It came to a halt just at the edge of the inner circle, in front of the altar stone. Unknown to the Swarm, an alarm system built into the fence was activated, and a warning light went off at the local constabulary.

Inside the pod, Garlin had put the crown back on Duncan's head during the recon and hooked it up to the Ark leads.

The ground-penetrating radar hadn't revealed the presence of the craft that had been displayed in Duncan's memory. However, during the probing of Duncan's memories, the Swarm had noted the red netting that had been spread over the surface of the spaceship before it was buried and had to assume that it was some sort of shielding.

The issue was how to get into the stone elevator.

Garlin directed the probe into Duncan's mind, searching for more memories of when she had come here in the past.

The screen flickered, then came alive with an image. Stonehenge. The circles intact, indicating it to be thousands of years ago. It was nighttime, but the stones were bathed in a red glow. Several hundred meters beyond the stones, a massive wicker figure was burning. It was over fifty feet high and made of wicker branches woven onto a stronger wooden frame. Stuffed inside were dozens of people, screaming as the flames ate at their skin.

In a circle around the burning "man" were hundreds, if not thousands of people dressed in various-colored robes, watching the horrific display, the glow flickering off their rapt faces. At the back edge of the crowd were two people, edging away, heading toward Stonehenge. They were alone when they reached the monument and threw back their hoods. Duncan and her partner. She walked up to the left standing stone in the center of the complex and put her right hand out, pressing it against a spot on the stone, and the door appeared, opening.

Garlin disconnected the leads, the screen going black.

Looking down, he could see that Duncan was conscious for the first time in quite a while, her dark eyes staring at him. Her body had had enough time during the flight to recover from the damage that he had inflicted on her.

"Who are you?" Her voice was rough, her throat parched and ragged from her earlier screams. Her eyes were deep-set, weary, and worn, the memories of the pain etched on her face.

Garlin didn't answer. He reached down and tightened the strap around her right hand, pinning it securely to the table palm up.

"What are you doing?" she asked.

Garlin remained silent as he turned to the black bag and pulled out a strange-looking device, the key feature of which was a long, thin blade. He pressed a button and the blade began moving back and forth a very short distance, picking up speed until it became a blur. Duncan's eyes grew wide as he turned toward her and lowered the device toward her hand.

"Don't!" she yelled.

With a blur of flying blood, flesh, and bone, Garlin pressed it down against the wrist. Duncan's undulating scream echoed through the pod. In less than four seconds, an eternity for Duncan, the blade had cut completely through. Blood spurted out of the arteries that had been severed, and Garlin didn't bother to make any attempt to stem its flow.

He released the button, and the only sound was Duncan's pained moaning. He put the machine down and picked up her severed right hand. A section of the outer wall of the pod opened, lowered to the ground, formed a ramp, and Garlin walked out.

Behind him, Lisa Duncan lay on the table, hovering between consciousness and unconsciousness, her lips moving in a wordless babble. Blood no longer surged out of the severed artery at the end of her right arm as the virus sealed the wound. Slowly, the body began to regenerate the lost appendage.

Constable Martaugh quietly cursed as he drove the police Land Rover along the M-34 toward Stonehenge. The security system had been put into the fence by a private organization to help deter young revelers who often congregated at the monument late at night, drinking, carousing, and, in some cases, damaging the stones with graffiti. Martaugh had already run them off twice this month.

If he caught those damn kids again—Martaugh spun the wheel, directing his car onto the turnoff. He didn't mind them having fun, it was the desecration of the stones that bothered him. He'd lived here all his life and like most who'd spent their time near the henge, he'd always felt a reverence for the stones. Locals cared little when they were built or who had built them—the important thing was that they were here.

When his headlights illuminated the crushed fence, his foot instinctively went to the brake and the car quickly came to a halt. He blinked as he noted the large round orb floating a few feet off the ground near the inner circle. There was a man walking toward the center stones. And he was carrying something. Martaugh began to open the car door when the man lifted the object and placed it against the left upright stone, then the policeman recognized it: a severed human hand.

Martaugh ducked back into the car and grabbed for his radio, missing the mike on his first attempt, then fumbling with it for a few seconds. During that time everything went from the bizarre to the surreal, as a door opened in the stone and the man walked in, the door shutting behind him. For a moment Martaugh held the mike in his hand, not sure if he had seen what had just happened or if this was some nightmare he was acting out. But the large round black orb still floated a few feet above the ground not far from him.

Martaugh pressed the key on the mike.

CAMP ROWE, NORTH CAROLINA

The mothership was a black mass against a dark, overcast night sky as it descended onto the old airstrip. The Delta Force commandos stared in awe as it came to a hover, the bottom of it just a few feet above the pitted concrete. A cargo door near the front slid open and a metal gangway extended down to the ground. A green glow highlighted the opening and silhouetted two men as they exited the craft. One was huge, towering over his partner, but the smaller man walked with an air of confidence, despite shoulders stooped in exhaustion. It was the same silent confidence all the Delta men guarding the location had.

Major Quinn felt a wave of relief, recognizing Yakov and Turcotte. The relief turned to concern as the two came into the circle of light surrounding the hangar. Both men looked haggard, Turcotte particularly so. There were blisters on his face from the cold, his eyes were bloodshot, and he had gray stubble across his chin. He was absently rubbing the back of his head.

"I think we've found Duncan," Quinn led with.

Turcotte didn't react as the major had expected. No smile, no lifting of the weariness. "Where?"

"Stonehenge."

Turcotte didn't stop walking, heading past Quinn, Yakov at his shoulder, and into the hangar. Turcotte slumped into a folding chair and Yakov did the same. A soldier came over with a steaming cup of coffee, which Turcotte gratefully accepted. His hands cradled the warm cup and he leaned over, his nose just above it, breathing in deeply.

"Stonehenge? England?" Turcotte finally looked up. "How do you know?"

Quinn knelt in front of Turcotte and spoke softly and slowly. "A craft was tracked from the Gulf of Mexico to Stonehenge. It was too fast to be a jet. Strange thermal signature. They thought it was a bouncer, but all are accounted for. On top of all of that, we got a call from an Israeli sniper who said Sherev took the Ark of the Covenant to an oil rig in the Gulf of Mexico. And something, some sort of pod, took off from underneath the rig and flew away to the northeast not long ago. Now whatever took off there is at Stonehenge."

Turcotte had closed his eyes halfway through Quinn's explanation. "Sherev is dead then?"

"I don't know—" Quinn began, but Turcotte held up a hand, halting him.

"Why Stonehenge?"

"We don't know."

Turcotte slowly turned half-lidded eyes toward Yakov. One eyebrow lifted very slightly. The Russian was leaning back in his seat, long legs sticking out.

"Does anyone have some vodka?" Yakov asked. When there was no answer he let out a deep sigh and got to his feet. "You Americans are never properly equipped. I assume we must go to England."

Turcotte also stood. "Call the Brits," he said to Quinn as he headed for the hangar door. "Get someone there. SAS if they can."

"Yes, sir."

Turcotte paused. "What about Tesla and Tunguska?"

"I've got quite a bit of information," Quinn said. "I also have some more info on the way here."

"Did Tesla shoot down a Swarm ship?"

"Yes. He invented—" Quinn began, but Turcotte held up a hand.

"One thing at a time. We're going to England to get Duncan. Then we'll be back. Have the Space Command guys here and ready to go when we return. And whatever Tesla invented—find someone who can duplicate it."

STONEHENGE, ENGLAND

Martaugh's tongue nervously snaked over his lips as he considered the scene in front of him. The black sphere hadn't moved and the ramp the man had obviously come out of was still down. There was no sign of the door the man had gone through in the standing stone. Martaugh had called it in, been acknowledged, then put the mike back and sat paralyzed for several minutes of indecision.

Martaugh slowly opened the door and went to the Land Rover's rear door. He lifted it open and retrieved an old Sterling submachine gun that had been issued to him during the recent turmoil. He grabbed a flak vest, put it on, then made sure he had a round in the chamber of the sub. He made his way forward, the stock of the Sterling tight against his shoulder. His eyes shifted between the ramp and the standing stone the man had entered.

He turned toward the ramp.

Colonel Spearson, British Special Air Service (SAS) was heading toward Stonehenge within ten seconds of receiving the alert from Quinn in America. He'd been with Turcotte in Ethiopia when they'd found the cavern with the ruby stone in it. He knew Turcotte was a solid soldier. A man you wanted by your side.

They'd already been in the air as part of a training mission south of Hereford, where the Twenty-first Regiment, which Spearson commanded, was headquartered. They were now heading southeast at the helicopter's maximum speed.

Spearson considered the message and the destination. Stonehenge. Perhaps the heart of ancient England. Predating all the others—the Tower, the kings, the queens, all of them. From before the time of Arthur even, who it now appears was of alien origin in some manner. Now something was there. Something unknown, tracked across the Atlantic. Most likely alien in origin. It bothered him greatly that the aliens seemed to have corrupted every legend and myth, even something as noble as Arthurian legend. And now they were at Stonehenge.

"Faster," Spearson ordered the pilot. In the rear of the Westland Lynx helicopter sat a dozen Special Air Service troopers. The elite of England's soldiers. They had weapons in their hands and steely looks in their eyes. They were all sick of it. Aliens. Servants of aliens. Humans being manipulated, infected, changed. They'd watched the reports of Taiwan being devastated, Seoul being assaulted first by North Korean chemical agents, then American nuclear bombs, and somehow they knew, they just knew that while humans had always fought among themselves, it was the aliens behind things. Acting from the darkness, from the shadows. And they were all sick of it.

AIRSPACE UNITED STATES

Turcotte was in the pilot's seat of the mothership racing across the Atlantic. How fast neither he nor Yakov knew, but the ocean far below was going by at a dizzying speed. Excalibur was leaning against the control console nearby.

"My friend," Yakov said.

"Yes?"

"Are you all right?"

"No."

"Me neither." Yakov placed a large hand on Turcotte's

shoulder. "Do not let what Aspasia's Shadow said cause you to doubt yourself."

Turcotte didn't respond, staring at the display screens.

Yakov didn't remove his hand. "And"—he drew the word out, sure he had Turcotte's attention—"as far as Ms. Duncan goes, you must remember that no matter what her past, she is different now even from the person you knew very briefly the last few months."

Turcotte nodded, very slightly. "I know."

"We sometimes do things when we are in stressful times," Yakov continued, "that in retrospect—"

Turcotte interrupted the Russian. "I know I wasn't thinking straight."

"Neither was I when I got involved with Katyenka," Yakov said, referring to the woman who had betrayed them in Moscow.

Normally Turcotte would have bridled at the comparison, but too much had happened in the past few days for him to argue anything. "I was a lumberjack."

Yakov removed his hand and sat down. "What?"

"I was a"—Turcotte hesitated—"a man who worked in the forest, cutting down trees."

"Ah, yes." Yakov waited.

"It always struck me as very strange what I did. Cutting down living things. Trees. Beautiful big trees. That had been there for much longer than I would be on Earth. The other guys didn't think like that—I don't know why I did. But then I would reconcile it with the thought that the wood would be turned into valuable things. A kid's bed, maybe." Turcotte gave a thin smile. "Bull, I know. But hey, I had to deal with it somehow. So I dealt with it."

"And this?"

"I don't know how to deal with it."

Yakov slammed a large open palm into Turcotte's chest.

"You're human." His hand thumped his own chest. "I'm human. That's it. That's all. I spent all my life, while you were cutting down these trees you care so much about, tracking these aliens and their creatures. They killed my friends, they destroyed my country. Destroyed many other countries and killed millions—billions of people most likely—over the thousands of years they have been here on our planet. We know they caused the Black Death. Tried to bring a version of it back that we were barely able to stop.

"All those years I spent in the dark, tracking them, I had to, how do you say, deal with it in some manner. Make my mind"—Yakov searched for the words—"wrap around what I was doing, understand it. Just as you had to understand what you were doing. And do you know what I decided? What it came down to?"

Turcotte shook his head.

"I am human," Yakov said. "They, and those who work for them, aren't."

"That simple?" Turcotte asked,

"It is that simple."

STONEHENGE

Martaugh slid his feet up the ramp. He didn't dare take a step, afraid his boot would make too much noise. He'd watched the BBC. He knew about the aliens, Area 51, the world war. Everyone did. He had no doubt somehow that this was involved. How he had no idea.

He moved inside. There was a green glow. Martaugh swallowed, but continued forward. The ramp went up to a metal door that was half-ajar. Using the muzzle of the Sterling, he slowly pushed the door open, revealing a chamber. The first thing he noticed was the pale woman covered with blood strapped to a gurney, her right arm ending in a stump.

"Good Lord," Constable Martaugh muttered.

He sensed, rather than heard, someone behind him and he swung about. His finger froze on the trigger the shock was so great. He saw it wasn't a person, but a thing, an unspeakable thing, even as the tentacle wrapped around his throat. He opened his mouth to scream, and that was a mistake.

AIRSPACE

The coast of England appeared ahead and Turcotte looked down at the GPS navigational screen to check their location and the direction to Stonehenge. He adjusted course and the mothership turned slightly to the left.

"One minute out," the pilot informed Spearson via the intercom.

The colonel pulled back the bolt on his MP-5 submachine gun and made sure a round was in the chamber. Seeing that action, the rest of the men in the helicopter's cargo bay did likewise.

The Lynx flared as it slowed, losing altitude.

"Talk to me," Spearson ordered the pilot, who he knew was flying with night-vision goggles and had a clear view of what was ahead. Spearson also had night-vision goggles attached to his helmet, but he couldn't see past the pilot.

"There's some sort of black sphere, about five meters in diameter, hovering just in front of the center ring of stones. There appears to be a doorway of some sort, emitting a green light. There's also a police Land Rover parked nearby. No sign of whoever drove it."

Black sphere? Spearson had kept up with the torrent of intelligence reports about the recent world war, fought primarily in the Pacific and Middle East and he could recollect no such description. Something new. Something different.

Spearson had been under fire many times, in Northern Ireland, during the Gulf War, in Ethiopia—but he felt a shiver of unease as the Lynx's skids hit the ground with a slight thump.

He didn't have to yell any commands. He knew the men would be right behind and spread out tactically. That was the difference between the SAS and a regular line unit. He ran from the chopper toward the black sphere, shoving his night-vision goggles down on their slot on his helmet. He blinked for a second as the darkness gave way to a bright green scene. The black sphere was perfectly still, hovering a few feet above the ground, part of the outer shell forming a ramp to the ground.

Spearson froze as a figure carrying a Sterling submachine gun came out of the opening. He had the muzzle of the MP-5 centered on the man, when he stopped his finger, just short of firing, as he recognized the uniform.

"Over there!" the constable yelled, pointing to the left, away from the monument.

Spearson turned, as did all his men. Nothing.

Spearson heard the sound of an automatic weapon going off as the first rounds hit him in the chest, knocking him backward. The police officer was moving toward the SAS troopers, weapon to his shoulder, firing.

Spearson landed on his back, his chest aching from the impact on his Kevlar vest. He lifted his head as his men returned fire. He watched in disbelief as the cop was riddled with bullets, yet kept firing. Two more SAS men went down, one fatally shot in the face.

The cop's weapon—an old Sterling, Spearson could see through the goggles—clicked on an empty chamber. The SAS troops kept firing, literally tearing the cop to pieces until his body collapsed.

Spearson got to his feet. One of his men ran forward and checked the body. Spearson indicated for the rest to follow him. He edged around so that he could see into the pod. A door blocked the way just inside.

"Blow it," Spearson ordered.

One of his men pulled a small shaped charge out of his pack and ran up to the door, placing it in the center. He pulled the fuse.

"Fire!" the demolitions man yelled as he exited the craft and dived for cover. Spearson hit the ground, tucking his head down. There was a sharp crack. He got up and cursed. Only a two-foot-wide hole had been blown in the door.

He heard shots behind him and spun about. The man who had been with the cop's body had shot another SAS trooper right in the face. The second man screamed, hands to his face, blood pouring between his fingers. The SAS man fired at his comrades, head shots as he'd been trained.

"Goddamn," Spearson cursed as two more of his men went down. He squeezed the trigger, the bullet hitting the man in the head, just above the right eye, below the edge of the helmet. Blood and brain flew out the exit wound in the back of his head. And still he fired. Another SAS man was down.

Spearson sensed something overhead, but didn't take the time to look up. He fired, pulling the trigger as quickly as he could, head shots all, hitting his own man repeatedly until he finally collapsed.

"What the hell was that, sir?" one of his few surviving men demanded as they converged on the body. It was unrecognizable. Spearson had literally blown the man's head off.

Spearson glanced up. The stars were gone.

Then he was blinded as a brilliant light filled the sky.

Turcotte was waiting right by the cargo door and as soon as Yakov opened it, he rushed down the still-extending gangway to the ground. He had an MP-5 in one hand and Excalibur in the other. The Russian must have also found some way to illuminate the ground below, because it was as bright as if it were high noon.

Turcotte took in the tableau. The large stones were right in front of him, the black pod, a Land Rover, bodies. A few men in uniform still standing, ripping off overloaded night-vision goggles. He recognized one of the men—Spearson—from the mission in Ethiopia.

"Colonel," Turcotte called out as he headed for the SAS commander.

Spearson blinked, trying to reorient himself, still confused and dismayed by the insane actions of his own man.

"Colonel, what do you have?" Turcotte was next to him, noting the bodies. "What happened?"

Spearson shook his head, confused and shocked. "I don't know. The police officer shot at us. Then one of my men—I don't know why."

Turcotte looked down at the headless body. Something was stirring in the area of the stub of the spinal column that poked above the neck. Something gray.

"What the hell is that?" Spearson took a step back.

The three-fingered tip of a Swarm tentacle emerged, grasping, searching for a new host. It was slithering out of the body, a foot now exposed. Turcotte swung Excalibur and sliced the tentacle in two, just below the "fingers." The severed portion fell to the ground, and then began to "melt," producing a foul smell.

"What the hell is that?" Spearson demanded.

Turcotte ignored the question. "Duncan? Have you seen Dr. Duncan?"

Spearson shook his head, still staring where the tentacle had been. "We just got here. The copper shot at us. Then my man went crazy. What *was* that thing in him? What is going on?"

Turcotte continued to ignore the questions, as there was

no time to explain. He moved toward the pod, both weapons
at the ready. It didn't even occur to him to feel strange holding an ultramodern submachine gun in one hand and a legendary sword in the other. He stepped onto the pod ramp and
saw the hole that had been blasted in it. He paused for a moment, then leaned over and poked his head inside. The skin
on the back of his neck prickled as he waited for a tentacle to
lash out at him. In the green glow he saw Duncan strapped to
a table. He took in the massive amounts of blood under and
around her; the half-regenerated hand; the Ark of the
Covenant on a table next to her along with the crown.

Duncan turned her head and met his gaze. Turcotte could
see the pain in her eyes.

"Mike." She said it so softly, Turcotte wasn't sure whether
there was an actual word or he was interpreting the way her
lips moved.

"I'll get you out of there," Turcotte said. The hole was too
small for him to fit through. He would need more demolitions.

"Mike."

He definitely heard her this time. He took a quick look
around, half-expecting to see one of the creatures he and
Yakov had found in the ruins of Section IV. "What?"

"I'm sorry."

Turcotte staggered as the pod moved beneath his feet. "I'll
get you out." He wondered if it were taking off. He pulled his
head out of the hole and stepped back. It wasn't the pod. It
was the ground itself moving. The nearest standing stones
were leaning precariously. A lintel stone fell off, slamming
into the ground with a loud thud. Spearson was yelling orders, ordering his men to pull back.

Turcotte turned back to pod, just as the door he was standing on began to lift. He knew he had just a few seconds. "I'll
be back!" he yelled toward the opening, then he dived to the

side, narrowly avoiding being crushed as the door sealed. The pod rose and moved to the side, out of the way of the hovering mothership. It stopped about fifty yards away.

Turcotte stood, then had to dash out of the way as another tall stone came crashing down, missing him by a few inches. He felt the rush of air displaced by the stone as it hit the ground with a solid thud.

Turcotte's fingers scrambled to grab hold of solid ground, but the dirt was sliding away beneath him. Then he felt metal, warm metal, which was strange. The mothership overhead was still illuminating everything and he looked down. Gray metal. More and more of it. The surface Turcotte lay on was slightly curved. He realized he was on some sort of craft, a type which he hadn't seen before. And it was going up.

On all fours, Turcotte scuttled toward the edge he could see about ten yards away. He heard a loud, echoing thud, which he could only imagine was one of the standing stones falling onto the skin of the craft.

By the time he made it to the edge, the craft was clear of the ground. It was saucer-shaped with a large protrusion near the front and two more near the rear. Turcotte didn't spend much time checking it out. He gathered himself and jumped off, the airborne training he'd received at Fort Benning so many years ago taking over. Black Hats with megaphones yelling: Feet and knees together, knees bent, arms tucked. Hit. Roll.

Turcotte lay on his back and saw the outline of the strange craft against the mothership's lights. Then it darted off to the west, the Swarm pod following.

CHAPTER 11: THE PRESENT

EARTH ORBIT

Artad stepped up, placing the front of his feet into the toe openings in the front half of the space suit and pressing himself against the interior padding. The rear half swung forward, locking shut. He scanned the display just below his visor, making sure all systems were working correctly.

The report from the scouts he had sent over to the derelict mothership had intrigued him. He felt little sense of time pressure as the last reports he had checked indicated the array on Mars was not yet completed. The humans might attempt to fly the mothership to Mars, but then what? He doubted they had more than the most rudimentary understanding of the craft. In fact, as he considered the options, he hoped the humans *would* fly the mothership there, so he could assault it and regain control. That would look much better when the fleet arrived. He paused—certainly it would be better to send the first message with the mothership under his control. As it stood now, he was calling for help in a situation that had gotten far out of control.

Secure in the suit, he went to the Talon's airlock. Locking one door behind, he waited as the outer door slid open. They were adjacent to the main cargo bay of the mothership. A massive explosion had torn the doors off and ripped a quarter-mile-long gash along the side of the craft. Artad jetted across to the larger ship. Entering the large cargo bay, the first thing he noted was the devastation. While the rip in the outer hull was bad, the interior had been gutted, as the interior bulkheads weren't quite as strong as the external skin.

There were also the smashed remains of several Talon craft—Aspasia's fleet from Mars. Artad headed toward one of the Talons, where several of his suited Kortad waited for him. They shepherded him inside, through a hatch and into a corridor. There were several Airlia bodies floating inside, perfectly preserved by the vacuum of space. Artad ignored them, even though he recognized some, as one of his Kortad led him forward to the control room.

A half dozen dead Airlia were strapped to their chairs. They weren't even in their space suits, indicating they had met disaster unexpectedly.

And in the command seat—Aspasia.

Artad came to a halt in front of his old nemesis. Over ten thousand years had passed since they had first fought. Their Shadows and their followers had continued the fight through the millennia. He had never expected that it would end like this, with Aspasia dead by human hand, depriving him of his revenge.

Artad reached a gloved, six-fingered hand forward and grasped Aspasia's chin. He lifted the drooping head. The red eyes were cloudy, vacant.

Artad turned his head toward another Airlia body, behind Aspasia's, still holding his adversary's chin. A female. Artad's fingers tightened on Aspasia's chin, digging into the dead flesh. He remembered her. Remembered when she had left on the mission to this forsaken corner of the universe. Remembered their time together so long ago.

His arm jerked, snapping Aspasia's neck.

Artad looked once more at the female's body, and then turned for the exit. Without a backward glance he departed.

•   •   •

MARS

Mars Pathfinder was launched on December 4, 1996. On July 4 the following year, Pathfinder reached Mars, taking an orbit that did not overfly or even come close to Cydonia. The lander entered the atmosphere and five miles from the surface its parachute deployed. Sixty-nine feet above the surface near Ares Vallis, the parachute was cut loose and Pathfinder, surrounded by airbags, fell to the surface and bounced. It continued bouncing for over half a mile before coming to a halt. The airbags deflated.

Four petal-like blue solar panels slowly unfolded. A weather mast extended upward along with the IMP, the Imager for Mars Pathfinder. Resting on one of the solar panels was a small vehicle, the Sojourner Truth, named for a nineteenth-century African-American antislavery crusader. The Rover was twenty-six inches long by nineteen inches wide and twelve inches high, weighing in at twenty-two pounds.

As dawn came to Mars on July 5, 1997, the IMP, which actually had two slightly offset cameras that produced a three-dimensional image when used together, took the first pictures of the surface of the planet from the surface. Sojourner's wheels, retracted while in transit, slowly extended and locked into place. It rolled down onto the Martian surface, the first human moving vehicle on another planet since the last Apollo missions to the moon. Sojourner moved about sixteen inches to a rock, which controllers had given the name Barnacle Bill, and analyzed it using the APXS, Alpha Proton X-Ray Spectrometer. The APXS bombarded the rock with alpha particles and measured the radiation that bounced back. The resulting data was relayed to Pathfinder, which then transmitted it back to Earth. Analyzing the results, scientists were able to get a very good idea of the rock's composition.

One of the problems with moving Sojourner about was that it took two and a half minutes for images and data to make it to Earth and then the same amount of time for controlling information to be sent the other way. Thus, the controllers only could see where the vehicle had been and had to plan future movements very carefully. So fascinated was the American public with this accomplishment that forty-four million people logged onto NASA's web site the first day Sojourner moved.

Designed to last only seven days, Sojourner continued to function well past that limit. In August it was moved to a spot about thirty-three feet away, where it measured the composition of several rocks. On September 26, with power indications down to 30 percent, Sojourner was sent off on its greatest journey, a 165-foot trek around the Pathfinder lander. However, the next day, the signal from both Sojourner and the Pathfinder lander were lost. Scientists believed that the onset of the Martian autumn had caused Pathfinder's temperature to fall below the point where the transmitter could function.

Still, scientists continued for several weeks to send orders to Sojourner, on the chance that while it could not relay data back through Pathfinder, it still might be able to receive orders and function with power from the solar panels.

Unknown to the scientists, their orders were indeed relayed through Pathfinder to Sojourner, and it continued its journey, moving across the Martian surface at a very slow pace, using the rudimentary laser guidance system that allowed it to avoid obstacles directly ahead. Sojourner traveled almost a quarter of a mile, over four hundred yards away from the lander, before its batteries finally gave out. It came to a halt in the center of an open area, a small symbol of mankind's ability to travel to other worlds.

It was still dead in that spot years later when a plume of red dust on the horizon indicated something was headed toward it. The main Airlia convoy was almost to the base of Mons Olympus. Miles behind it, the vehicle that had recovered the crystal from the rubble of the Face hurried to catch up. Huge treads tore into the Martian landscape, spewing a long plume of red dust behind them.

A track pad on the Airlia vehicle approaching was larger than the entire Rover.

And one of those track pads ground the Rover into the Martian soil as a man might step on an ant without noticing.

The Pathfinder lander, a quarter mile away, wasn't even noticed as the Airlia crew hurried to catch up with the rest of the convey headed toward Mons Olympus.

AIRSPACE SOUTHERN UNITED STATES

Aspasia's Shadow had the Talon flying at an altitude of over eighty thousand feet, well above the paths crisscrossed by commercial airlines, as he pondered his current situation. He wasted no time on anger or regrets, but simply reviewed the facts.

The nanovirus no longer functioned, and those who had once been his unwilling slaves were now free.

By his own hand Easter Island was no more.

The Mission in Mount Sinai was crawling with Israeli forces.

Aspasia had died in space.

Artad was free, currently being tracked in a Talon by the humans, apparently on his way to Mars.

Aspasia's Shadow had lost much. And all he had was a Talon, incapable of warp speed.

Unacceptable.

Aspasia's Shadow had known that even as he made the deal. He would not spend eternity slowly flying between star systems at sub–light speed. He would not do so even in suspended sleep. He had waited too long to accept such a fate.

He still had some options. The Guides. He had recruited many people over the years, bringing them to Sinai and forcing them to make direct contact with the guardian. The machine had literally "rewired" their brains to make them his servants without the necessity of infecting them with the nanovirus. And since the programming was imprinted on their minds, it would still function even without Aspasia's Shadow having control of a guardian. He had sent these people back to wherever they had come from, agents ready to do his bidding when given the proper code word.

Always have a backup plan. That was a lesson Aspasia's Shadow had learned over the millennia in his various reincarnations. The ultimate backup had always been to have a cloned body in the *ka* tube and his memories up to his last visit loaded into the computer. Thus if he were somehow killed, as had happened on occasion, the *ka* machine would activate on a preset date, load memories into the clone, and he would be "alive" once more. Of course whatever had happened from the last time he updated the machine until his "death" would be lost, but he had always tried to keep the machine relatively current, rarely letting more than ten years elapse before an update. The Israelis controlled the machine now, as it was deep inside the base at Mount Sinai, but that didn't concern Aspasia's Shadow at the moment. He had something much better as the ultimate backup— immortality.

He also had a backup emergency plan for support in case things went terribly wrong, which they had. Aspasia's

Shadow checked his location. He was over west Texas, where the Rio Grande took a long turn, near Big Bend National Park.

He dropped the Talon down through the atmosphere at high speed, decelerating only when he was just above the desert floor. There were no lights in sight, no sign of civilization. That wasn't unusual, as Big Bend was the least visited national park in the United States, sprawling across over eight hundred thousand acres. The Indians had called the area the Great Spirit's rock storage facility, giving one an idea of the terrain. The early Spanish explorers had called it El Despoblado, the uninhabited land.

The Talon landed at the base of Chilicota Mountain, a four-thousand-foot-high mountain with no road within forty miles. Once the Talon was securely on the ground, Aspasia's Shadow turned on a strobe light near the top of the vessel. The beacon flashed across the darkened terrain, visible for over thirty miles where it wasn't obstructed by the mountain.

Then Aspasia's Shadow leaned back in the command chair and waited.

TRIPLER ARMY MEDICAL CENTER, OAHU, HAWAII

A steady stream of doctors entered the room, checked the charts, examined the patient, then left. Not because they thought that there was anything more any of them could do, but because no one could believe she was still alive, and they had to see with their own eyes.

Kelly Reynolds weighed about eighty pounds, a significant drop from her normal 165. Simply getting intravenous feeds into her emaciated body had proven an almost impossible task. But since there was no other way to get essential nourishment into her body, the doctors had persisted until finally they had two lines directly into arteries.

She had not regained consciousness since being transported here from Easter Island and there was little hope she would. Not a single one of the doctors who were amazed she was alive was willing to wager that she would still be in a few days. She had lost too much critical body mass and there was too much damage to vital organs. They couldn't explain why she wasn't dead already.

But she lived. And one nurse on the intensive care ward thought differently than the doctors. Terry Cummings had worked at Tripler for over thirty-five years. She'd cut her teeth on the planeloads of wounded brought in from Vietnam near the end of that war. She'd seen people who should have lived give up and die and she'd seen those the doctors had written off fight their supposedly fatal wounds and live.

She believed Kelly Reynolds was one of the latter. After all, she'd survived so far. That indicated a strong will. So while the doctors gaped at the bony body and shook their heads, Cummings treated her as a person, holding her hand, talking to her even though there was no reply.

Deep in her mind, in the part she had escaped to when hooked up to the Easter Island guardian, Kelly Reynolds was more than alive, she was thinking. Reviewing the torrent of data she'd accumulated while in symbiosis with the guardian. So much history, most of it very different than what she had learned in school or read in books.

And the beginnings of it all, going back to the time when the Airlia first arrived on the planet. The guardian had shown her some of that, but every time her mind went to it, she recoiled, terrified of seeing the truth. And because of that, she couldn't break through the coma she was in.

STONEHENGE

Turcotte stared at the crater in which the massive stones that had once formed Stonehenge lay tossed like a child's building blocks after a tantrum. He keyed his radio.

"Yakov?"

"Yes?"

"Where are the two craft?"

"They headed off to the southwest. I've contacted Major Quinn and told him to get your Space Command to track them as much as they can."

"I saw Duncan."

There was only static in reply.

"I couldn't save her. The Swarm still has her. She looked to be in pretty bad shape. One hand had been cut off. She said she was sorry."

Yakov finally replied. "For?"

"I don't know."

"We need to go," Yakov said. "Come on board."

Turcotte turned and saw the gangplank extending from the mothership. Spearson was ordering his men to make a perimeter around the site. The SAS colonel came over to Turcotte.

"What just happened?"

"I don't know." Turcotte had neither the time nor the inclination to explain the Swarm and Duncan or Mars. "I have to go."

"Do you need help?" Spearson asked.

Turcotte gave a tired smile. "I appreciate the offer. But the next battle isn't going to take place here"—he pointed down—"but rather there"—he pointed up.

AIRSPACE NORTH ATLANTIC

The pod hung in the air next to the spaceship five thousand feet above the ocean, hidden in the darkness. A hatch on the top of the spaceship opened and Garlin climbed out onto the craft, moving carefully but with no safety line. He moved to the center of the top of the ship and waited as the pod maneuvered closer. He stepped back as the pod descended and landed on the top of the ship itself. Garlin then opened a couple of small hatches on the deck of the ship, retrieved high-tensile mooring lines, and secured the pod to the ship.

The ramp on the side of the pod came down and Garlin entered. He soon exited with Duncan in his arms. He carried her into the ship, tying her down in one of the seats inside. He then made a second trip, dragging the Ark of the Covenant on board. On his third he brought the priest's garments and crown. The pod sealed and Garlin reentered the spaceship, shutting the hatch behind.

The spaceship slowly accelerated, heading upward, passing through the atmosphere until it was in Earth orbit. Once more the hatch on the pod opened. The Swarm orb, with only two full-sized tentacles attached, now moved.

No intelligent species in the cosmos knew the origin of the Swarm. Scientists of those races that survived contact with the species and managed to inspect the corpses recovered after battle had only been able to determine a few things. One was that the orb was basically a large skull containing a massive four-hemisphere brain. The tentacles contained a basic brain stem at the base that could communicate with the main brain when attached and control any organism it entered when separated. Another interesting thing that those species familiar with space travel had discovered was that it appeared as though the Swarm had developed in zero gravity.*An orb could move only with great difficulty on a planet's surface, and that required almost all tentacles to be attached.

However, in zero gravity, the Swarm could move swiftly and with great efficiency even with just one tentacle attached to the orb. It also could survive for a limited amount of time without oxygen. With eyes spaced equidistant around the body, the Swarm could navigate in any three-dimensional direction with equal dexterity and ease. There was no forward or back, up or down, for the Swarm. On those rare occasions in space battles where ships were boarded, the Swarm were vicious and practically unbeatable antagonists. There was some speculation among Airlia scientists that the Swarm had not evolved naturally, but rather were a race manufactured to be a weapon—one that had consumed its own originators and become a plague on the universe.

Here the task was simple. The Swarm crept along the surface of the spaceship until it reached the airlock. The hatch swung open and it entered, the hatch shutting behind it.

Inside, Lisa Duncan heard the outer hatch opening. She recognized where she was—the inside of her own spaceship. And she knew she was in space because of zero gravity. She was tied to a seat near the rear of the pilot's chamber. She was coated with dry blood, her hair in knotted tangles.

She turned her head as the inner hatch opened. The orb swung in smoothly. Duncan's skin crawled as she watched the grotesque creature. It floated to the seat next to where Garlin sat and grasped hold with one tentacle. After it settled into place, Garlin unbuckled from his seat and came over to Duncan.

"Are you there?" she whispered. "The real you?"

Garlin stared at her blankly for a moment, then opened the lid to the Ark of the Covenant. He picked up the crown and set it on Duncan's head.

"Haven't you got everything you need?" Duncan asked. "What more do you want?"

"We want to know why you came to this planet in this ship," Garlin said.

"Who was Garlin?" she asked. "I know you're in there somewhere, some part of you. Some human part."

"He is in here." Garlin pointed at his head. "But we control everything. You will get no aid from him."

"Why didn't you take me then?" Duncan was stalling, anything to keep it from activating the probing.

Garlin shook his head. "We can't. The virus that is in you. From the Airlia's Grail. It attacks anything that infiltrates the body." He turned to the Ark and put his hands on the controls.

Duncan screamed as the probe sliced into her brain.

BIG BEND NATIONAL PARK

Aspasia's Shadow had prepared this operation years earlier and had given the initial implementation order when he first arrived at Easter Island. It was one of many orders he had dispatched, unsure how many of them he would actually have to follow up on.

So he wasn't surprised as a dozen headlights appeared in the distance, heading toward his location. He'd planted thirty Guides, all ex-military, in sleeper cells here in this remote part of Texas to wait for his call, which he had hoped he would never have to make.

The twelve off-road vehicles drove up to the base of the Talon and the men exited. They pulled weapons and backpacks out of the trucks. Quietly they walked up the narrow stairs Aspasia's Shadow had extended from the Talon. Once all were inside, he shut the hatch and took off. For step two in his emergency plan.

CAMP ROWE, NORTH CAROLINA

Things were different. That was Turcotte's impression as Yakov brought the mothership down toward the side of the landing strip, where there was a large open field. There were many lights blazing and activity all over the place.

Helicopters flitted about, getting out of the way of the descending alien ship. A half dozen C-130 cargo planes were lined up off to one side.

As soon as Yakov brought the ship to a halt, just above the ground, the two walked back to the nearest hatch and exited. Turcotte carried Excalibur, wrapped in a cloth. Major Quinn was waiting, flanked by Colonel Mickall and another man wearing a very nice suit.

"Major Turcotte, Mr. Yakov"—Quinn had quickly stepped forward to make the introductions—"this is Deputy Secretary General Kaong, the new director of UNAOC."

Turcotte almost laughed. UNAOC—United Nations Alien Oversight Committee—had been practically a nonentity ever since it was formed after he and Duncan publicized what had been hidden at Area 51. Kaong had a very serious demeanor as he stiffly held out his hand. Turcotte shook it briefly.

"What can we do for you, Secretary Kaong?"

"We are trying to determine what threat remains," Kaong said. "We know that Aspasia's Shadow is still on the loose, as is Artad."

Turcotte tried to figure out if there was a tone of accusation in Kaong's voice. "Major Quinn could tell you more about that than me."

"What happened at Stonehenge?" Kaong asked. "We received only the barest sketch of details from the British. They aren't quite sure themselves."

"The Swarm recovered some sort of spaceship there," Turcotte said. He was looking about, over Kaong's shoulder, searching for the Space Command troops who should be here.

"And this Swarm's goal?" Kaong asked.

"I assume the same as Artad's. Get to Mars and take over the transmitter. Call home and ask for reinforcements."

"Most grave," Kaong said.

Turcotte brought his attention back to the United Nations representative, again not sure of his tone—was he being factitious? "Yeah. Grave. That's a good word to use."

"How can we help?"

Turcotte wondered where all this help had been while he was on Everest. "There's not much you can do right now." He turned to Quinn. "Are the Space Command people here?"

Quinn nodded. "A full team with equipment and TASC suits. Ready to go."

"And status of Artad's ship? The Swarm's?"

Quinn directed them toward the hangar. "Artad stopped at the derelict mothership for a while. His Talon only just left it about twenty minutes ago. Based on how long it took Aspasia to come here, we estimate around two days for him to reach Mars. The Swarm ship just broke orbit. We don't have a speed for it yet, so we don't know who will get to Mars first."

"And Aspasia's Shadow and *his* Talon?" Turcotte asked as they entered the hangar. He saw a man standing nearby wearing a black jumpsuit with the Space Command patch on the shoulder.

"We lost track of him somewhere over Texas."

That gave Turcotte pause. "Texas? He's not in space?"

"We haven't spotted anything else escaping the planet's gravity."

"Damn," Turcotte muttered. He slumped down in a chair. "All right. Talk to me about Tunguska and Tesla. I want to have something with a bit more punch than this"—he held up the sword—"when we go after them."

MARS

The Airlia convoy was well up on the hundred-mile-long ramp that led to and through the four-mile-high escarpment surrounding the Mons Olumpus Aureole. A long plume of red dust trailed behind the convoy. The actual cut in the escarpment, even with the ramp, was two miles deep, a testament to the efficiency and immense capabilities of the mech-machines. A dozen of those machines were scattered about in the midst of whatever task they had been about, their system crashing when the Cydonia guardian went off-line.

The lead vehicle cleared the escarpment and rolled onto the slope of Mons Olympus. The volcano was so large, that the angle of ascent was actually relatively gentle, only about five degrees. Far ahead, and near the summit, the arcs of two completed pylons and a third incomplete one were visible. And fifty miles behind the convoy, reaching the beginning of the ramp, was the trail vehicle carrying the core element of the transmitter.

CHAPTER 12: THE PRESENT

CAMP ROWE, NORTH CAROLINA

"Nikola Tesla." Quinn held up a black-and-white photograph of a young man with pale skin, dark hair parted in the middle, and sporting a thick mustache. "He was an electrical engineer and scientist who was born in 1856 and died in 1943. He's known for some very innovative work on electricity and magnetism." Quinn put the photo down and picked up another old black-and-white image, someone Turcotte recognized. A savage-looking man with scars on both cheeks and intense black eyes. "Tesla met Burton."

"How do you know that?" Turcotte demanded.

Quinn held up a leather-bound manuscript—the lost manuscript of Burton that Professor Mualama had tracked down. "It's in here."

Yakov spit. "Another thing Mualama didn't tell us."

"And?" Turcotte gripped the arms of his chair, trying to keep his anger toward the archaeologist under control. The man, after all, had been infected by a Swarm tentacle. His actions had not been of his own volition. And he had paid the ultimate price. Turcotte could still see the archaeologist tumbling from the face of Everest in his final act of resistance against the Swarm's attempt to use him to stop Turcotte from reaching Excalibur.

"I found a scholar who could translate Akkadian," Quinn continued, "and had her work on the manuscript via fax. Do you want Burton's words verbatim, or do you want my summary?"

"Summarize," Turcotte said, checking his watch.

"Burton was being chased by the Watchers, who were afraid his investigations might cause problems and upset the truce. Also, he was being tracked down by the Ones Who Wait and Aspasia's Shadow."

"Sounds like he wasn't making any friends," Yakov said.

"Because he thought for himself," Turcotte said. "That's been a rare commodity throughout history, it appears."

Quinn continued. "Shortly before his death, Burton ran into Tesla in Paris, acting on a tip he received. It turns out that Tesla was a member of a group that traced its beginning back to Myrddin—Merlin as he is more commonly known."

"But I thought Merlin had been a rogue Watcher?" Yakov pointed out. "A onetime thing?"

"True, Merlin was a rogue Watcher," Quinn said. "But it doesn't look like it was a onetime thing. It appears that Burton was occasionally aided by a clandestine group of rogue Watchers who actually claimed the mantle of being the *real* Watchers."

"What?" Turcotte asked irritably. Another thing that wasn't as it had originally appeared.

"Like the Roman Catholics and the Protestants," Quinn said, "it appears there was a schism among the ranks of the Watchers precipitated by Merlin's actions or perhaps even earlier. Burton himself wasn't really sure about the timing, but he does write that there was a split between those who believed in the original edict as decided at Avalon after the destruction of Atlantis, to remain a neutral group dedicated simply to watching, and a more progressive group, initiated perhaps by Merlin, that dedicated itself to more active measures against the aliens."

"They haven't been very helpful," Yakov muttered.

Quinn shrugged. "How do you know that?" He didn't wait for an answer. "Both sides of the Airlia have committed terrible atrocities against the human race over the millennia but we're still here. Maybe some of that is due to the active Watchers."

"Tesla. Burton." Turcotte shot the words out like bullets. If there had been active Watchers, it didn't appear they were still around—he checked that thinking. There had been the man in South America—whom Turcotte had thought a Watcher—who had warned of the plague the Mission had let loose. And the destruction of the shuttle Columbia. Perhaps Quinn was right—more had been going on behind the scenes than he realized.

"Burton wrote that Tesla was one of these rogue Watchers. Tesla questioned Burton about his expeditions to northern India. And he told Burton he had made contact with a guardian computer."

"Where?" Turcotte asked.

"Mount Ararat."

Yakov nodded. "The Kurds did say some people came there now and then. And if they had a Watcher ring or medallion, the Kurds would let them in the mothership cavern."

Turcotte leaned forward. "So Tesla found the mothership, got into it, and found the Master Guardian?"

"It appears so," Quinn said.

"Why?" Turcotte asked.

"To learn about the Airlia," Quinn said.

"To copy from them?" Yakov wondered.

Quinn shook his head. "Burton is pretty adamant that Tesla wanted nothing to do with taking knowledge from the Airlia. He wanted to learn about their technology in order to counter it."

Turcotte nodded. "Good. And?"

"That is all that's in the manuscript about Tesla," Quinn said. "Burton died—was killed, basically—by Aspasia's Shadow shortly after that meeting."

Turcotte rubbed his forehead, feeling the painful pounding of a growing headache. The back of his head still hurt and he wondered if he might have sustained some permanent damage from his time in the death zone on Everest. "OK. Exactly who was Tesla? And how is he connected to Tunguska and the Swarm scout? How did he shoot it down?"

"Nikola Tesla," Quinn said as he referred to his notes. "He was a Serb, born there in 1856. He was formally trained as an engineer. He came to America in 1884, arriving in New York City with just four cents in his pocket."

Yakov snorted. "Sounds like the typical American immigrant story."

"Tesla was anything but typical," Quinn said. "He went to work for Thomas Edison, but the two soon parted ways over differences of opinion. Edison was an advocate of direct current electricity and Tesla of alternating current. Tesla invented the induction motor, fluorescent lights, and many other things for which others took subsequent credit. However, his obsession was the wireless transmission of power."

Turcotte had never heard of either Tesla or his theories and inventions. Which was strange considering the everyday things Quinn was saying the man had invented. He thought of the alien shield and how it stopped power and—his train of thought came to a halt as Quinn continued.

"In 1899 Tesla moved to Colorado Springs. There he made a most strange discovery—terrestrial stationary waves."

"Which are?" Turcotte prompted.

"Tesla believed the Earth itself could be used as a conductor for electrical vibrations of a certain pitch. During his experiments he lit two hundred lamps *without* any wires between them and the power source, which was twenty-five miles away from the lamps. He also created man-made lightning. He even claimed to have received signals from another planet, a claim that was one of the many reasons he wasn't taken seriously despite an astounding list of inventions and accomplishments."

"That claim would be taken seriously now," Yakov noted.

"The bouncers," Turcotte realized. "The best Majestic could figure was that they used some sort of field that the planet itself generated, right?"

"Right," Quinn said. "I think Tesla was tapping into the same thing. In fact, I know that some of the scientists who Majestic brought in were using research that Tesla had done. I've back-checked and they were trying to make a connection between the Earth's magnetic field and the bouncer's propulsion system. Even more basic, they felt there was a tremendous amount of untapped energy in the Earth itself, deep beneath our feet."

"What else?" Turcotte asked.

"I just read Tesla's journal," Quinn continued.

"His journal?" Turcotte asked. "How did you get that?"

"Tesla died in New York City in 1943," Quinn said. "His notes and letters were in a large trunk, which became the property of his nephew"—there was a short pause as Quinn checked his notes— "one Sava Kosanovich, a citizen of Yugoslavia, where the trunk was shipped. It appears that somehow, at the end of the Second World War, the trunk fell into the hands of the intelligence arm of the military there."

"No surprise there," Yakov said. "Knowledge is power."

"Once you told me to check on him, I had a friend in the NATO peacekeeping forces in Sarajevo search the archives and find the trunk. Turns out in all the turmoil at the end of the Cold War a lot of material disappeared from the secret police files and ended up in the public domain. He e-mailed me a copy of the scanned journal just ten minutes ago."

"What did it say?" Turcotte asked.

"If you read between the lines concerning the supposed

messages from the planets, I think Tesla definitely tapped into either a guardian or transmissions between guardians."

"Go on," Turcotte said.

"He gained some understanding of how Airlia technology functioned and also saw that his own research was along similar lines. Because of his status as a rogue Watcher, he understood we—humans—needed weapons to counter the aliens. I think, perhaps, that is why many people have never heard of him—whereas Edison used his genius for practical inventions for day-to-day living, Tesla's focus was on something that has never been publicly acknowledged until recently. Because of that, he had to use misdirection when pursuing much of his work.

"Tesla worked on using his nonwire electrical beam transmission as a weapon. He went to New York in 1900 where, with the financial backing of J.P. Morgan, he began construction of what he said was a wireless broadcasting tower that could make contact around the world. It appears from reading his papers that Tesla was not entirely forthcoming to his financial backer. While the huge tower he was building at a place called Wardencliff could transmit radio waves, that was not its primary purpose.

"In his papers Tesla writes that he developed a wireless transmitter that could produce destructive effects at long distances using a certain frequency of radio wave propagated through the Earth itself. Indeed, he claimed he could touch any spot on the globe by sending a transmission through the planet, and even have the inherent energy inside the Earth magnify the power. He claimed that the high-end effect would be the equivalent of the detonation of ten megatons of TNT."

"Could this new form of power get through a shield wall?" Turcotte asked. "How powerful was it really?"

"Well—" Quinn paused. "That brings me to Tunguska."

Yakov cut in. "Do you remember General Hemstadt's last words to me on Devil's Island?"

"I remember you telling me he said something about Tunguska," Turcotte agreed.

"Yes," Yakov said. "We never really followed that up."

"We've been a bit busy saving the world," Turcotte said. "There was a file in the archives we recovered about a German expedition to Tunguska, wasn't there?"

"I have it here," Quinn said. "Part of what we were able to rescue from Area 51." He held up a thin leather portfolio with a swastika on the cover. "The report is dated 1934. In summary, it appears the Germans uncovered remains of an alien craft from Tunguska. That's where those creatures that Section IV had in the tank, the *Okpashnyi* came from, which we now know are Swarm. At the end of World War II, the Russians recovered what had been taken."

Turcotte suppressed a shudder as he remembered the strange object floating in the tank at the underground base on the island of Novaya Zemlya, where Russia's Area 51 had been. A central orb several feet in diameter and six arms separate from the main body. Each arm had been approximately six feet long, twelve inches thick at one end, tapering to three "fingers," each about six inches long. While the center orb had been yellowish, the arms had been grayish blue. There were lidded, protruding eyes spaced around the center orb.

Quinn's voice cut into Turcotte's remembering. "The Russians formally called it *Otdel Rukopashnyi* which means 'section of hands.' *Okpashnyi* was the shortened version. There were two recovered—one of which the Germans had done an autopsy on. They found that the center orb housed a four-hemisphere brain surrounded by a very hard skull. The arms, or legs, or tentacles, or whatever you want to call the six appendages, had a nervous system with a complex stem on the end that attached to the orb. The German scientists guessed that the arms were detachable and could function in some manner on their own, away from the orb or perhaps even mate with another orb, either in a sexual manner or to exchange information.

"The Germans took casualties on that mission," Quinn continued. "Five men dead. Cause—an alien infection after thawing out one of the *Okpashnyi* bodies. The Germans shot the men to stop the infection from spreading."

"Could one of the Swarm have survived the crash?" Turcotte asked.

"I don't know," Quinn said. "It appears so now, though."

"OK," Turcotte said. "Tunguska."

"Many people have wondered what really happened at Tunguska in 1908. I've got photos here from the German expedition. You can see that the trees have all been blasted outward from a central point. The most commonly accepted explanation has been that a meteor struck at the epicenter, but the problem with that was that no one could find any remains of the meteor. Given what we know now, and the results of this German expedition, there's no doubt that an alien craft crashed at Tunguska.

"You think Area 51 was desolate, Tunguska is in the middle of nothing. It's located in the Central Siberian Upland. If it had not been for the Trans-Siberian Railway, which was built in 1906, the exact site of the crash would probably never have been found. Siberia is half again as big as the United States. Yet at the time the railroad was built and the crash occurred, the population in that region was less than one million."

"What exactly happened with the crash?" Turcotte asked, checking his watch once more. He was anxious to get going after Artad and the Swarm, but he knew he had to go prepared.

Quinn consulted his notes. "In 1908, on June 30, just after seven in the morning, passengers on the Siberian railroad saw something bright race across the sky and disappear below the horizon to the north. There was an enormous explosion.

"Thirty-seven miles from the epicenter, at the trading station called Vanavara—the nearest place where people were, at least people who survived the explosion—no one knows how many trappers or hunters might have perished closer to the blast—the shock wave knocked buildings down and those in the open were burned by radiation. That was only determined decades later, when original reports from the time were studied by scientists who had the data from Hiroshima available. At the site itself trees were blown outward for dozens of miles.

"It was quite a worldwide event. In London, five hours after the explosion, measuring instruments picked up the shock wave in the air after it had already traveled around the world several times. At first, the English scientists thought perhaps they had recorded a large earthquake somewhere on the planet. But that night there was a strange glow, bright red, in the eastern sky, something they had never seen before. For two months afterward the night sky over England was much brighter than normal. It was so bright in some places that fire wagons were called out by people thinking there was a blaze just over the horizon.

"If it had not been for the sighting from the Siberian railroad, the whole source of the event might have been lost. Even with that, the cause of the explosion was not formally investigated by the Russians for nineteen years."

" 'Nineteen years'?" Turcotte repeated.

"Ah," Yakov growled, eager to explain. "You have to remember that that was a turbulent time in my country's history. The czar in 1908, well, one could not expect much from him, then we went through revolution and civil war not long afterward. You also have to understand the remoteness of the Siberian tundra. I have been in Siberia many times. Thousands upon thousands of miles of nothing but trees with bog underneath. A most desolate and isolated place."

"So what exactly occurred?" Turcotte asked, eager to get back on track.

"What do we know for certain happened?" Quinn checked his notes. "Those on the train, Tungus tribesmen, and fur traders in the area who were interviewed later reported seeing a fireball streaking through the atmosphere toward the trading post of Vanavara and leaving a trail of light some eight hundred kilometers long. The object approached from a heading of 115 degrees and descended at an entry angle of thirty to thirty-five degrees above the horizon. The fireball—as most described it—continued along a northwestward trajectory until it seemed about to disappear over the horizon. There followed a rapid series of cataclysmic explosions."

"Not one explosion?" Turcotte asked.

"No. Numerous witnesses reported hearing several blasts in succession."

"That's strange," Turcotte said.

"The site was centered on coordinates one-zero-one east by six-two north near the Stony Tunguska River, ninety-two kilometers north of Vanavara. The power of the blast felled trees outward in a radial pattern over an area covering over two thousand square kilometers. Closer to the epicenter, the forest was incinerated, causing a column of flame visible several hundred kilometers away. The fires burned for weeks, destroying a thousand square kilometers of forest. The fires were so vast and intense that they caused tremendous winds, sucking up ash and tundra so violently that they were caught up in the high-altitude air circulation pattern and carried around the world. The initial explosion and aftershocks were heard as far away as eight hundred kilometers.

"From this data it was calculated that the explosion was at least twenty megatons and may have been as high as forty, depending on the altitude of the initial blast." Quinn looked at Turcotte and Yakov. "To give you an idea of the size, the explosive force that formed Meteor Crater in Arizona was figured to be only three and a half megatons."

"Was there a crater then?" Turcotte asked.

"Ah, a good question!" Quinn was in his element, working with data he had uncovered and giving it to others. "I'll get to that. A most strange recording was made of the earth's magnetic field at the Irkustk Observatory nine hundred kilometers from the epicenter. At the time they did not know what they were picking up, but comparing those 1908 data with modern records of atmospheric nuclear test explosions shows a remarkable similarity."

"You're saying a nuke went off in the atmosphere?" Turcotte asked, confused. "That's what caused all this? I thought you said an alien ship crashed there. And Tesla caused it? Did he develop a nuke?"

Quinn quickly backpedaled. "I'm saying the results were similar to a nuclear explosion. Just as when you exploded the ruby sphere inside the mothership it added to the force of the nuclear explosions you also initiated. All I have told you are the known facts.

"Now let us move on to current speculation before getting back to what you recovered from the Moscow Archive. Current—before the discovery of the Airlia that is—explanations for the cause of the 1908 Tunguska blast have been numerous. Some say a nuclear blast, which of course necessitates involving aliens, as humans did not posses nuclear weapons at that date."

"But Von Seeckt did recover the Great Pyramid nuke in

1941," Turcotte noted. "So we not only know the Airlia had nukes, we know they left at least one sitting around."

Quinn continued his story. "Others have said it was a black hole striking the planet. Or a small piece of antimatter. Even before the discovery of the Airlia there were those who did say the explosion must have had an extraterrestrial cause—the nuclear power plant of a spacecraft malfunctioning."

"The mothership wasn't powered by a nuclear reactor," Turcotte said. "The UNAOC scientists don't know what the ruby sphere was exactly, but it wasn't nuclear. Although as you said, when it exploded it certainly acted like a nuke."

"The biggest problem with knowing what happened at Tunguska—and no insult to you or your country, Mr. Yakov— is that it took nineteen years before the site was actually first examined," Quinn said. "A Soviet scientist named Leonid Kulik was the one who organized the first expedition. He'd heard rumors of the explosion from the local tribesmen, the Tungus, and that they had closed off the area, saying it was 'holy' land and they were afraid of further enraging the gods who had caused the explosion."

"Primitive thinking, or perhaps they knew more than the scientists," Turcotte noted.

Yakov agreed. "I learned traveling around the world to trust in the words of the so-called primitive people."

Quinn went on. "With backing from the Soviet Academy of Sciences, Kulik and his party traveled to the area in 1927. Kulik discovered the epicenter of the blast by the straightfor-ward method of working his way in against the knocked-down trees.

"He also discovered several cleared oval areas that he assumed to be old meteorite craters that had been filled in by time. However, not only were those 'old' meteorites never discovered, they never found any remains of the large meteorite everyone assumes caused the 1908 blast.

"There are several curious aspects to Tunguska," Quinn said. "One is very strange. It was discovered not long ago that there was accelerated growth of biomass material in the area surrounding the epicenter and that accelerated growth has continued to this day. There have also been a number of mutations of animal and plant life in the area. Among the local Tungus tribesmen, it was found that their Rh blood factor is abnormal, even now, almost a hundred years later."

"What could affect life like that?" Turcotte asked.

"Perhaps radiation," Quinn said. "But even at nuclear test sites, there haven't been biological data collected like these. Perhaps," he ventured, "the Swarm bodies did have some alien-type viruses and they infected the local area—and the Germans when they arrived years later. Or, maybe the craft itself or the weapon used against it propagated a field that affected bioforms.

"The common explanation for the Tunguska event has always been that it was caused by an asteroid," Quinn continued. "However, we run into the problem of not being able to find the crater and asteroid fragments that would be necessary parts of such an occurrence. Making that explanation even more difficult is that aerial surveys in the 1960s discovered four smaller blast epicenters within the confines of the larger one. That also backs up the claims of witnesses that there were multiple explosions. So what caused the smaller blasts?"

"Secondary explosions from a craft," Turcotte suggested.

"Perhaps," Quinn said. "But what caused the primary explosion?" He didn't wait for an answer. "Another, bigger expedition was sent to Tunguska after the Second World War. They found signs of an airburst nuclear explosion, now that they knew what the results of such an event would be. Using the data, the men with their slide rules again estimated the equivalent of a twenty-megaton blast. One thousand times the size of the bomb that destroyed Hiroshima. You can be assured that generated some interest.

"The Soviet scientists also found traces of the radioactive isotope cesium 137 in the ring structure of trees on the outskirts of the blast that corresponds to the year of the explosion. And still no sign of a crater.

"One of the scientists on the expedition—Gregori Kazakov—said that the explosion at Tunguska had definitely been nuclear and he suggested that it was caused by the nuclear engine of a spacecraft exploding. He said that traces of metallic iron found in the area were fragments from the skin of the spaceship. Other metals found there were from the ship's wiring. He based his theory on the fact that a spacecraft exploding in midair would leave no crater and form the circular effect of blown-down trees that was noted in the area. They also found traces of metal that they couldn't identify."

Turcotte waited, the information coming full circle as Quinn continued.

"Then an aerodynamics expert carefully examined eyewitness reports of the object that had been moving across the sky and concluded that it had to have been under intelligent control. Based on the various reports, the object slowed to around .6 kilometers per second prior to explosion, indicating an attempt to perhaps land—a meteorite would have continued at the same terminal velocity to detonation. He laid out the route according to the various accounts and it appeared—if the accounts from 1908 were to be believed—that the object actually made a significant course change prior to exploding, definitely ruling out an uncontrolled object.

"With this new information the team decided to expand the resources and dig. The thought is that whatever exploded fell to the ground, melted the permafrost, then sank into the melted ground. Then the permafrost refroze, effectively burying—and preserving—whatever was there. However, the expedition that went after World War II did extensive digging and found nothing."

"Because the Nazis had already recovered whatever was there." Turcotte supplied the missing piece.

"It appears so." Quinn said.

"How were the Germans able to operate so freely in Russia?" Turcotte asked.

"Ah, the 1930s." Yakov's voice sounded sad. "A black time for my country. If you remember history, Stalin had signed a nonaggression pact with Hitler that decade. A most foolish decision given subsequent events."

"Could there be more to that treaty than meets the eye?" Turcotte suggested. "Perhaps the influence of either the Mission or the Ones Who Wait?"

"That is possible with every event in man's history," Yakov said. "Who knows even who Stalin was? Single-handedly he almost destroyed my country. We still struggle to recover from all the policies he enacted; and the millions he killed, they will never be replaced. What he did made no sense."

"Major Quinn, what did the Germans find?" Turcotte asked. "How intact was the wreckage?"

"It was in many pieces," Quinn said. "The Germans took out as much as they could uncover."

"And it wasn't a Talon, bouncer, or mothership?"

"Apparently not."

"Well, what was it exactly? What kind of ship does the Swarm have?" Turcotte asked.

"The Germans never really determined the structure of the craft," Quinn said. "They didn't have enough to work with."

"What was Swarm doing on Earth in 1908?" Yakov asked.

"That's a very good question," Quinn said.

"An even better question," Turcotte said, "is how did Tesla destroy their ship in 1908?"

"At the same time as the Tunguska explosion," Quinn said, "the most significant event occurring in the news was Admiral Peary's expedition to the North Pole. There are some who speculate that Tesla, desiring to gain publicity for his new device, wanted to send a transmission through the Earth to Peary's camp, where it would light the entire area."

"Wait a second." Yakov was confused. "You said it was a weapon?"

"It depends on the amount of energy transmitted. At a certain low level it could transmit a radio message. At other low levels it could produce a glow. Indeed Tesla claimed shortly after the *Titanic* disaster that his device—located in the Azores—could prevent similar accidents by lighting the entire Atlantic Ocean at night with a low-level glow."

Turcotte wasn't sure how much of this he should believe. A month ago he would have thought it all nonsense, but he had seen so many strange things in the intervening weeks that very little was out of the realm of what he now thought possible. And he desperately needed a weapon, a human weapon, one that was powerful enough to attack the Talons and destroy the Mars transmitter.

"Most of what I am telling you is easily checkable," Quinn said. "You can look them up in the library or on the Internet. Anyway, these people who believe Tesla was trying to contact Peary speculate that Tesla's experiment went tragically wrong.

"If you look at a global projection, from Tesla's tower site on Long Island to Peary's camp near the North Pole and continuing on a line around the planet, you strike Tunguska straight on. The theory is that Tesla mistook both the power and the direction of his beam and instead hit Tunguska with a powerful electromagnetic pulse, causing the explosion."

"You sound as if you do not believe that," Turcotte noted.

"Tesla was a brilliant man," Quinn said. "Reading his journals convinced me of that. I do not think he made a mistake. I believe the North Pole information was a cover story that was put out to hide the real mission. I think he did exactly what he set out to."

"And that was?" Yakov prompted.

"Destroy the Swarm spacecraft."

"How did he develop such technology?" Yakov asked. "And how could he know the Swarm craft was inbound, then target it?"

"That I don't know yet," Quinn said. "I've got more research to do. But if he had contact with the Master Guardian in Turkey, he might have been able to find out about the Swarm spaceship being inbound. I'm just telling you all I've found out so far."

"Can we duplicate his weapon?" Turcotte asked. "Can it cut through the Airlia shield?"

"I'm speculating that the Swarm craft must have been guarded by some sort of similar shield," Quinn said. "Tesla's weapon seems to have worked on that."

"Can we duplicate it?" Turcotte asked once more.

"I'm working on the data and construction details," Quinn said. "His energy projector doesn't appear to be very complicated."

"Why has no one tried to duplicate it then?" Turcotte asked.

"No one really appears to have looked," Quinn said. "As I said, his papers were taken by the Yugoslavian intelligence service and locked away. I've put out some feelers for experts on Tesla's science. There's one more thing," Quinn added.

"And that is?" Turcotte asked.

"Tesla traveled to England in 1924."

"So?"

"That's the same year Irvine left England to try to climb Everest. Tesla mentions in his journal that he met Irvine prior to his departure, but he doesn't say why."

"That's not just a coincidence, is it?" Turcotte asked.

"I don't think so."

Turcotte leaned back in the seat and closed his eyes. "Where are they now?"

"Excuse me?" Quinn asked.

"These other Watchers," Turcotte said. "Where are they now? How come they haven't done anything?"

Yakov shrugged his large shoulders. "I have not met any of them or seen the results of any of their actions in my years tracking the aliens. Perhaps Tesla was the last?"

Turcotte turned back to Quinn. "Can we make this weapon?"

"I've got someone coming—a professor from MIT who has done a lot of work with things Tesla worked on." Quinn checked his Palm Pilot. "A Professor Leahy. Should be here very soon."

Turcotte stood. "I hope so. Because we're taking off within the hour."

CHAPTER 13: THE PRESENT

BARKSDALE AFB, LOUISIANA

The two Air Force officers walked to the surface entrance of the Final Option Missile Launch Control Center (FOM-LCC). Both were dressed in black one-piece flight suits. On their right shoulders each wore a crest with a mailed fist holding lightning bolts and the words Final Option. A Velcro tag on their chests gave their names, ranks, and units. One was Major Bartlett, the other Captain Thayer.

The surface entrance to the LCC was set in the middle of an open grassy space, about a hundred meters square, surrounded on all sides by thick forest. Twenty meters from the edge of the forest on all sides surrounding the surface building was a twelve-foot-high fence topped with razor wire. One gravel road led to the building. NO TRESPASSING and DEADLY FORCE AUTHORIZED signs were hung every ten feet on the fence. Video cameras, remote-controlled machine guns, a satellite dish, surface-to-air missiles, and a small radar dish were on the roof of the building, the latter three pointing at the cloudless sky.

The two officers had arrived moments ago in a pickup from Barksdale Air Force Base, where the 341st Missile Wing was headquartered. The pickup was parked right behind them, waiting to take the off-shift crew back to base. The LCC was located eight miles from the main air base, one of a dozen launch control facilities scattered about the post. Each control facility was in charge of six silos, each housing an intercontinental ballistic missile.

One of the officers punched a code into the panel next to the outer door and it opened. They stepped into a short hallway and approached a massive vault door guarding the elevator. The Final Option Missile crest was painted on the elevator door. The first officer put his eyes up to the retinal scanner on the left side of the door. A mechanical voice echoed out of a speaker.

"Retina verified. Major Bartlett. Launch status valid."

The second officer followed suit, raising his glasses so his eyes could push up against the rubber.

"Retina verified. Captain Thayer. Launch status valid."

There was a brief pause, and then the computer spoke again.

"Launch officers on valid status verified. Please enter duty entry code."

On a numeric keypad next to the vault door, Bartlett entered the daily code they'd been given when departing Barksdale.

The unemotional voice of the computer echoed in the lobby. "Code valid. Look into the camera for duty crew identification."

Bartlett and Thayer stepped back and looked up into a video camera hanging from the ceiling. The image was relayed below them to the current crew on duty.

"On-duty crew identifies," the computer intoned. "Opening door."

The vault door slowly swung open. They walked into the elevator and the door shut. The elevator hurtled down a hundred feet and abruptly halted, causing them both to flex their knees.

The elevator doors opened to the rear of the launch control center. To the left of the elevator, a door went to a small area that contained enough stores for the crew for three months. To the right another door went to a small room that held two bunks, a bathroom, and a kitchen area. The two men walked into the Final Option Missile Launch Control Center, a forty-by-forty room filled with rows of machinery. The entire facility was a capsule resting on four huge shock absorbers, theoretically allowing it to survive the concussion of a direct nuclear strike. Like the Space Command facility at Cheyenne Mountain, it had originally been built early in the Cold War, when there were those who thought such a thing was possible. Even with retrofits of stronger armor and better shocks, the crews of the LCC knew their survivability rate would be very low given an all-out nuclear exchange.

The dominating feature of the control room was a wide console at the front of the room, divided in half by a bullet-proof glass wall that went from floor to ceiling and extended back eight feet. A chair was on either side of the glass, the duty stations for the crew. The glass prevented one crewman from access to both key controls and also from holding a gun on the other crew member to get him to turn the key.

In front of the console, various screens showed scenes from the surface directly above and the silos the center controlled. Many of the screens had the brightly colored display that indicated thermal imagery. The LCC crews, along with the rest of the military, had been on the highest alert during the recent world war, and the status had only been downgraded one level since the apparent end of hostilities.

A lieutenant stood up and saluted Bartlett. "FOM-LCC is yours. Nothing of note in the duty log. Status green. Still at stage three alert. Targeting matrices are still hot." He reached inside his flight suit and removed a set of two keys, one red, one blue, on a steel chain from around his neck and handed it to Bartlett. His partner did the same with Thayer.

Bartlett looked over at the large red digital clock overlooking both consoles. "You stand relieved as of zero-six-zero-four."

He looked over at the consoles as he passed over the pickup truck's key. "How's the computer acting?"

On top of the main computer console there was a sign spelling out the acronym:

FINAL OPTION COMMAND MATRIX TARGETING AND EXECUTION

The relieved officer pocketed the truck key, anxious to be gone. "Fine. No glitches. Have a good shift."

He and the other officer walked to the elevator and got on board. The doors shut and they were gone. Bartlett and Thayer took the seats at their respective terminals, separated by the glass wall. Bartlett watched the video screens, seeing the two crewmen get off the elevator in the upper facility. One screen showed the pure video feed, the other the thermal. On the thermal screen the two men were glowing red figures against a blue background. When they got in the truck the thermal sight picked up a perfect outline of their sitting forms. Then the engine started, showing up as a bright red glow in the front of the truck.

"Surface door secure," Thayer reported. "Hatch secure."

On the screen, the pickup truck pulled away. The gate in the fence closed behind it automatically.

"Fence secure," Thayer said. "LCC secure."

"Turn the sensors, missiles, and automatic guns on," Bartlett ordered.

Thayer threw a switch activating the machine guns and surface-to-air missiles on the roof of the LCC building. The former were slaved into motion sensors and would fire at anything moving inside the perimeter. The latter were directed by the site radar and could be launched by the crew against any air infiltration.

There was a moment of quiet and, in the background, the two men could hear the rhythmic thump of the powerful pumps that drained the water that flowed from the high water table in this part of Louisiana into the space outside of the LCC. They were only thirty miles from the coastal swamp that extended for sixty miles before hitting the Gulf of Mexico. Not the smartest place to build underground control centers and silos, but pork-barrel politics had determined the location, not military practicalities. It was theorized that if the pumps ever broke down or lost power, the LCC would be submerged within four hours. However, there were backups to the pumps and two powerful generators standing by in case power was lost.

Bartlett pulled out a binder. "Let's run through our checklist and make sure we're running smoothly." He flipped open to the first page. "Cable link to National Command Authority?"

Thayer looked at his console. "Cable link check."

"Satellite dish link to MILSTAR?"

"Satellite dish check."

An alarm chimed, and Bartlett paused.

Thayer looked at the radar feed. "Incoming craft. Range five miles, altitude six thousand feet. Closing fast. It's big."

"Damn," Bartlett muttered as he picked up the microphone for the FM radio. "Unidentified aircraft, you are entering restricted airspace. Veer off on a heading of one-six-zero degrees immediately."

There was no reply.

"Still coming," Thayer reported.

Bartlett flipped a switch, arming the Stinger missiles deployed on the roof of the LCC. "Unidentified aircraft, you will be shot down if you do not immediately veer off."

"I've got a visual," Thayer said.

Bartlett looked at the video display. A lean black form was approaching, definitely not of human origin. "What the hell is that?"

Bartlett hit the button and two Stingers launched. He watched the two missiles roar toward the Talon and hit with no effect.

Bartlett picked up the red phone that linked them with headquarters at Barksdale. He paused as he heard the distinctive sound of a gun's hammer being pulled back. He turned to look right down the barrel of Thayer's 9mm Beretta. The other crew member had left his station and come around the wall.

"What the hell—" Bartlett didn't finish the sentence as Thayer pulled the trigger.

The round hit Bartlett in the forehead, plowing through and exploding out the back, taking with it blood, brain, and bone, producing a gory splatter on the bulletproof glass.

Thayer glanced at the video display. The Talon had landed inside the fence. A door slid open and a gangway extended to the ground. Several heavily armed men wearing an assortment of camouflage uniforms and carrying a spectrum of weapons sprinted off, taking up defensive positions. Then a tall, pale-skinned man walked off and headed into the LCC. Thayer put the gun down on his console and typed an override command into the computer. The steel doors in the surface entrance slowly opened.

Thayer heard the elevator rumble. He turned and faced to the rear as the doors slid open. Aspasia's Shadow walked in. No greetings were exchanged. Thayer was responding as the guardian computer underneath Mount Sinai had programmed him to upon receipt of the proper code word—which had arrived via e-mail less than three hours earlier.

Aspasia's Shadow went to the other console and reached inside Bartlett's jumpsuit, retrieving a red key on a metal chain and placing it around his own neck. Then he pulled Bartlett's body out of the seat, sending it tumbling to the

floor. He sat down, ignoring the blood and brain matter staining the back of the chair.

"Are you ready?" Aspasia's Shadow asked. He grabbed a
three-ring binder that had a red cover and TOP SECRET
stamped in large letters. He had learned of the Final Option
Missile from one of his Guides secreted high inside the
United States intelligence community. He had targeted several of the crew members for imprinting and succeeded with
three, one of them Thayer, ensuring a good chance that he
would always have a Guide on duty in this LCC. It had been
a backup plan, one of many that Aspasia's Shadow had put in
place around the world, but this was perhaps the most powerful and most desperate.

Thayer looked over his panel. "Final Option Missile silo
on-line. Missile systems show green."

"Open silo," Aspasia's Shadow ordered.

"Opening silo."

Four hundred meters from the surface entrance to the Final
Option Missile LCC was another fenced compound. Inside
the razor wire topping the fence, two massive concrete doors
slowly rose until they reached the vertical position. Inside a
specially modified LGM-118A Peacekeeper ICBM missile
rested, gas venting.

"I've got green on Final Option Missile silo doors," Thayer
announced, verifying what one of the video screens showed.
He had trained so often to do this that he was acting almost
instinctively. The only difference from his training routine
was that he was acting under the motivation of the imprinting, not an order from the National Command Authority.

"Green on silo," Aspasia's Shadow confirmed, reading the
checklist. He thought it very nice of the United States Air
Force to have a step-by-step list of actions to be taken to

launch the missile. It always made him feel superior to use humans' own inventions against them.

The tower at Barksdale Air Force Base served two functions. In the top, air traffic controllers ran the day-to-day operation of the airfield itself. On the floor below the top, the duty staff for the 341st Missile Wing ran the day-to-day operation of the LCCs and missiles under their control.

The opening of a single silo door was indicated by a lone red light going on among a cluster of green ones. The duty officer immediately picked up the phone and punched in the number for the Final Option Missile LCC. When the other end rang ten times with no answer, the duty officer put the phone down and hit the large red alarm button. A Klaxon wailed from the top of the tower as the duty officer picked up a different phone that had a direct line to the wing commander.

"What's the targeting matrix for Final Option Missile?" Aspasia's Shadow asked.

Thayer had already checked that information. Since the end of the Cold War the United States and Russia had reached an agreement where all ICBMs would no longer rest in their silos targeted at each other's countries. Instead, the standing targeting information programmed in each warhead was for a site in the middle of an ocean, called a Broad Ocean Area. Its purpose was to prevent disaster in case of accidental launch. In the event that a launch was actually desired and the missiles used in a conflict, a target matrix would be fed by computer into each missile, and they would be quickly reprogrammed with the new destinations for the warheads.

"Resting matrix is the Broad Ocean Area. However, a broad range of firing options was programmed in at the start of recent hostilities," Thayer said. "Primary standby matrix is against mainland China. Secondary matrix is for North Korea. Third priority is the Middle East."

"We can reprogram, correct?"

Thayer nodded. "After we launch the FOM, we can access it through MILSTAR. You can then program the targeting matrix once the missile is up." He tapped a laptop computer that had wires running from the back into the main console. "I've got this on-line and we can use it from a mobile spot as long as we can access MILSTAR." He held up a small green box with a small dish on top. "This is a secure SATCOM link."

Aspasia's Shadow smiled. "Oh, where I have in mind, we most definitely can access MILSTAR." He pulled the red key from under his shirt and inserted it into the appropriate slot. "Insert key." Thayer did the same.

"On my three," Aspasia's Shadow said, staring through the glass at Thayer. "One. Two. Three."

They turned their keys at the same time.

The solid rocket first stage of the LGM-118A ignited. Umbilicals fell away and the rocket slowly began lifting on a tail of flame, clearing the silo.

Thayer was already moving before the rocket emerged from the silo. He disconnected the laptop computer from its port and slid it into a briefcase. Aspasia's Shadow led the way to the elevator and they headed for the surface.

The wing commander stared in disbelief at the flashing red lights indicating a missile launch. He looked out the tower window and saw a plume of smoke heading up into the morning sky.

"What launched?" he demanded.

The answer was the worst one he could have received. "Final Option Missile silo is empty, sir."

"Get me the LCC," he ordered the duty officer.

"Our link with the Final Option Missile LCC is down. Everything else shows secure." The duty officer reported.

The wing commander turned to the duty officer. "Get me Final Option Missile command computer on MILSTAR."

"I'm not getting an answer, sir."

"Status on Final Option Missile LCC other silos?"

"All other missile silos are still secure and in place."

The first stage of the Peacekeeper finished its sixty-second burn and separated, the second stage immediately taking over. The missile had been going straight up, simply absorbing the upward thrust of the first stage, but the second stage had some thrust vector and the rocket turned slightly to the north and west, ascending at over a thousand miles an hour and still accelerating.

The second stage burned out and explosive bolts fired, causing its large metal casing to fall away. The Peacekeeper was now almost out of the atmosphere as the third stage fired cleanly.

The third stage stopped firing but did not separate. There was still fuel left, enough for the payload to be further maneuvered if needed. The Peacekeeper was in space, at a point above the middle of Kansas. Small thruster rockets fired as the onboard computer checked its position with various satellites to settle the rocket into a geosynchronous orbit.

After a few moments of firing they too fell silent and the Peacekeeper was in position.

Aspasia's Shadow's Talon lifted off and headed directly upward, moving even faster than the missile that had just been launched.

• • •

The wing commander grabbed the red phone. "Space Command, are you tracking an ICBM launch from out site?"

"Roger that. We also have another controlled craft heading upward at escape velocity."

"What kind of craft?"

"Profile fits with an alien ship."

"Oh my God," the wing commander muttered. He clicked the phone off, then dialed the war room.

The capsule on the end of the Peacekeeper rocket split in two, both shells falling away. Bolted inside, the Final Option Missile payload activated itself. It was not a warhead. Instead, solar panels slowly unfolded, gathering the energy of the sun to complete the boot-up of the computer and communications system. A boom mast extended, a half dozen satellite dishes attached to it.

One of the satellite dishes twisted and turned, seeking out the closest MILSTAR satellite. It found one that was in its own geosynchronous orbit two hundred miles away. An inquiry burst was transmitted from Final Option Missile to the MILSTAR satellite on a secure link. A positive link burst was sent back by the MILSTAR computer, indicating that Final Option Missile was now on-line with MILSTAR. The other satellite dishes were oriented toward Earth and they sent out their own checks, linking with submarines, bombers, and launch control centers.

Inside, the master computer checked itself and found all systems to be functioning.

Final Option Missile was ready.

CHAPTER 14: THE PRESENT

CAMP ROWE

Turcotte returned Captain Manning's salute. The Space Command team had loaded all their gear in one of the cargo bays near the front of the mothership. The dozen men were stowing equipment and performing last-minute checks to make sure they had everything they would need. There were numerous pallets of equipment scattered throughout the bay.

"Are you ready?" Turcotte asked Manning.

"Yes, sir. We had everything packaged on pallets. We flew it here on a C-17 and just rolled it all in here."

Turcotte noted several containers marked with an atomic symbol. "Nuclear warheads?"

Manning nodded. "Yes, sir. Ten tac nukes loaded into Tomahawk cruise missiles."

"What if the target is shielded?" Yakov asked.

Manning shrugged. "Maybe they'll have to turn off the shield when they turn the array on. If so, we might be able to drop one of these in during that window of opportunity."

"That's not good enough," Turcotte said. "I don't think it's going to take them very long to get a message out. If we destroy it *after* a message is sent, we're wasting our time."

"That's the best I've got, sir."

"That's why we're waiting on this Professor Leahy." Turcotte checked his watch. "He ought to be here any minute."

Manning indicated a large medical device with a table extended in front of it. "We need to MRI you in order to prepare your SARA link."

Turcotte wasn't thrilled with the idea of using the SARA links, but Manning had insisted that they had found it to be perfectly safe and it would allow them to use the suits to their maximum capability. He reluctantly climbed onto the table as Yakov and Manning stood on either side.

"Try to remain perfectly still," Manning said. "This will only take a few minutes." He hit a button and the table slid into the machine.

Turcotte fought the feeling of claustrophobia. He closed his eyes and forced his breathing back to a normal cadence as the machine made strange noises. He was sure it was more than just a few minutes before the table vibrated and slid him out of the machine. He swung his legs down to the ground. Manning was standing next to a small laptop, looking at the display with one of his men and Yakov.

"Do I still have a brain?" Turcotte asked as he walked over. He sensed something wrong in the way both men were leaning over the screen, staring at it.

"You've got a brain," Manning said. He touched the screen, indicating a small round black spot. "You also have something implanted in it."

WAR ROOM, PENTAGON

Three hundred fifty feet below the lowest level of the Pentagon proper was the Joint Chiefs of Staff's National Military Command Center, commonly called the war room by those who worked there. It had been placed inside a large cavern carved out of solid bedrock. It was ten times larger and over three times deeper than the LCC Aspasia's Shadow had been inside of in Louisiana, but it was designed along the same principles. The complex could only be entered via one secure elevator and the entire thing was mounted on massive springs on the cavern floor. There were enough food and supplies in the war room for the emergency crew to operate for a year. Besides the lines that went up through the Pentagon's own communications system, a narrow tunnel holding cables had been laboriously dug at the same depth to the alternate National Command Post at Blue Mountain in West Virginia.

When it was built in the early sixties, the war room had been designed to survive a nuclear first strike. The advances in both targeting and warhead technology over the subsequent three decades had made that design obsolete. There was no doubt in the minds of anyone who worked in the war room that the room was high on the list of Russian and Chinese nuclear targeting and that it would be gone very shortly after any nuclear exchange. Because of that, it had been turned into the operations center for the Pentagon.

Since the start of the Third World War, the war room had been fully staffed and it was still operating at nearly peak level. The main room of the war room was semicircular. On the front, flat wall, there was a large imagery display board, over thirty feet wide by twenty high. Any projection or scene that could be piped into the war room could be displayed on this board, from a video of a new weapons system, to a map of the world showing the current status of US forces, to a real-time downlink from an orbiting spy satellite.

The floor of the room sloped from the rear down to the front so that each row of computer and communication consoles could be overseen from the row behind. At the very back of the room, along the curved wall, a three-foot-high railing separated the command and control section where the Joint Chiefs and other high-ranking officers had their desks. Supply, kitchen, and sleeping areas were off the right rear of the room, in a separate cavern. The war room had had its first taste of action during the Gulf War, when it had operated full-time, coordinating the multinational forces in the Gulf.

The elevator in the left rear opened and the president's national security adviser, and the chairman of the Joint Chiefs of Staff strode into room.

"What the hell is going on?" the national security adviser demanded as they walked to the center desk and stood behind it.

"Give me a status report," the chairman of the JCS ordered, ignoring the adviser for the moment.

The senior duty officer, a full colonel, turned. "We've got a red, level-four serious incident, sir. Final Option Missile has been launched without authorization."

"Go through MILSTAR and get ahold of the Final Option Missile LCC to determine status and gain positive control," the chairman ordered.

The duty officer shook his head. "We've tried, sir. Someone's overridden an external link. Barksdale Wing Command can't get ahold of it on land line either. They're sending a reaction force out to the site. Final Option Missile's MILSTAR link is locked into its LCC computer and we have no contact with it."

"Who's in the Final Option Missile LCC?" the chairman demanded. "The crew?"

"We don't know, sir." The colonel cleared his throat. "Maybe no one. Space Command is not only tracking Final Option Missile in orbit, but also picked up an alien spacecraft at the LCC and now on its way into orbit."

" 'An alien spacecraft'?" the chairman repeated. "What kind and from where?"

"We've got a report from Area 51 that Aspasia's Shadow has control of one of the Talons that was on the second mothership. Space Command lost track of it somewhere over Texas. The signature of the craft lifting from the LCC vicinity fits the profile for a Talon. I've got a message to the Area 51 people to find out if it might be one of theirs, but it's hard getting through to them since they've relocated to North Carolina."

"Good Lord," the chairman muttered as the implications of Final Option being in the wrong hands sank in.

"Will someone please tell me exactly what the Final Option Missile is?" the national security adviser demanded. "Obviously something I haven't been briefed on yet."

The chairman of the Joint Chiefs turned to the civilian. "Final Option Missile is a special payload loaded into a Minuteman ICBM. Final Option is the code name for what we used to call the Emergency Rocket Communication System."

The national security adviser held up his hands. "General, since I don't have a clue what you're talking about, why don't you tell me what the hell is going on in plain English?"

The chairman took a second to collect his thoughts. "Final Option Missile can communicate through MILSTAR with every nuclear launch platform this country has. Subs, missile launch facilities; it can even scramble strategic bombers and get them in the air."

"What?"

"Final Option Missile is an automated command and control system that can alert, specify targeting matrices, and actually send an emergency action message—EAM—to launch any nuclear system our military has."

"You're joking."

"No, sir, I wish I was."

"Why did someone design something like that?" the national security adviser demanded. "Only the president can order a launch—not a machine."

"That's why we call it the Final Option." The general's face was stone. "FOM was designed to be used if every other normal mode of communication was knocked out and the president can't issue the orders or if the National Command Authority is wiped out. It's the last-gasp means by which the National Command Authority can transmit an order so that launch codes and target matrices can get to America's nuclear forces if all other communication means are destroyed. FOM is basically a last-ditch device and a deterrent."

"Deterrent to what?"

"To keep someone from thinking they can wipe out our leadership in one strike and we couldn't strike back. There's even an automated system in Final Option designed around sensors that if a negative code isn't transmitted from this war room, Space Command, the White House, Air Force One, or another classified location every day, it begins a countdown to launch. Thus if someone does wipe all those locations out—which basically means there is no leadership left in this country, Final Option will launch and transmit a target matrix and launch authorization for whatever nuclear platforms have survived."

"That's insane."

"No, sir, that's the reality of deterrence."

The security adviser rubbed his forehead. "OK, so this thing has been launched and it appears by Aspasia's Shadow. But *we* can still communicate with all our launch platforms also, can't we? Our National Command Authority *hasn't* been wiped out. We can still transmit this negative code, correct?"

"That's true, sir, but—"

"Then get on the radio and tell all launch platforms to

ignore any orders from Final Option Missile. And transmit this negative code."

The chairman of the Joint Chiefs began to show some emotion as he ran a nervous hand across his chin. "It doesn't work that way. The point of all our training is for the crew never to ignore an emergency action launch order from a valid source. Final Option Missile is a valid source. In fact, it is the ultimate and final valid source. Did you ever see the movie *Fail Safe*?"

"Yes."

The general continued. "Just like in the movie, any launch officer, pilot, or sub commander will believe Final Option Missile before they believe us. They would ignore even a direct order from their commander in chief, as Final Option actually has a higher authorization code. And a launch code supersedes a negative code."

"Bull," the adviser snapped. "If we get the president on the horn, he'll stop this in its tracks."

"No, sir, he won't be able to."

"Why don't you just jam the damn thing then?"

The general spoke slowly. "The system in the payload consists of two parts: a sophisticated computer and a powerful transmitter. The computer holds all—and I mean all—the nuclear launch codes, targeting matrices and authorizations, while the transmitter on launch becomes part of MILSTAR, a high-tech, frequency-jumping, secure global satellite network by which those codes and matrices are sent. It cannot be aborted or jammed by anyone else. That's the way we designed the thing in order for it to be secure from enemy jamming.

"The computer that runs everything, the Final Option Command Matrix Targeting and Execution computer, was developed to be totally self-sufficient for each nuclear weapon. Whoever has the proper code word for it has complete control and can't be superseded by anyone else even if they have their own launch computer. In fact, once a target matrix and authorization is transmitted by Final Option there is only one way it can be stopped—by Final Option itself transmitting the stop codes to each individual launch platform. No other source can stop an FOM launch.

"We have to assume that Aspasia's Shadow has control of the Final Option Missile and the onboard computer. Therefore, in essence, he has his finger on the button of this country's entire nuclear arsenal."

"Why is he doing this?" the national security adviser asked.

To that, there was no response.

"Can we shoot it down?" the national security adviser pressed.

"We can try," the chairman said, "but I doubt if we'll get it in time."

"What do you mean?"

"As I just said, once it transmits a target matrix the only thing that can stop the launches is the same transmit source—i.e. the only way to stop a Final Option launch is Final Option. If it transmits before we shoot it down, then we're destroying our only means of stopping any launches it's ordered."

"Just great," the national security adviser muttered. "What genius thought this up?"

"Our only hope is to seize computer control back," the chairman said.

"And how do we do that?"

"Ordinarily it would mean regaining control of the LCC for Final Option, but since this Talon has taken off, I have to assume they've made computer control mobile."

A voice near the front of the war room called out. "Sir, we've got a signal coming in. It's Aspasia's Shadow."

CAMP ROWE

"What does it do?" Turcotte demanded. He felt sick to his stomach, staring at the small object on the screen. Now he knew what the cause of his recent headache had been, but more importantly: What had the thing been doing before that? Manning had put him back in the MRI to take more images, focusing on the small round object they'd discovered. It was about a quarter inch in diameter and located in the rear of his brain, just above the stem.

"I don't know," Manning said. "I've never seen anything like it." The image displayed was magnified ten times normal size. He traced a line coming out of the object going toward the top, forward part of the brain. "This is a very thin, almost microscopic wire, much like our SARA link uses. It's running into this part of your brain."

"And what does that part of my brain do?" Turcotte asked.

"It's in your cerebrum." Manning typed a command into the computer and an overlay of the brain came up. "It's going right into the border between the area that has your memories and the part where psychologists think emotion resides."

"So this thing could be messing with my memories and what I'm feeling?" Turcotte asked.

"I don't know," Manning said. "It doesn't appear to be doing anything right now. Maybe it's just a recorder."

Turcotte tried to remember when the orb could have been implanted, then he felt a sharp stab of fear—he couldn't necessarily trust his memories. Whoever had done this to him had most likely covered up the event. The fear grew worse. Was he who he thought he was? He tried to think through the fog of confusion and anxiety. "We haven't seen this before"—he turned to Yakov—"have you?"

The Russian shook his head. "Nothing like this." He stroked his chin. "It is not the way Aspasia's Shadow operated—he used either Guides imprinted by a guardian or the nanovirus. The Ones Who Wait are clones. So—"

"So this is something new," Turcotte summarized. "What about Majestic? They were working on that EDOM stuff at Dulce. Could they have done this to me when I reported for security duty there? I don't remember anything like that, but if this messes with memories, then maybe they wiped out my memory of it?"

"But you destroyed Majestic," Yakov noted. "I don't think—"

He was interrupted by the appearance of Major Quinn in the entrance to the cargo bay. From the look on the major's face, Turcotte knew more bad news was forthcoming.

"Aspasia's Shadow has shown up."

"Where?" Turcotte demanded. He realized he was rubbing the back of his head, and forced his hand back to his side.

"He infiltrated a launch control center at Barksdale Air Force Base."

"What did he launch?" Turcotte asked.

"Final Option Missile."

"That just doesn't sound good," Turcotte said.

Quinn quickly briefed him and Yakov on what the Final Option Missile was. By the time he was done, Turcotte knew exactly what was going to happen next, but he let the major finish.

"He's contacted the Pentagon," Quinn said. "He's threatening to launch every nuke the US has, at a variety of targets blanketing the world. Given we have enough warheads to destroy the world a dozen times over, there's not going to be much left if he follows through."

"Unless we give him the mothership, correct?" Turcotte asked.

"Correct."

"Where is he now?"

"Space Command has tracked the Talon into orbit."

"How about taking out the satellite?" Turcotte asked.

Quinn quickly explained.

"So in other words we have to seize control back?" Turcotte summarized.

"Unless we can get to Final Option before he sends out a targeting matrix," Quinn said.

"Has our Tesla expert arrived yet?" Turcotte asked.

"Chopper's inbound, five minutes out."

"We can't wait. We're lifting now." Turcotte grabbed Quinn as the man turned to go. "Did Majestic use implants?"

" 'Implants'?"

Turcotte tapped the back of his head. "Did they put something in my head?"

Quinn shook his head. "No, sir. I never heard of Majestic doing that to anybody. They used the EDOM device to mess with memories, but no implants."

"Great."

ORBIT

Aspasia's Shadow looked over Thayer's shoulder at the laptop screen. A map of the world was displayed. He pointed as he spoke.

"New York, Mexico City, São Paulo, Tokyo, Osaka-Kyoto, Los Angeles, Buenos Aires, Rio de Janeiro, London, Moscow, Calcutta, Bombay, Seoul—scratch that last one"—he said with a laugh—"already taken care of. Let's see. Chicago, Lima, Paris, St. Petersburg, New Delhi, Tehran, Shanghai, Bangkok, Cairo."

As Aspasia's Shadow listed each city, Thayer moved the small pointer on the screen to the spot and clicked. A small red triangle appeared over each.

Aspasia's Shadow smiled. "Let's throw in Sydney, Athens, Baghdad, and Atlanta just for fun and an even twenty-five."

Thayer marked each of the additional cities. "All programmed into the target matrix for five nuclear warheads each."

"Send it."

CHAPTER 15: THE PRESENT

AIRSPACE CAMP ROWE

"What do you have?" Turcotte asked Kincaid. They were in the control room, watching the computer display that the JPL man had rigged, which was currently forwarding information from Space Command tracking Aspasia's Shadow's Talon. It was currently in orbit, moving to the east.

"Give me a second," Kincaid said. He tapped the screen. "He's heading somewhere. No need for him to be moving."

"Where?"

Kincaid hit the touch pad and made a few adjustments, extending out the flight path of the Talon. "There."

A small dot was directly on the flight path.

"What's that?" Turcotte asked.

"The International Space Station."

"And Final Option?"

"The platform is here. Directly above Kansas."

"Seal us up," Turcotte ordered Yakov. He turned to Manning. "Get your men ready. We've got an immediate mission."

"Sir—" Major Quinn was holding his hand up, almost like a schoolchild, the other hand pressing the earpiece tightly to his head so he could hear whatever was being transmitted.

"What?"

"Space Command has copied a target matrix that was just transmitted by the Final Option Mission."

"Targets?"

"Twenty-five cities around the world." Quinn was looking at his Palm Pilot. "It looks to me as if he's targeted them by population." Quinn rattled them off quickly. "New York, Mexico City, São Paulo, Tokyo, Osaka-Kyoto, Los Angeles, Buenos Aires, Rio de Janeiro, London, Moscow, Calcutta, Bombay, Chicago, Lima, Paris, St. Petersburg, New Delhi, Tehran, Shanghai, Bangkok, Cairo, Sydney, Athens, Baghdad, and Atlanta."

Turcotte just stared at Quinn.

"All targeted," Quinn said, not sure if Turcotte had understood him.

"By our own weapons."

Quinn couldn't tell if it was a question or statement.

"Yes, sir."

"So it's too late to take out the platform."

"Yes, sir. The only way we can stop those nukes is to regain control of the computer."

"Which is where?"

"I would say in the Talon with Aspasia's Shadow. Barksdale confirms there is no one in the LCC and the mainframe there is off-line. Aspasia's Shadow must have a laptop on board the Talon with a satellite link."

Turcotte turned to look at Yakov. The Russian had a bottle of some clear liquid, from which he took a long drink, then held it out to Turcotte. The Special Forces officer shook his head. "My head hurts enough already."

"I always tell you things can get worse," Yakov said.

Turcotte ignored the Russian's comment.

"Also—" Quinn dragged the word out.

"What?"

"Kaong"—Quinn glanced at his laptop screen—"he wants to speak to you."

"About?"

"Aspasia's Shadow has issued the UN an ultimatum."

Turcotte walked over stood next to Quinn, looking down at the face on the screen.

"Deputy Secretary General, what can I do for you?"

The Deputy Secretary General was listening to someone to his left, the sound muted. He reached forward and fiddled with something, then his voice came out of the small speakers. "We have received an ultimatum from Aspasia's Shadow. If we give him the mothership he will relinquish control of the Final Option Missile."

" 'We'?" Turcotte asked. "You don't have the mothership, sir." He indicated the space around him. "We control it. Area 51 controls it."

Kaong frowned. "I don't understand what you are saying, Major. You work for UNAOC."

"I didn't see anybody from UNAOC when I was on Everest," Turcotte said. "Or helping Yakov on Ararat. Or when Quinn and Kincaid were being attacked at Area 51. You, sir, don't have a clue what you're talking about. You don't know Aspasia's Shadow. We do. He cannot be trusted."

"But he contacted the United Nations," Kaong said. "And he is threatening your country along with many member nations. I am—"

Turcotte shook his head. "We'll deal with Aspasia's Shadow first. Then we'll deal with the others."

"The others?"

"I don't have time for this." Turcotte reached down and cut off the transmission. He walked back to the pilot's seat and took his place. "Are we sealed?" he asked Yakov.

"Yes."

"All right." Turcotte put his hands on the controls and the mothership lifted.

INTERNATIONAL SPACE STATION

Who would have thought a lock was needed on the airlock hatch for the International Space Station?

Aspasia's Shadow jetted across the narrow space between his Talon and the space station and simply spun open the manual latch on the outside lock. He slid inside and shut the hatch behind him. He removed his space helmet, then opened the inner airlock. There was a man floating in the narrow corridor, blocking his way and holding a crowbar, apparently the only weapon the crew of the station could come up with on short notice.

Aspasia's Shadow tucked the spear he had retrieved from the Talon's armory under his arm and pressed the indentation set in its haft. A golden bolt hit the man, knocking him unconscious. Aspasia's Shadow flexed his legs and pushed off, swinging the airlock hatch shut behind him. He let go and floated through the center of the chamber, shoving the unconscious man out of the way. The far hatch was closed and when he reached it, Aspasia's Shadow discovered the latch wouldn't move. He peered into the small glass and saw a woman looking back at him. He knew there was a crew of three on board the station, two Americans—a man and a woman—and one Russian.

He didn't have time for games. He edged back slightly from the hatch and aimed the spear at it. He adjusted the power setting and fired, keeping the trigger pressed. The golden beam hit the center of the door. After a couple of seconds, the metal began to buckle. Aspasia's Shadow let go of the button as the hatch crumpled open. He heard the airlock behind him open and glanced back as Captain Thayer entered, his laptop and small satellite radio tucked under one arm.

Aspasia's Shadow entered the end module, the US Destiny

laboratory. The woman had backed away from the hatch and was next to the other male member of the crew, who was desperately making a radio call to mission control. Aspasia's Shadow wasted no time, firing the spear twice, knocking both out.

He directed Thayer into the module. As the officer hooked his computer and satellite radio to the space station's power and antenna array, several of the Guides Aspasia's Shadow had gathered in Texas boarded the station. He had them take the three unconscious astronauts and unceremoniously dump them in the airlock and purge it.

Aspasia's Shadow stood near the lock, peering out a port at the three bodies floating nearby. He glanced at a clock. Forty-five minutes since he'd issued his ultimatum to the United Nations. A few minutes until Thayer was ready to launch the salvo of nuclear warheads. Aspasia's Shadow looked past the bodies, down at the planet below. "Your move, Mr. Turcotte," he said, before putting his helmet back on.

SPACE

Garlin watched the Ark of the Covenant's screen impassively. Now that the Swarm had the ship and knew where Duncan had come from, she was no longer a priority. The major purpose of continuing the probing was to learn as much about humans as possible so that a complete report could be rendered once they reached Mars and took over the communications array.

As the Ark probed into Duncan's brain, the artery gave way once more. The shunt kept her alive and the brain functioning, and soon Garlin was rewarded with a vision of a cluster of men dressed in armor gathered at a circular table set in the center of a wooden hall.

And in the shadows of the hall stood Duncan, dressed in a white robe trimmed with silver.

INTO ORBIT

Turcotte was feeling more comfortable flying the mothership. The controls he used were quite simple, although there were a number of displays and controls whose function he had no clue about. He could see the curvature of the Earth now, indicating they were very high up. He indicated for Yakov to take his place.

"I'm heading forward to join the team."

The Russian was less than happy. Once more he was being kept out of the action because none of the TASC suits were large enough for his bulk. He reluctantly took the pilot's seat. "How do you want me to approach the space station?"

"It's not like we're going to be able to sneak up on them," Turcotte said. "Just get us close. About a hundred meters away will work."

"What if Aspasia's Shadow uses the Talon to attack the ship?"

"He wants this ship," Turcotte said. "He won't take a chance of damaging it."

Not wasting any more time, Turcotte ran from the command room to the forward cargo bay. A half dozen commandos were already suited up and waiting. He forced himself to be still as the SARA link pad was carefully wrapped around his head. He then stepped back into the rear half of the suit. The front portion swung shut, and he was sealed in. He could feel the flow of oxygen from the pack on the back.

Turcotte had worn a TASC suit before, during the mission into the Giza Plateau to rescue Duncan. As soon as the suit was sealed, he was ready to move; but Manning's voice echoed inside the helmet.

"Hold on."

"What?" Turcotte demanded. He could see the interior of the cargo bay on the curved screen directly in front of his eyes.

"It takes a minute or two for the SARA link to get in synch with both your mind and the computer."

Turcotte forced himself to remain still. He felt nothing different.

He had an MK-98 attached to his right arm. It looked like a jackhammer with an open tube at the end instead of a chisel. It had a laser sight on top and, like the suit, it was painted flat black. A two-foot-long cylinder was loaded in the magazine hold. It held ten depleted uranium darts, each six inches long and an inch in diameter. Each tip was sharpened to a point. The darts were fired by a compressed high-tension spring. When fired, the darts lost no speed to friction going down the barrel because an electromagnetic field kept them in the exact center and on course. It was the best the Space Command had been able to come up with to use as a weapon in a zero-g, no-atmosphere environment. Since there was no atmosphere in space, the rounds would keep going until they struck something.

On his left he had a fully functional oversize replica of a hand, with eight-inch-long fingers. Two of the commandos had MK-99s, which were similar except they fired larger rounds, about the same length but two inches in diameter, that contained high explosive.

"Can I move now?" Turcotte asked.

"Go ahead," Manning said.

It was different with the SARA link, Turcotte quickly learned as he brought his "hand" up in front of his visor. The suit's arm was moving *with* his own arm, not in response to it. A small, but significant difference, he realized. The last time he'd worn the suit, the ever-so-slight delay until the suit reacted to interior movements had been something he had just taken as the price to be paid for the additional armor and strength. But now—all he had to do was move as he normally would and the suit was in synch.

Turcotte picked up Excalibur and slid it into a leather sheath he'd had one of Manning's men rig, attached to the side of the suit with a Velcro strip.

Yakov's voice echoed inside the helmet. "Space station is directly ahead, about five kilometers away. I'm closing on it. No sign of the Talon. It is not answering hails."

Turcotte had fought Aspasia's Shadow several times now. He had learned that nothing was as it seemed and to expect the unexpected in such encounters. He doubted Aspasia's Shadow would abandon the Talon, even if he left Guides on board the spacecraft. But he also knew that the alien creature's goal was the mothership. There was the added factor that Aspasia's Shadow had shown a strong inclination for vengeance, such as rigging Easter Island, and subsequently the entire Pacific Rim for destruction, and now targeting twenty-five major cities for destruction.

"We're a kilometer away," Yakov said. "Closing slowly. I'm going to open your outer hatch. Is everyone suited?"

"Roger that," Manning replied.

The lights in the bay went off, leaving them in pitch-blackness for a few seconds, then a sliver of starlight appeared at the cargo bay door, growing larger as the door opened. The bay decompressed with a puff of air. Manning and his men moved forward, weapons at the ready. Turcotte followed right behind them, switching his display over to night vision, amplifying the starlight.

The space station was directly ahead, three connected modules and the large solar panels extended. And three bodies floated nearby, dressed in blue jumpsuits.

"What was the crew of the station?" Turcotte asked.

Quinn quickly responded. "Three—two American, one Russian."

Three more dead, Turcotte thought. A small number when considered against the toll from the recent world war, but still—why had Aspasia's Shadow taken the space station? Turcotte wondered. He didn't need it. And Turcotte also knew that Aspasia's Shadow knew him.

"The crew are dead," Turcotte said.

"We can see that," Manning said.

Turcotte realized he shouldn't have pointed out the obvious to Manning, but he wanted the captain to realize that only hostiles were on board the space station now.

"Holding in place," Yakov said as he brought the mothership to a halt less than one hundred meters from the space station.

"On me, circle wedge," Manning ordered. The dozen commandos jetted out of the cargo bay, spreading out, left and right, up and down. Turcotte realized this was a very different venue for combat, one where three dimensions had to be considered constantly. He held back, on the edge of the cargo bay. He waited until the lead commando reached the space station.

Then Turcotte activated his jets, moving out of the cargo bay. But he didn't head across to the space station. Instead, he moved up, right next to the surface of the mothership, following it around to the side away from the space station.

The other eleven men held back as the first man to reach the space station moved to the left of the airlock. He placed a shaped charge against the side of the module, and then backed off.

The charge blew, peeling back the side of the module. A

pair of commandos jetted in through the hole, weapons at the ready.

Turcotte watched as the Talon came in fast from directly behind the mothership. It had been hiding to the north, behind the curvature of the Earth. As it closed on the mothership, the lean form rotated, so that the thicker stem was forward. The slightly curved ship decelerated abruptly, so that when it reached the mothership, it was barely moving. The Talon angled against the end of the mothership perfectly but didn't make contact, holding just a few feet away.

Turcotte was in the shadows near the top of the mothership, a shadowy figure that was almost invisible against the black skin of the craft. He saw a flash of light that lasted for a few seconds. On night-vision mode he could see a spacesuited individual leave the Talon and move forward toward the mothership.

Turcotte raised the MK-98 and sighted it at the figure. He waited until it was abreast of him, farther down the ship. Then he fired as quickly as the gun would cycle through the magazine, emptying half of it.

The first depleted uranium dart hit Aspasia's Shadow in the right side, punching through his space suit, through his body, and out the other side. The impact sent his body spinning. The second round missed because of that, but Turcotte was adjusting and the next three all hit, torso shots, tearing apart flesh and bone. Small puffs of red surrounded the body.

Turcotte ceased firing with six rounds still in the chamber. He jetted "down" toward the tumbling body. He had to accelerate to catch up to it as the rounds had not only torn through the body, but also given it velocity. Reaching out with his articulated hand, Turcotte grabbed hold of the lifeless figure.

He was now almost a kilometer from the mothership, so he held on to the body as he arrested his vector.

Holding still in space, high over Earth, Turcotte used the hand to rip into the pack on Aspasia's Shadow's back. He located oxygen lines and pulled them out, keeping a grip on the lines, while turning the body around.

Turcotte brought the figure in close in front of him. He lifted the dark visor and saw Aspasia's Shadow's face. A thick trail of blood leaked from the mouth. The eyes were vacant. Turcotte waited. The eyelids flickered, intelligence showed briefly in the face.

Turcotte closed his "hand," ripping through the oxygen lines. Aspasia's Shadow's mouth opened, gasped for air for several seconds. Then death came once more.

Turcotte considered lashing Aspasia's Shadow to the outside of the mothership just like this. Having him die every few minutes. It seemed a fitting retribution for all the sorrow the creature had inflicted on mankind.

Turcotte looked toward the planet. The demarcation line between day and night was halfway across the United States. He could see a swirl of clouds in the Caribbean, a storm brewing.

Yakov's voice startled him out of his reverie. "My friend? Are you all right?"

"Yeah, I'm fine."

"Where are you? I've had a message relayed from the men on station outside the station. Captain Manning has taken the shuttle back. His men have seized the computer and are working on stopping the launches."

Turcotte had forgotten about the target matrix. He realized he'd forgotten about it because he'd adjusted his thinking to outsmart Aspasia's Shadow—he knew the creature would not be concerned with the matrix either. It had simply been a ploy to lure Turcotte and the mothership here. That's not to say that the launch wouldn't have happened, but rather that Aspasia's Shadow only considered the destruction of all those cities a sideshow to his primary objective, which had been to get the mothership.

He was thinking like his enemy. It was advantageous in battle, Turcotte allowed, as he shifted his view once more to the body he held, noticing the face come to life once more, struggle for air, then die, but it made him feel as if he had a hole drilled clear through his chest. To think like his enemy he had to put aside his humanity.

A thump on the side of his helmet made Turcotte start, then he realized it was his own hand, unconsciously moving up to touch the spot over the implant. That brought him back to the current situation. Aspasia's Shadow. Immortal.

But.

The word echoed in Turcotte's mind. Checks and balances. He doubted very much that the Airlia had designed the Grail to give immortality to humans without having a way of taking back the gift. In his mind he replayed the scene when he had first met Aspasia's Shadow in the mothership, inside Ararat—the first time he'd met the creature after it had partaken of the Grail. Only one thing had seemed to disconcert Aspasia's Shadow.

Turcotte drew the sword from his side and grasped it gingerly with his mechanical hand. He drew the arm back, the stars glistening off the blade.

Aspasia's Shadow's eyes came alive with intelligence. His mouth opened, struggling for air, the pain etched across his features. He focused on the sword above Turcotte's head, and his eyes widened in fear.

Turcotte swung, and the sword sliced through Aspasia's

Shadow's neck, parting head from body in one smooth stroke.

Blood flowed out of the neck for a moment, then stopped. Turcotte waited to see if there would be any change.

After a minute nothing.

Aspasia's Shadow was finally dead.

CHAPTER 16: THE PRESENT

SPACE

Turcotte turned toward the mothership. "Yakov?"

"Yes?"

"How are they doing on stopping the launches?"

"I haven't heard from them since the initial transmission," Yakov said. "FM radio won't reach through the side of the station."

"Damn it," Turcotte cursed.

With one last glance at Aspasia's Shadow's severed head and torso, Turcotte jetted around the mothership toward the space station. He spotted two suited men flanking the tear that had been blown in the side of the station. Turcotte passed between them.

Lights were flickering as the station's power struggled to continue running. There was no one in the module. Turcotte twisted and went headfirst into the connecting corridor. He bumped into one of the commandos as he entered the next module.

He was assaulted by a blast of FM communications. It sounded like everyone was trying to speak at once, the radio waves contained inside the module. Six men in TASC suits were crowded inside along with four dead Guides. They were all gathered around one of their own, who was seated at a laptop computer, trying to type with great difficulty, given the limitations of the oversize hand he was using.

"Shut up!" Turcotte yelled.

The airwaves fell silent.

"Status?"

"I can't get the codes entered," Manning said. Turcotte saw the name tag on the man at the computer and realized it was Manning.

Turcotte checked the chronometer display inside his helmet. Less than three minutes until the matrix was fired. He'd counted on Manning and his men to take care of this. He wouldn't have floated above the planet contemplating Aspasia's Shadow's fate if he'd known there was a problem.

"Why not?"

Manning held up his artificial hand, now with a screwdriver grasped between two large fingers. "Too big."

"Why didn't you bring it back to the mothership?"

Manning was still trying to type in codes using the screwdriver. "By the time we took it off-line from the station's SATCom system, transported it over, hooked it back up and got it on-line..." Manning didn't finish the statement as he continued to peck at the keyboard... "I've got five of the targets off the matrix."

Turcotte found it so amazing he almost started laughing. After all he'd been through, to have the planet devastated by a nuclear strike from his own country—and to fail to stop it because they simply couldn't type in the proper code to stop it in time.

He did a time check. Two minutes.

Turcotte turned toward the side of the module closest to the mothership. He raised the MK-98 and fired his remaining six rounds, tearing a gap in the wall so he could communicate on the local FM band—line of sight.

"Quinn."

"Sir?"

"If we can't get all the stop codes entered in time—options?"

There was silence.

"Seven," Manning announced.

Eighteen to go, Turcotte thought. No way will Manning will make it.

"Quinn?"

"Ten," Manning was poking with the screwdriver.

Turcotte wondered which cities had been saved and which were still doomed as he waited for a response.

"Send a new matrix," Quinn said.

"What?" Turcotte asked.

"It's the quickest way. One new entry instead of deleting all the old entries."

Turcotte reached forward and tapped the commando's commander on the shoulder. "Manning, you get that?"

"I got it, but how do I do it? And the nukes will still go off somewhere."

"Not if you reset to target their own launch sites," Quinn said. "The data is already there—it has to be in order for a matrix to work. Just turn it against itself."

Quinn rattled off a series of numbers and Manning pecked at the keyboard. Turcotte floated in the background, feeling quite useless. He checked the time. Under a minute. The seconds clicked off.

Quinn fell silent. Ten seconds.

"Quinn?" Turcotte asked.

"It's done."

Turcotte grabbed hold and moved himself to the opening he had created. He pushed out of the hatch and looked down at the planet. He could imagine the turmoil on board submarines, inside bombers and launch control centers as crews realized they would be destroying themselves if they launched their weapons. He watched the United States, now almost all in daylight, waiting for the telltale burst of a nuclear weapon exploding as there would be no transit time.

Nothing.

TRIPLER ARMY MEDICAL CENTER, OAHU, HAWAII

It was early morning, a few hours before the sun would come up. Terry Cummings carefully unhooked the various monitoring devices from Kelly Reynolds. Cummings knew that other than the intravenous drip providing nourishment, none of the gear made any difference. The doctors had done all they could and the consensus was that it was a miracle Reynolds was alive and no one had any faith that she would ever recover.

Cummings rolled the bed into the quiet hallway to the elevator. Once on board, she pressed the button for the roof. When the doors slid open, she pushed the bed onto the roof of the center tower of Tripler. Since the hospital was already high up on top of Moanalua Ridge, she had a commanding view of the south side of the island of Oahu. An offshore breeze gently blew across the rooftop. Cummings turned the crank on the side of Reynolds's bed, raising her frail upper body so that she was half-sitting. The lights of Honolulu were off to the left. The island was still in the throes of recovering from the nanovirus assault but life was slowly getting back to normal. Cummings looked down at Reynolds. Her eyes were closed, the skin taut against her cheekbones.

Cummings leaned over, her mouth near Reynolds's ear. "Feel the breeze?" She reached down and took the clawlike hands in her own, rubbing the leathery skin. "Do you feel my hands on yours?"

Cummings moved from the hands up the arms, working Reynolds's entire body, slowly and with great diligence so that when the sun began to rise, she had just finished. Throughout she had spoken to Reynolds, keeping up the conversation as if the other woman were replying. Cummings stretched, then cranked the top half of the bed back down. Focused on pushing it back toward the elevator, she failed to notice a muscle on the side of Reynolds's face twitch as if the woman were trying to speak. The muscle moved for several moments, then subsided.

CAMP ROWE, NORTH CAROLINA

Turcotte was actually looking forward to the journey to Mars. It would be an opportunity to rest and recuperate. As far as what would happen when they got to the Red Planet, he blocked thinking about that right now, shutting down his thought projection as effectively as if a steel door had come down through his mind. He was so tired he knew that any plan he came up with at the moment would likely have serious flaws in it.

They were touching down at Camp Rowe, returning from defeating Aspasia's Shadow—for the last time—a phrase that Turcotte savored. A creature that had led the Mission for generations and haunted the history of mankind had finally been vanquished. It was a victory, a clear-cut one. Yakov was by Turcotte's side as they went down the main corridor of the mothership.

"One down, two to go," Yakov said.

"Excuse me?"

"The Swarm and Artad," Yakov said.

Exactly what Turcotte didn't want to contemplate at the moment. The cargo door slowly slid open and Turcotte paused. There was someone standing by the ramp leading into the mothership, silhouetted by the lights ringing the airfield. A tall woman clutching an old leather briefcase to her chest with an overnight bag at her feet. She had wide shoulders and shoulder-length gray hair.

She extended one hand as Turcotte approached.

"Major Turcotte, I'm Professor Leahy."

"Can you duplicate what Tesla did?" Turcotte asked.

She didn't answer. She kept her hand extended, until Turcotte shook it.

"Yes."

Turcotte blinked, surprised at her confidence. "You only just saw his lost papers, how—"

"Do you want me to make his weapon?" Leahy asked.

Turcotte nodded. Yakov came up behind him.

"Then why are you questioning my answer?" she asked.

Turcotte smiled. "You'll do well with this gang. Welcome aboard." He introduced her to Yakov. The Russian picked up her overnight bag and indicated for her to follow him on board. She pointed where several forklifts were lined up, holding pallets.

"I gave Major Quinn a list of what I'll need. Pretty basic stuff, actually. It wasn't hard to find. And most of what I brought is material I already had. I've been working on Tesla's coil for over thirty years."

"Why?" Turcotte asked.

"Because of the potential." She smiled. "And I was right, wasn't I? You've called, haven't you?"

Turcotte nodded. "Good. Let's move then. We've got a long way to go."

MARS

The Airlia convoy reached the edge of the array. The large vehicles were dwarfed by the pylons arching overhead. They maneuvered around to the one that wasn't complete and came to a halt. Hatches opened on the vehicles and Airlia piled out dressed in black pressure suits. All the survivors that Aspasia had left behind.

Most began putting together prefab enclosures. A handful walked over to the thick base of the pylon. They looked up. The unfinished portion was far above them, but in the lesser gravity of Mars a half dozen Airlia began climbing up the slightly curving outer surface. As they climbed, others began backing up the tracked vehicles, leaving a space in between which they started covering with a heavy material to form a living area.

Twenty miles away, on the ramp, the last vehicle, the one bearing the crystal, was approaching.

SPACE

Garlin was near the Swarm orb, waiting placidly as his tentacle, now attached to the orb, made a report.

On the gurney, Duncan slowly opened her eyes, the virus having repaired the physical damage done to her mind. She lifted her right arm—a fully formed hand with smooth skin was at the end.

There was a throbbing noise inside the spacecraft, something she vaguely recognized. She stared up at the ceiling for several seconds, trying to orient herself. It too was familiar although she couldn't immediately place it. Her head hurt and it was hard to concentrate.

Her last conscious memory was of Garlin cutting off her hand. She stretched the fingers of the new hand. It was strapped to the table at the elbow, limiting her movement. Another strap ran across her ankles, thighs, and chest. She lifted her head, noting the dried blood encrusted on the robe she wore.

Immortal.

The word echoed in her consciousness as her head slumped

back on the table. What good was immortality in the current situation? Where was she? That was the question that bothered her as this place seemed familiar, almost comforting despite her predicament.

Her spaceship—the *Fynbar*. It came to her with a wave of sharply conflicting emotions. A warm, familiar feeling, spiked through with the realization that the Swarm was in control of it. Memories poured through her mind in an overwhelming cascade. Her conditioning had been broken. If she could remember, then the Swarm knew what she did. She felt despair, then, as she was able to sort through the memories, she was crushed with a flood of grief.

Duncan turned her head as tears streamed from her eyes. Two cloning/sleep tubes were at the edge of the room, pressed up against the bulkhead. Her hand closest to them strained against the strap as she reached toward one.

"*My love*," she whispered in a language she had not spoken for over a thousand years. "*My love*."

Ten thousand kilometers behind Duncan's ship, the mothership was moving away from Earth. Yakov was in the pilot's seat, directing the ship onto the vector that Larry Kincaid had programmed in order to intercept Mars. On his lap he had the thin instruction manual containing all the material that Majestic had managed to assemble on the workings of the mothership after studying it for fifty years.

"How long until we get there?" Yakov asked.

Turcotte was seated behind Yakov, eyes closed, head back, apparently asleep. A slight opening of one eye indicated he was awake and also waiting for the answer.

"Just over a day at this speed," Kincaid said.

"And the Swarm and Talon?" Yakov asked.

Kincaid checked his laptop. "The Talon will get to Mars

about two hours before us. The Swarm ship about two hours after that."

"At the same time we arrive?"

"Roughly," Kincaid said. "We're faster than the Swarm ship, but moving at pretty much the same speed as the Talon. I think we might even get to Mars before the Swarm ship."

Two hours. Turcotte considered that. "When will the array be done?" he asked, still without opening his eyes.

Kincaid shrugged, the motion lost on Turcotte. "Hard to say. The convoy just arrived at the construction site."

"What we need to know," Turcotte said, emphasizing the last word, "is whether it will be done before the Talon arrives. If it is, I'm sure Artad can get a message out in two hours."

"We should get an idea pretty soon," Kincaid said. "I think it's going to take them a while. They've got to complete the third pylon by hand, and then who knows what else they have to do to get operational."

Turcotte opened his eyes and wearily got out of the seat. "I don't know much about space travel, but since Mars is moving around the sun, our track isn't exactly a straight shot, right?"

Kincaid brought up an image of the inner four planets of the solar system's orbits on his laptop. "We're heading for this intercept point right here." He indicated a location on Mars orbit ahead of where the planet currently was. He tapped the touch pad and a green dot was fixed in that spot. "The Talon will reach Mars when it's here." Slightly before the mothership intercept a red dot appeared. "And this is its vector." The Talon's path was to the "right" of their track.

"What about the Swarm ship with Duncan?" Turcotte asked.

"Here." A third track and dot appeared, this time to the left of the mothership's.

Turcotte rubbed the stubble on his chin. "You said we're going faster than that ship, right?"

Kincaid nodded. "Somewhat."

"If we change our path to intercept it, where would that happen and how much time would we lose?" Turcotte asked. Yakov had left the pilot's seat and come over during the conversation.

"What do you have in mind, my friend?" the Russian asked.

Turcotte ignored Yakov for the moment as Kincaid calculated.

"We would intercept here." He indicated a spot well short of Mars orbit. "Because we'd change vectors slightly and then have to redirect to intercept Mars, we'd lose a little time, but not much. A couple of minutes, give or take."

"How far out from Mars would the intercept be?" Turcotte asked.

"Three hours."

Yakov cleared his throat. "We must stop Artad first. That is our primary mission."

Turcotte shook his head. "We have to stop both. They're equally important. Artad is first because he gets to Mars first. But"—Turcotte dragged the word out—"if the array isn't complete, then it doesn't matter. And if it is complete, then it doesn't matter if we get there a couple of minutes late."

Yakov frowned. "Are you suggesting that we intercept the Swarm ship first?"

"Why not?" Turcotte asked in turn.

"But what if the array is completed during that few-minute window?"

"Then we screwed up," Turcotte said. "But if we intercept en route, then we have three hours after that to get ready for Artad. If we go straight to Mars, we have to attack Artad and the array, then have the Swarm ship show up a couple of min-

utes later. Things could get very busy." Something had occurred to him as he spoke. "And we have three, not two,
groups we have to stop. Artad and the Swarm aren't enough.
We also have to stop the Airlia on Mars. Even if we stop
Artad, the Airlia on the surface can still send a message. And
let's remember something else. The Airlia on Mars were
Aspasia's. We can't be sure that Artad is going to be welcome
when he shows up. That might gain us some time." Turcotte
turned to Yakov. "What do you think?"

"It is taking a chance intercepting the Swarm ship. I agree,
though, that having the Swarm show up right after we get
there could be a problem. We could be battling the Talon and
it could go straight to the array to send a message. If we do
intercept the Swarm ship en route, how do you propose to
stop it?"

"The old-fashioned way," Turcotte said. "We board it. Just
like pirates used to in the old days."

Yakov shook his head wearily. "Pirates in the old days.
Another great plan."

Artad was lying on his back, his command chair enclosed by
a curved display. He brought up the tactical situation, noting
his ship's projected course to the fourth planet. He also saw
the two spacecraft chasing him.

The mothership he expected. The humans were nothing if
not persistent.

The other ship, though, was a puzzle. There was no record
of its type in the Talon's database. Of course, much might
have happened in the universe during the ten thousand plus
years that he had been disconnected from the Airlia Empire.
There was even the possibility that the empire no longer existed.

That was something Artad choose not to dwell on. The
empire had existed for millions of years. There was no reason

to believe that something drastic had happened in the relatively short time span Artad had been in deep sleep to change that. Even the war with the Swarm had gone on for such a long time, more a war of attrition along a front encompassing galaxies than one of vanquishment. The universe—and empires involved—were simply too large for decisive strategic victories. It was a bitter lesson the Airlia and other species had discovered when they moved out among the stars.

The second ship bothered him. Could it be a human one? Historical records downloaded from the guardian indicated that the humans had achieved minimal space travel, barely able to reach their own moon with a manned mission. This craft was clearly beyond the technological level of the planet. They had barely managed to launch a few primitive probes toward the fourth planet and his Ones Who Wait had sabotaged most of them.

While he knew there was nothing he could use effectively against the mothership, this spaceship was another matter. Artad slid his hands into holes on either side of the command chair. His six fingers made connections with the controls.

A portal opened amidships on the Talon. In rapid succession, a half dozen small pods were ejected. The portal shut as the pods moved through space on an interception course with the third spaceship.

CHAPTER 17: The Present

SPACE

Turcotte walked down the main corridor, taking note of the activity on board the mothership. He had Excalibur in one hand and the sheath in the other. Directly behind the control room, the Space Command troops were billeted in one of the many large holds. The doorway was open and Turcotte could see that most of the men were asleep, lying on pads they had rolled out on the floor. That seemed like a good idea to him.

On the other side of the corridor, through the open door, he could see Professor Leahy and Major Quinn holed up with their pallets of equipment. He was tempted to go in and ask about the weapon and whether they could do it—and if so, when it would be done. But he held back, knowing his asking wouldn't make any difference. Either they would get it done in time and it would work, or they wouldn't. He'd deal with it when the time came.

Turcotte continued down the corridor and stopped at the entrance to the Master Guardian room. The door slid open and he entered. He walked across the narrow metal bridge to the platform on which the red pyramid rested. The surface glowed from within.

Turcotte slid the sword into the sheath and the glow faded. He put the sword down, leaning it against the pyramid. Then he turned to the other objects in the room: the Grail and the thummin and urim.

Turcotte sat down cross-legged, his back against the

Master Guardian, Excalibur by his side. He picked up the Grail. It was surprisingly heavy. He placed it right in front of him.

When he reached for the thummin and urim the stones began to give off a green glow and he paused, his hands over them. Gingerly he picked them up, feeling their warmth seep into his flesh. He held his hands out in front, as if weighing the stones. He lowered his left hand toward the Grail and the top irised open, revealing a slight depression in which the stone would fit snugly. His hand hovered over the opening, then he shook his head, putting the stones back down.

"My friend."

The words startled Turcotte, who had not noticed Yakov entering the chamber. The Russian walked across the gangway until he was right in front of Turcotte, towering over him.

"What are you doing?" Yakov indicated the Grail.

"I don't know."

"It draws you, doesn't it?" Yakov asked as he also sat down.

"It is a dangerous thing."

Yakov nodded. "All powerful things are dangerous. And this"—he reached out and tapped the Grail—"this is the most dangerous thing."

"I believe what I told Aspasia's Shadow," Turcotte said. "This will destroy the world if we bring it back to Earth."

"Yet here you are," Yakov said.

"Yes."

"What should we do with it?"

"If we partake, it will give us an advantage in our upcoming battles," Turcotte said.

Yakov frowned. "But you said you believed what you told Aspasia's Shadow. If we go back to Earth after partaking and *don't* bring the Grail then"—Yakov paused as the implications sank in—"you don't plan on returning to Earth?"

"The thought has crossed my mind. I don't think any of this"—Turcotte indicated the mothership, the Master Guardian, Excalibur, the Grail and stones—"should be brought back. It's caused so much trouble over the years and will cause much more in the future now that some of the truth is out. And if we partake, then we don't belong either."

"Then we will not partake," Yakov said simply.

"We might need the advantage immortality will give us."

"We haven't yet. It did not help Aspasia's Shadow much, did it?" Yakov stood. "My friend, do not doubt yourself now."

Turcotte tapped the side of his head. "What about this thing inside?"

"It hasn't impaired you yet, I would not worry about it."

Turcotte laughed. "You have very easy answers."

"It is the Russian way." Yakov reached down and offered his hand to Turcotte, who took it. Yakov pulled him to his feet. "I say we rest."

"Agreed."

She had failed.

More than failed.

Duncan numbly watched the tentacle detach from the Swarm orb and enter Garlin's mouth. He walked over to the gurney and picked up the crown, setting it on her head. Through the dried blood on her face, her tears had cut their own course, leaving tracks of uncovered skin.

She looked over at the tubes. Despite her best efforts, her chest began to heave as uncontrolled sobs tore through her. Garlin noted this reaction and went over to the tubes. He hit a button and the lid swung up on the one that was occupied. A puff of air escaping indicated the tube had been sealed against the outside environment. A body lay inside, wrapped tightly in linen bandages from head to toe. From the form, it was a human male.

"Leave him alone!" Duncan screamed.

Garlin ignored her, taking a pair of scissors and cutting through the cloth covering the head. He peeled back the linen exposing the man's face. He was the same one from the early images, except very young, with unmarred skin. The man who had escaped the planet with Duncan. His eyes were blank and the body was perfectly preserved. His features bore a striking resemblance to Mike Turcotte, but younger.

Garlin walked over to Duncan, tossing the scissors onto a table. "We destroyed your home world."

Duncan closed her eyes. "When?"

"Seventy-two revolutions around the star after you departed on the mothership."

She could only hope her son had been dead when the Swarm arrived. The scientists' calculations had said it was doubtful many of those left behind would still be alive that many years into the future.

"We will show you, through your own memories and records recovered from your planet." He took one of the lines from the top of the Ark and connected it to a small black circle. Duncan felt a spike of pain and then she "saw," beginning with what she now knew were her own memories:

Hard times require hard choices. A simple and easy to understand maxim until the time comes and the choices are personal. For those who still survived on the ravaged planet located in the Centaurus Spiral Arm of the Milky Way Galaxy, forty thousand light-years away from the Sol System, the hard times had brought about many hard decisions, and the current one being implemented was not only the latest but also the most far-reaching.

Set in what had once been a desert area, but now resembling most of the planet, a massive alien spacecraft—an Airlia mothership—rested on large struts. Military forces patrolled the perimeter while thousands on the inside of the barriers that surrounded the ship waited on the final lots to be chosen to separate the select few who would be on the mothership from the greater majority who would stay behind. It was hotly debated among the inhabitants of the planet which of the options was the more desirable.

It was a harsh planet, made even harsher by the ravages of war and revolution. Those who had survived had made the difficult decision to launch the mothership the previous year and there was still much argument about the wisdom of the act. There were many who wished to do nothing—except hope. That despite the billions who had already died.

Two things had forced the action—one was logical, the other emotional. The cold facts laid out by the scientists indicated that the devastated planet could not sustain the current population beyond another generation. They had won the war but lost the following peace in the process. The burning emotion was to ensure that what had happened to them would not happen to others. And there were others out there. That startling fact had been uncovered when they gained control of the alien mothership and accessed its star map. There was also the unspoken fear that others from the alien race they had defeated would come to investigate the lack of communication from their kin. They had defeated those who had come on the ship at the cost of their own planet. Another ship, with more Airlia, would be too much to fight.

Those who were in the running for the final selection were the best the planet had to offer. Men and women who were at the pinnacle of their chosen fields whether they were scientists or soldiers—and the selection was heavy with the latter, based on their experiences.

Besides people, the mothership would be loaded with ships and weapons that those on the planet had developed under the dire necessity of combat along with scavenged technology from the aliens against whom they had successfully rebelled.

When the final countdown for liftoff began, troops were needed to encircle the launch site to keep out protestors who wanted to stop the launch and those not chosen who desperately fought to be on the ship. Over a mile long and a quarter mile in beam at the center, the black craft rested in a cradle made of the same practically impenetrable metal. Despite the excellent construction of the ship, there were scars on the skin where heavy weapons fire had played along the surface, indicative of the brutal fighting the inhabitants of the planet had waged against those who had flown the ship here. They had captured the mothership during the final assault, overwhelming the last of the aliens who had taken refuge aboard it before they could escape. The war had been savage and the costs almost beyond bearing. For every alien they'd killed, tens of thousands of their own had died.

Among those who crowded onto the interstellar craft, was a young woman, a scientist by training and a mother by love. Also with her was her husband, a soldier who had fought in the Revolution. Their young son was among those who ringed the departure field. The decision to leave their son had not been easy, but where they were going and the mission they had been given precluded the presence of children. That was the cold reasoning of those in power, but the tears streaming down the scientist's face as the cargo door slowly closed, cutting off her view of the distant crowd, indicated *emotion warred against intellect. She knew no matter what her destiny, she would never see her child again.*

She had had many long discussions with her husband about the future of both the mission and their planet. He had been blunt and honest, as was his nature, hiding any emotions with a focus on preparing for the upcoming mission. But she noted his chest moving rapidly as the door shut and their world disappeared from sight. He kept his face averted from hers as he reached out and put his arm around her shoulders. All on board had left loved ones behind, and they were merely an island of misery among a sea of pain. Large as the ship was, the five thousand chosen were tightly packed on board along with their supplies.

At the appointed moment, the ship lifted out of its cradle without a sound. It moved upward, accelerating through the planet's polluted atmosphere until it was in the vacuum of space and out of sight of the millions of eyes on the planet's surface who watched it with mixed emotions. It continued to accelerate conventionally away from the planet and the system star's gravitational field.

After two years of travel, the star's field was negligible and the mothership was moving at three-quarters of the speed of light. It was also far enough away that those on board hoped any sign of its passage would not be linked back to their home world.

At that point the mothership's interstellar drive was engaged. With a massive surge of power as great as that of a brief supernova, the ship shifted into faster-than-light travel and snapped into warp speed.

As had been feared by those left behind on the planet, the warp shift was eventually noted by sensors on board a Swarm scout ship over twenty light-years away. The scout

*immediately turned in the direction of the disturbance. It rec-
ognized the pattern as that of a mothership belonging to a
race it had fought against for millennia.*

*Star maps were brought up on the scout's control room
display and all nearby star systems were marked for recon-
naissance. An alert was sent to the nearest battle core.*

*The planet had circled the star over sixty times since the de-
parture of the mothership, which was equal to the now average life span of those who survived there. Those who
remembered its launch were few and far between and their
words little heeded by their offspring, who struggled to eke
out their survival among further diminished resources. The
civilization, what was left of it, was barely at a subsistence
level, so there was no technology sufficient to notice when the
Swarm scout ship finally entered the star system, the fourth
on its list to be checked. Signs of intelligent life were immediately noted on one of the planets. The small ship swung
around the star and took a long time to decelerate so that
when it reached the planet it could move into a stable orbit.*

*Once in position, probes were sent down to the planet's
surface. The population of the planet was by then less than
twenty million, a small number on the intergalactic scale, but
the crew of the scout ship didn't concern itself with numbers,
only with the fact that there was intelligent life on the planet.
The scout descended to the planet and secreted itself beneath
one of the seas while the crew did a closer and more intimate
inspection of the populace.*

*While the crew continued to gather information and infil-
trate the population, a probe was launched. It moved into
space a sufficient distance from the planet, then transmitted a
message into the vastness of space from which the scout had
come. The nearest battle core had already been alerted when
the scout had picked up the mothership transition and it was*

already on its way. This message updated the strategic situation and pinpointed which star system and planet was to be targeted.

The Swarm orbs and tentacles sent to the planet's surface to infiltrate the people learned some things of value. That there had indeed been a mothership, of a type they were familiar with, but there was no sign of the race—the Airlia—that had built the mothership. They also learned that the mothership had departed just prior to the time of the interstellar shift nearby so the logical assumption was that the mothership had departed, abandoning the planet for some reason. They also learned that the remaining population—not Airlia, but rather an apparently rudimentary intelligent species—was not currently capable of spaceflight and offered no interstellar threat.

The son of the couple who had departed on board the mothership had only vague memories of his parents. He was a grandparent. He worked the land, his body bent and worn by the physical labor of trying to produce enough food to survive. Once in a while he told his own offspring of watching the mothership depart, but with each passing year the story became more myth than real. Even the Revolution that had preceded the launch seemed distant, though the ruins of a city destroyed during the fighting could be seen on the western horizon. For those who lived in grass huts and caves, even the ruins of the city were overwhelming.

There were even those who wondered if their forbears had been right to revolt against the "gods." Things must have been better when man could inhabit such glories as the ruined city indicated had once existed. The word freedom lost much of its strength when one's back was weighted down with field work. Even the son wondered once in a while why his parents had abandoned him. What was out there among the stars that was more important than family?

Twelve years after the scout ship had landed on the planet, the Swarm Battle Core arrived. The couple's son's wife had died several years previously, her heart giving out as she worked in the fields. The son was confined to a chair and daily considered taking his own life rather than be a burden to his family.

When the Core appeared overheard, at first he thought it was the mothership returning, but then seeing how high up it was, he realized with a shudder that whatever was overhead dwarfed the size of the mothership. The shadow of the Battle Core covered half the planet, causing an unnatural eclipse.

The son remembered tales he had been told as a child and he spoke of the Ancient Enemy in whispers, but such babble meant little to his children and grandchildren who had not seen the mothership depart with their own eyes or remembered the wars and devastation that had preceded that event. Still, a feeling of dread swept over the surviving people as they gazed up at the behemoth.

The scout ship left the planet's surface and rendezvoused with the Battle Core. The Core was in essence a self-sustaining mechanical planet with a star drive. Over six thousand miles long, by four thousand high, and two hundred wide, it was massive enough to generate a discernible gravity field.

The scout's report indicated there was only one thing of value on the surface of the planet and that the inhabitants were no technological threat given the regression that had occurred. The report also said that the planet's ecosystem had been so damaged by war that the intelligent life would not last beyond another two generations.

Report done, the scout was dispatched toward the site where the faster-than-light shift had occurred so many years previously and instructed to follow the track of the mother-ship.

Warships deployed from the Battle Core. The fleet spread out in equidistant orbit, bracketing the planet. Each capital ship was twice as large as a mothership and shaped differently, in the form of massive orbs with eight protruding arms bristling with weapons and launch portals. What was coming was exactly what they had been designed to do. The scout's estimate that the intelligent life would be extinct in what was for those in the fleet a relatively short time mattered little. There was intelligent life there now.

Every arm on each ship launched planetary craft, spewing them out, smaller versions of the larger interstellar craft until there were over two million of them dropping down toward the planet's surface. Like large black rain they descended, through daylight on one side of the planet and in darkness on the other, targeted toward population centers that had been mapped out by the scout's infiltrators.

At precisely the same moment around the world the attack ships landed and portals opened.

The son saw one of the ships land in the field where his wife had died. When he caught a glimpse of what came out of the invading ship, it was worse than the horrible stories his father had once told. His heart gave in to the shock and he died in his chair.

He was one of the lucky ones.

When the rest of the inhabitants of the planet saw what came out of the invading craft the shock and fear paralyzed most. Some fought but were quickly overwhelmed. Then the harvest began and the screams reached into the heavens.

Duncan realized she was screaming in concert with what the Swarm had just shown her. The images disappeared and she opened her eyes, blinking away tears. She wondered how much of what she had seen was her memories, Swarm information, and her imagination. She knew the images of her son grown were her mind, projecting forward, as it had done so many times. But she also knew all she had seen was true in essence.

"Why do you do this?" she demanded. "Why do you kill and destroy?"

"We keep the universe clean."

" 'Clean'?"

"Species like you are a disease that must be eradicated before you infect and destroy us."

"And the Airlia?"

"Yes. If we did not fight the Airlia, they would have destroyed us. We have found it is the way of all intelligent life. It centers on itself and sees all others as threats."

"As you do."

"Yes. And as you do."

"Can't species coexist?" Duncan asked.

"The history of the planet we just left indicates humans can't even exist peacefully within their own species on a single planet. What do you think they would do with other species from other planets? They are a disease that must be stopped quickly before it infects us."

"How much of Earth's history has been due to interference from the Airlia?" Duncan demanded. "Have humans ever had a chance to make it on their own?"

"We do not care."

Duncan wondered if she had led the Swarm to Earth. If the scout ship had successfully followed the mothership she and her husband, Gwalcmai, had been on. And her son? She had abandoned him to a terrible fate.

Garlin turned on the Ark and the probe blasted into

Duncan's brain, ending her ruminations as her head slammed back on the gurney from the pain.

The round table reappeared on the screen. But this time there were no knights sitting around it. Just a single man in battered armor seated facing the door to the chamber. A sword was on the table in front of him, the blade covered with dried blood.

The door opened and Duncan entered, walking around the table. She was in the same long robe with silver fringe as the previous vision. She took the seat next to the man, turning it so that she faced him.

The screen suddenly went dark and Garlin turned to the table. Lisa Duncan was staring at him, a muscle on the side of her jaw twitching. "No more. My memories are mine."

Garlin turned back to the machine and upped the power for the probe.

Tension filled Duncan's face as she consciously fought the invasion of her mind. Sweat poured down her forehead.

The screen flickered with color but no coherent images.

Garlin continued to raise the power level.

The battle became so intense, the sweat was replaced with blood.

But still no image appeared.

Mike Turcotte slept. And for the first time in months, he had no dreams. It was a deep, body-and-mind-replenishing slumber.

In the mothership control room, Yakov was carefully checking out the instruments, assuming that anything as drastic as a self-destruct for the mothership wouldn't be easily accessible. He used the Majestic binder as a guide as much as he could. He was particularly focused on the part of the control panel that Aspasia's Shadow had accessed. Weapons would be a useful thing to have ready when they reached the ship the Swarm was on and then Mars.

In the forward left hold, Major Quinn held a roll of duct tape in one hand and an eight-foot-long crowbar in his other. His fatigue shirt was soaked with sweat and his short hair was plastered tight against his skull. Doctor Leahy was leaning over a set of diagrams, running her finger along a circuit, occasionally looking up to compare the diagram with the device that she was directing Quinn to build.

So far, all he had done was lay out a set of plastic "footprints" as Leahy called them, in an elliptical configuration, twenty feet long by ten wide.

"One of the problems people have had with Tesla coils," Leahy said, "is that they were using the wrong material for the wire and they were simply wrapping it in a standard, circular coil. However, the major problem is that they used the wrong material to support the coils. When you produce an electromagnetic field of such intensity, most material will draw off some of the power. More importantly, though, is the frequency."

Quinn nodded, as if he had a clue what she was talking about.

Leahy left the plans and went to a large plastic case. She undid the latches and threw the top open.

"I've been working on this off and on for the past twenty-five years."

"Why?" Quinn asked as he walked over to see what was in the box.

"Because I studied Tesla and his inventions in college and I realized he was on to things, but for some strange reason, the scientific community had never followed up on his theories."

"What is that?" Quinn asked. A complex series of different-colored wires, woven about six marble posts was inside the box. He had never seen anything like it.

"The core of a modified Tesla coil—pretty close to what you uncovered, but I see now I was wrong about a few things."

"Can you modify it?"

Leahy smiled. "Hell, yeah."

CHAPTER 18: THE PRESENT

MARS

Six space-suited Airlia clung to the top of the quarter-mile-high third pylon. Below them was the bowl the mech-machines had dug out, covered with black mesh laid on top of struts. Other Airlia were in the center of the bowl, having secured cables from the tops of the other two pylons and awaiting the last set of cables from this one.

The final piece of pylon was secured in place. The six Airlia stood on a narrow platform to the side and activated a control. Cables inside the pylon spun out, slowly descending in the weak Martian gravity.

Once the cables reached the bottom, they were secured by the waiting Airlia to a large wire mesh basket. Then they turned and looked toward the lip of the bowl, where the track that carried the green crystal had been parked. With a lurch it began to move, heading down toward the center, moving very slowly underneath the metal array.

SPACE

"I think Aspasia's Shadow disabled the mothership's weapons system."

Turcotte kept his eyes closed. He recognized Yakov's voice and assumed it was the Russian's large hand on his shoulder that had just woken him.

"I've been trying to work the console he was using," Yakov continued, "and it's dead."

Turcotte sighed. "So even in death he still tries to foil us." He opened his eyes and swung sideways, putting his feet on the deck. "We didn't know if we could use the mothership's weapons anyway. So we stick with our original plan. How is Leahy doing with Tesla's weapon?"

"I don't know."

Turcotte stood. He felt better but still tired. It would take a week of sleep for him to make up for all he had recently been through. "How far from intercept with the Swarm ship?"

"An hour."

Turcotte left the room and turned right down the main corridor. The hatch to the hangar Leahy and Quinn were in was open and Turcotte paused in the opening, taking in the strange device that the two were laboring over. It looked more like a power substation than a weapon. A center twenty-foot tower stood among a series of looped coils. On top of the tower was a platform with six marble columns and wires wrapped around them.

"Is it ready?" Turcotte asked, not expecting a positive response.

"Almost," Leahy replied.

"We're less than an hour out from the Swarm ship," Turcotte said. "Will it be ready by then?"

"Theoretically." Leahy had a wrench in her hands and was tightening something down at the base of the tower.

" 'Theoretically'?" Turcotte repeated. "Why doesn't that give me a warm and fuzzy feeling?"

Yakov cleared his throat. "Do we have a plan B for intercept if we can't use that?" He indicated the Tesla weapon.

"I wasn't too clear on the details of plan A," Turcotte said. "Never mind come up with a plan B. Theoretically," he continued, loudly enough so that Quinn and Leahy could hear

him, "plan A should be ready by the time we make intercept."
He turned toward the main corridor. "I'm going to suit up."

"What kind of weapons does this ship have?"

Duncan stared at Garlin. "None."

"You lie."

"Why do you need weapons?" Duncan asked.

"What kind of weapons does this ship have and how are
they activated?"

Duncan shook her head, trying to clear the pain of the
most recent probe. "This ship has no weapons."

The drip of blood from Garlin's left ear was a steady
trickle. His skin was paler than it had been. The side of his
face was constantly jumping as if from a nervous tic.

"Nothing? Particle beam? Plasma? Arrayed pulse?"

Duncan laughed bitterly. "Those were all beyond our capabilities."

"Then how did you overthrow the Airlia on your planet?"

"Blood. Lots of it. And we helped them defeat themselves."

Garlin remained still as the tentacle inside absorbed this
information. Her answers were not acceptable. The orb had
detected a mothership closing on this ship with an intercept
coming shortly. A scan of the oncoming craft revealed its
weapons systems were off-line, which reduced the threat
considerably. The Swarm was evaluating options.

"Defensive capabilities?" Garlin asked.

"Is someone chasing us?"

"If this ship is destroyed," Garlin said, "you will be adrift
in space. You will die, come back to life and die again. For
eternity."

"Who is after us? The Airlia?" Duncan's eyes widened.
"Turcotte. He's coming."

"It would do you well to tell me about the ship's capabilities."

Duncan laughed. "I will never help you."

"Then you will suffer until you tell us." Garlin picked up the saw he had used on her hand. He slashed down with it across Duncan's right arm, cutting through the forearm.

Duncan screamed and thrashed against the straps holding her down.

Just as Garlin finished cutting through her arm, there was an explosion, and the ship canted hard left. He fell forward, the saw cutting into his own chest, splattering his blood on top of Duncan's. Garlin staggered back from the gurney, looked at the hole in his chest, and died.

At the controls, the Swarm orb jerked the ship about to avoid hitting another mine.

"Range?" Turcotte asked.

"One thousand kilometers and closing rapidly," Yakov replied over the radio net. "Hold on. It's changing course. Taking evasive action."

"Then it knows we're coming," Turcotte said.

"Hard to hide this ship," Yakov said. "We're still closing."

Turcotte was in a forward cargo bay along with the rest of Captain Manning's team. They were suited and ready to go.

"Quinn," Turcotte said. "Status on the weapon?"

Leahy's voice responded, "I think it's ready."

Turcotte bit off his retort. He realized her life in academia had not exactly prepared her for the realities of their current predicament.

"Six hundred kilometers," Yakov announced. "Leahy's set up a remote firing system for the Tesla gun."

Gun? Turcotte wondered. They didn't even know if it would work. "What kind of range does she think we can fire from?" he asked.

"The closer the better."

Again, Turcotte choked down a smart-ass retort. He considered the situation and came up with the only possible solution. "We don't know what kind of armament this ship we're approaching has. Tell Leahy if it fires anything at us, she fires immediately. If it doesn't fire, let's get within five hundred meters. Then she fires, hopefully breaches the hull, and we assault."

"And if the weapon doesn't breach?" Captain Manning asked.

Turcotte shrugged even though no one could see the gesture inside the TASC suit. He was tired of being the one people turned to for plans in situations where there were no established parameters from which to work. "Then we back off and lob a Cruise missile at the damn thing."

"And Ms. Duncan?" Yakov asked.

"*Now* you're worried about her?" Turcotte didn't wait for a response. "We don't have any choice. We've got to stop the Swarm first. If we can rescue her, fine. I don't see any other way to do this. Do you?"

A long silence answered his question.

"One hundred kilometers and slowing," Yakov finally said. "It's no longer trying to evade."

"Open the cargo doors," Turcotte ordered.

A fifty-meter-wide door slid open in front of the team. Turcotte looked ahead but he couldn't see the Swarm ship, even when he shifted to night-vision mode. It was somewhere against the blackness of space.

"Fifty kilometers."

"Anyone see it?" Turcotte asked.

No answer.

"Ten kilometers."

"I see something," one of the team members called out. "Ahead and slightly to the right."

Turcotte oriented himself, went to maximum amplification, then he saw it too. The same ship that had escaped him at Stonehenge. He could tell Yakov was slowing the mothership as the objective got closer.

"Leahy?" Turcotte found he was almost whispering. He half expected some sort of weapon to be fired at them from the craft.

"Yes?"

"Are you ready?"

"Yes. I've got a lock on the target."

Why hadn't she said so? "Then fire now," Turcotte said. He saw no point in waiting.

For several seconds nothing happened, then the display inside his helmet went bright white and he closed his eyes as the computer shut down the night-vision mode to prevent it from burning out.

Duncan felt the throb of pain from her right arm. She turned her head and saw that Garlin was lying on the floor dead. Then the ship rocked once more. There was smoke billowing from several panels.

If the Swarm had wanted to know about weapons, then someone must be after them. Duncan looked down at the straps holding her to the gurney. Her right arm was severed halfway down the forearm. The spurt of blood ceased as she watched, but the jagged edge of the two bones poked out unevenly because of Garlin's aborted cut. She jerked back on the arm, slipping the shortened length under the restraints. She twisted her body and jabbed the end of the bone into the restraint on her other arm. The sharp end punctured the nylon. She began sawing, using her own bone to cut, ignoring the throb of pain.

She heard a cracking noise and turned her head to the left as she continued sawing. Garlin's mouth was wide open and the tip of the tentacle appeared, forcing its way out of the dying host.

Duncan sawed faster.

Turcotte opened his eyes and his screen slowly came to life. "Did we get a hit?" he called out.

"Dead on," Yakov yelled, causing Turcotte to flinch as the sound echoed inside the helmet.

Turcotte looked ahead. He saw the ship, not far away. "Range?"

"One kilometer and closing," Yakov said. "It was doing evasive maneuvers, but it's on a steady and straight trajectory now, no acceleration."

There was a black mark along the top of the craft where the Tesla gun had hit it. Turcotte didn't see a breach in the hull. "We need an opening. Leahy, can you punch a hole in it?"

"I can try," Leahy responded.

Duncan cut through the restraint across her chest and arms as the Swarm tentacle cleared Garlin's now-dead body. She sat up and used her good hand to unbuckle the other straps. The tentacle slithered to the floor and crept toward the Swarm orb, which was still at the controls.

Free of the gurney, Duncan looked about. She could see the display screen in front of the orb. A mothership filled the view. She could even see an open hatch near the front of the ship and several figures dressed in TASC suits waiting at the edge. There was another open hatch to the right of it and some sort of machine in the bay. A machine that suddenly began sparking.

A weapon, Duncan realized. Getting ready to fire. She looked about wildly, then made her decision.

Turcotte shut off the night vision for his helmet and watched the next bolt of power streak from the mothership to the other spacecraft. The blast knocked the craft sideways, sending it tumbling, a small hole punched in its top. The ship vented atmosphere and debris out of the hole, but no bodies that he could see. They were now within five hundred meters.

"Let's go," Turcotte said as he jetted out of the cargo bay.

He headed across, weapons at the ready. Checking his rear view, he could see the rest of Manning's team following. He concentrated his attention forward as he got closer. When he was less than fifty meters from the spaceship, he slowed as the team deployed on either side and above and below.

"Hold and cover me," he ordered.

The men spread out farther and jetted to a halt. Turcotte continued forward, toward the breach in the hull. He kept the reticule that aimed the MK-98 directed at the opening. His feet hit the deck and he slipped, then tumbled as he tried to balance himself. He slapped the barrel of the MK-98 against the hull to stop.

Turcotte got to his feet and edged closer to the opening. The plating had been torn up, leaving a six-foot-wide, irregular gap, just large enough for him to slip through. He went to night-vision mode as he entered the dark interior.

"I'm going in."

Turcotte stepped into the hole and jetted down, spinning so that as he entered, he was turning, weapon at the ready.

A tentacle coiled around the barrel of the MK-98, pulling it and him sideways. Turcotte fired, rounds ricocheting off metal. He pulled back, trying to regain control of the weapon as he saw the Swarm orb next to him, one tentacle on the gun, another tentacle holding something shiny. With his other hand, Turcotte grabbed Excalibur, using the MK-98 for leverage to swing around as a red bolt came out of the shiny object and just missed him.

He swung the sword, severing the tentacle holding the gun. He brought the barrel to bear as a second red bolt hit him in the chest and knocked him backward. An alarm was chirping and something was flashing on the display panel, but Turcotte ignored that as he fired, the depleted uranium rounds ripping into the Swarm orb and through it, splattering the hull behind with grayish fluid. Turcotte emptied the entire cylinder into the creature and when that was done he jetted forward, the point of Excalibur leading.

He slid the blade into the creature to the hilt and jerked upward, slicing through the Swarm as if it were butter. The blade came out of the top of the orb with a spray of gray blood and viscera.

Turcotte moved back. The Swarm orb was sliced open from midpoint to top. Neither tentacle moved and he had to assume it was dead. The eyes he could see were blank and dull, showing no sign of life.

He took in his surroundings, searching for Duncan. He saw the gurney she'd been strapped to, but she wasn't on it. He focused on an object floating next to the table—an arm severed at midforearm. A woman's arm to judge from the hand.

"We're reading damage to your suit," Captain Manning's voice filled the helmet. "You're venting oxygen."

Turcotte checked the readouts. He was down to 22 percent oxygen, and as he watched it went to 21 percent. He didn't feel any pain so he assumed the suit had taken the brunt of the Swarm's firing.

Where the hell was Duncan?

He scanned the interior of the ship but didn't see her. Had she been vented and he hadn't noticed? Then he saw the two tubes crammed in the rear right corner of the ship. He moved over and looked into the first. A body wrapped in white linen was inside, the face uncovered. He moved over to the other tube and looked in. Duncan lay inside, her eyes closed. There was a mist about her. Turcotte figured the tube was sealed and she had an atmosphere.

"You're well below safety levels," Manning announced. "We're coming in for you."

Turcotte was feeling a little light-headed. He looked about the interior of the ship. The command chairs were human-sized. Not Swarm. Not Airlia. Designed for a human.

"Strange," Turcotte muttered, then he passed out.

CHAPTER 19: THE PRESENT

MARS

The green crystal was set in the wire mesh basket and the Airlia climbed on board the vehicle. It headed out of the bowl as the cables began to retract, lifting the crystal upward above the array.

SPACE

Turcotte regained consciousness to find Yakov's bearded face leaning over him. He immediately closed his eyes. Yakov laughed.

"Wake up, my friend. We are getting close to Mars. Closer than anyone has ever been."

"Anyone from Earth," Turcotte muttered as he reluctantly opened his eyes and sat up. He was in the room they had commandeered for their sleeping area. "What happened?"

"Captain Manning brought you back just in time. You were out of oxygen." Yakov pointed. Turcotte's TASC suit was on the floor. There was a rip in the upper right chest. "You were lucky."

"Duncan?" Turcotte asked. Looking down, he saw a large purplish bruise on his skin, beneath the place where the suit had absorbed the force of the Swarm's weapon, another minor injury to add to all the others.

"She is still in the tube. She appears to be in some sort of deep sleep and I didn't see a need to disturb her."

Turcotte knew Yakov didn't trust Duncan and the reality was that he didn't see a need to have to deal with her right now. Turcotte thought differently.

"We brought the ship into one of the large cargo bays," Yakov continued. "The Swarm orb is dead."

That was one thing Turcotte had had no doubts about. Everything else, however, was up in the air. "How far out are we from Mars?" Turcotte headed for the door.

"Two hours."

"Artad's Talon?"

"Arriving at Mars in a few minutes."

"Kincaid got anything further on the array?"

"He thinks it's just about complete."

Turcotte felt a moment of panic as they headed toward the control room. " 'Just about'? How just about? Can they transmit?"

"There's been no indication of that yet, but Kincaid doesn't really know. He says all three pylons are complete and they are bringing something up in the center of the array on cables. Some sort of green crystal. Probably a power source or means of focusing power for the transmission is Kincaid's best guess."

They entered the control room. Captain Manning was there along with Kincaid, Quinn, and Leahy. Turcotte nodded at the Space Command captain, silently acknowledging his thanks.

Turcotte immediately turned to Leahy. "How far out can you hit the array with the Tesla gun?"

"I can't."

That stopped Turcotte. "What?"

"The second shot fried the central coil. I don't have the material on board to make another one."

Turcotte stared at her in silence for a few seconds, processing this piece of bad news. Then he shifted to Manning. "How far out before we can nuke it?"

The Space Command captain shifted his feet nervously. "The nukes weren't our idea. The Pentagon delivered them figuring we could use some firepower. They're actually Tomahawk cruise missiles and the problem with that is—"

"A Tomahawk has an oxygen-fueled rocket engine," Turcotte completed the sentence.

"We can lob them, using the mothership's velocity and direction," Manning suggested.

"I don't think Artad is just going to allow us to do a bombing run," Turcotte said. "The Talon could pick them off at will as they come in on a straight trajectory." He looked at Yakov. "Can you show us what we're facing?"

Yakov tapped the control panel and a large display came alive with a view of Mars. The Red Planet hung against the darkness of space. Yakov continued tapping the same key and Mars grew larger with each touch.

"It is the only way I know how to do this," Yakov said apologetically.

Soon the fourth planet filled the screen, but Yakov continued to zoom in. "I've got us heading directly toward Mons Olympus," he explained.

There was no mistaking the massive mountain as it first became visible. The base was hundreds of miles wide, gently sloping up to the top of the extinct volcano.

"What's that?" Leahy asked, as a line from the base extending inward became apparent.

Kincaid answered. "That's the track the Airlia mechmachines made from Cydonia to the transmitter site." He stepped closer and pointed. "There's the transmitter."

Yakov stopped hitting the controls as the large bowl carved out of the side of the volcano just short of the top became clear. The three pylons towered over the bowl. And in the center there was a glowing green dot.

"That's what they just put in place," Kincaid said, tapping the dot.

"So is it ready to transmit?" Turcotte asked.

"Hell, I have no idea," Kincaid said. "I don't even exactly know how it works. We use our version of this at Arecibo in Puerto Rico as a receiver, which is a passive activity. If this thing in the center is a power source, then they must be close. If it isn't, then they still need to get power from something. I would assume sending a message as far as they need to would require a tremendous amount of power."

Guesswork. Turcotte stared at the screen. Had he made a mistake going after the Swarm first? He realized the answer would be yes if Artad got a message off in the next two hours. He shook off his uncertainty.

"Anyone have other options than trying to lob some nukes on that thing?"

"We could land the mothership on top of it," Yakov suggested.

"While Artad attacks us with the Talon?" Turcotte threw back.

"Can a Talon hurt this ship?" Yakov replied in turn.

"Can we take the chance?" Even as he asked, Turcotte realized they were going nowhere fast. He stared at the array. "We've got two problems. The array and Artad. Our priority is destroying the array. Then we can deal with Artad. The problem is that Artad doesn't want us to do that, so we'll probably have to deal with him first."

There was no answer. Turcotte threw the variables up in his mind. Artad. The Array. The mothership. The nukes. The TASC suits. Then he realized they had an additional card up their sleeves.

"I've got an idea."

MARS

The cables pulled tight and halted. The green crystal was centrally located above the center of the dish. Along the crest of the dish, the Cydonia Airlia stood, looking down at what they had done.

Their sense of accomplishment disappeared, though, as a long, lean, slightly curving black form appeared overhead.

TRIPLER ARMY MEDICAL CENTER, OAHU, HAWAII

Nurse Cummings massaged Kelly Reynolds's left leg, making sure that blood got to the unused muscles. They were on the roof of the main tower of Tripler, with the south coast of Hawaii laid out in all its splendor. The doctors were still pessimistic about the possibility of Reynolds recovering, but Cummings saw no reason why the woman shouldn't. As far as she was concerned there was nothing wrong with Reynolds that more rest, nutrients, and sunshine couldn't cure.

A young doctor, one of the team that had basically written Reynolds off, came onto the roof to smoke. He saw Cummings with Reynolds and appeared embarrassed. Whether because he had given up on a patient, or she had caught him smoking, Cummings wasn't sure.

As he puffed furtively a short distance away, Cummings switched from the left leg to the right. The calf was barely larger than the bone, most of the muscle having been consumed by the body as it had attempted to keep itself alive during the stay under Easter Island.

Cummings pressed her fingers into the flesh, massaging what little muscle she could find. Out of the corner of her eye she caught a movement and she looked up quickly. But

Reynolds's eyes were still closed and she was still, a strap going around her chest and forehead, holding her upright in the wheelchair. As she went back to work, Cummings kept her attention split between leg and upper body.

"There!" Cummings cried out.

The startled doctor quickly stubbed out the cigarette. "What?"

"Did you see that? Did you?"

"See what?"

"Her hand. It moved. She lifted her forefinger."

The doctor shook his head. "She can't. Her brain has—" His words came to an abrupt halt as Reynolds's right forefinger lifted a half inch off the armrest of the chair. "I don't believe it."

Cummings leaned close to Reynolds's ear. "Do it again."

The finger lifted once more.

"She understands."

The doctor put his stethoscope to Reynolds's thin chest. "Her heart rate is accelerated."

"Of course," Cummings said. "She's putting everything she has into moving that finger." She peered at Reynolds's face, noting the quivering around the eyelids. "She'll be talking soon. Very soon."

MARS

Artad exited the Talon with a dozen Kortad backing him up. As soon as he was clear of the airlock, the ship rose into the Martian sky and took up an overwatch position ten kilometers above Mons Olympus.

The Airlia who had finished the array were in front of him. As he approached, they prostrated themselves. Their leader, whom Artad had known briefly many years previously, dropped to one knee.

"We have prepared the array for you."

They had prepared the array for him because they had no other choice, Artad knew. They could not call back to the empire and ask for help after their role in the civil war here so many years ago. They were criminals, traitors, who could only throw themselves on his mercy.

"Is it ready to transmit?"

"Shortly. It is powering up." The Airlia got to his feet and led the way to a tracked vehicle that was linked to the array with numerous cables.

Artad paused before following. He looked about. He saw the army of mech-machines that had been stopped in their tracks when the humans took over the Master Guardian and shut down the subordinate guardians. The magnitude of the loss of a master along with its Excalibur control was staggering. His reprimand when the fleet arrived would be great. And after over ten thousand years, what would his status be? He didn't even know what the status of the empire was. He assumed it was strong, as it had existed for many times that length of time. But what if—

Artad looked up. He knew the mothership was en route, with humans on board coming to stop him. And the Master Guardian was on board the mothership. Their arrogance was beyond belief.

It would be a much better message if it contained a more positive summary than the current status report, Artad realized.

SPACE

They had a plan. It wasn't the best, but Turcotte had served in Special Forces and he knew there was no such thing as a best plan, other than staying home and pulling the covers over one's head.

They were just under an hour out. Everyone else was in the control room, watching the array. Turcotte knew watching wouldn't make the time go by any quicker. He went down the main corridor until he reached the crossway leading to the hangar bay in which they had brought the ship with Duncan on board. Turcotte went into the bay and up the ramp into the ship.

Duncan was in the tube, eyes closed. A light on the side of the tube was green. Turcotte had to assume that meant it was functioning correctly, although he could not see her chest rise and fall. Her breathing must be down to an extremely slow rate, he figured.

Turcotte went over to the other tube. The light on this one was red. The man's face was slack, the eyes full of a dullness Turcotte had seen too many times before—he was dead, of that there was no doubt.

Turcotte swung the lid open and examined the body. The skin was flawless, with no scars or other marks. The man appeared to be in his late teens or early twenties, in excellent physical shape at the time of death. He didn't even have any calluses on the bottoms of his feet. It was as if the man had never left the tube.

Which he hadn't, Turcotte knew. He'd seen a tube like this before. Deep under Mount Sinai. The one Aspasia's Shadow had used to regenerate his new body. Apparently it had two functions, he realized, glancing over at Duncan's tube. It not only could regenerate a new body, it also could put someone in deep sleep—a necessary thing, he supposed, for travel in deep space.

Turcotte looked about. The interior was sparse, emphasizing function over comfort, much like a present-day submarine. He walked to the front, where two chairs faced a control console. He sat down in the right-hand seat. It felt familiar, which irritated him. What had been in his brain? He had a good idea who had put it there.

He scanned the console. If the seat felt familiar, then perhaps other things would strike a chord. A flat screen to the right, set at an angle in the console, caught his attention. There were five buttons with markings below it. He reached and tapped one. The screen flickered, then came alive.

In rapid succession a series of scenes played out on the screen. Turcotte saw Duncan and her companion aboard a mothership, leaving their homeworld and son. Departing the mothership outside the solar system. Landing on Earth. Burying the ship at what would become Stonehenge. Raising the first "stones" there.

Then he caught quick glimpses of the two of them throughout Earth history.

On a wonderful island with a huge palace in the center that he assumed had to be Atlantis. They were dressed in local garb and ambushing an Airlia in the streets and killing him.

On a ship, pulling away from the island kingdom as it was destroyed by a mothership.

Returning to the buried spaceship, regenerating new bodies, transferring their essences via the *ka,* and emerging.

In Egypt, sneaking around in the dark, again killing an Airlia in ambush. A confrontation along the Roads of Rostau with what appeared to be Ones Who Wait, Airlia-Human half-breeds.

Regenerating.

Greece. In the newly completed Parthenon, watching and listening to orators.

In a field, killing someone—a One Who Waits—who tried to ambush them.

Regenerating.

Rome. In the stands of the Coliseum watching gladiators hack at each other with swords.

The scenes began to flicker by so quickly he could barely comprehend a tenth of what he was seeing. Every forty years or so the two would return to Stonehenge and transfer to a new body. The same form of "immortality" that Aspasia's Shadow had had. So she had lied to him from the very beginning, which did not surprise Turcotte at this point.

He saw the two of them at Camelot. Aspasia's Shadow as Mordred. Artad's Shadow as Arthur. Duncan in the court, dressed in a white robe. The man in armor, next to the king.

Turcotte had an idea what was behind what he was seeing. Duncan and her partner had operated covertly, trying to manipulate the Airlia and their minions.

Then he saw a brutal battle, the dead and dying littering a field. Swords and spears covered in blood. Duncan's partner taking a sword blow to the chest from someone wielding Excalibur. His *ka* damaged. Duncan dragging him on a travois back to Stonehenge, unable to pass his essence on to the regenerated body. Turcotte glanced over his shoulder at the tube holding the dead man.

Looking back, he saw Duncan in the mothership cavern at Area 51, but it was unopened, dark. She was sealing it with explosives. So she had tried to hide the truth, Turcotte realized. Why? And the answer came to him as quickly as he posed the question—because man wasn't ready to challenge the Airlia yet.

Duncan in the ship. Standing over a man strapped to a table. Turcotte started as he recognized himself as the man on the table. She was doing something to his head. Turcotte's hand reached up and touched where the MRI had detected the implant.

Turcotte stopped the screen and turned toward the tube holding Duncan. Quinn was right—she had never been who she said she was. He felt betrayed—as close as the two of them had gotten, she had still lied. Of course, would he have been willing to accept the truth at any point? Hell, he still didn't know the entire story. Who were the Airlia? More importantly, who were we? Turcotte wondered.

He went over to Duncan's tube. He looked at the buttons, then hit one that seemed likely. There was a puff of air escaping the tube, and the lid slowly lifted. He checked his watch. They were twenty minutes out from Mars. Artad might have already sent his message.

Duncan opened her eyes. She blinked for a few moments, reorienting herself. The severed arm was already half–grown back, the edge a mixture of raw red and pulsing black as the Airlia virus reconstituted the cells.

"Mike—" Duncan sat up, reaching her good hand out.

Turcotte took a step back, shaking his head. "We're past that. You lied and manipulated me."

She sighed and sat still for a few moments, before replying. "I had to."

"Why?"

She glanced over at the other tube. "I am sorry. I was alone for so long. And I needed help. After the mothership was uncovered and Majestic formed, I knew I couldn't keep it under cover anymore. And that I couldn't do it by myself."

" 'It'?"

"The Airlia. The truth. I knew a battle, this battle that we've fought, was coming."

"And what is the truth?" Turcotte asked.

She shook her head. "I've blocked it from myself."

"What?"

She climbed out of the tube without his aid, using her one hand to support herself. "These tubes—we took them from the Airlia when we defeated them on my planet. They can grow a new body. Transfer memories and personalities—the essence of a person, via the *ka*. They also can be used for deep sleep. But you can program them too. After he"—she once more looked at the other tube—"his name was Gwalcmai, my husband, I buried him near Stonehenge—that's the body that couldn't be reborn, I knew it was all on my shoulders. I also knew where my home world was. And the Ones Who Wait, the Guides, they were after me. Aspasia's Shadow tried to track me down several times. So I blocked my own memory using the tube. Sealed off parts. My past. My home world. My memories of him. Of my son."

Turcotte suddenly realized the pain she'd been in to do such a thing. He understood the need to seal off the information she couldn't give up, but she'd also cut off memories that would cause her emotional pain.

"I want to know—" Turcotte began, but he was interrupted by Yakov appearing in the hatchway. "We're less than ten minutes out. You need to suit up." The Russian was staring hard at Duncan.

"What are you going to do?" Duncan asked.

"We need you to help us," Turcotte said.

"Of course."

Turcotte took a step closer to her. "Not 'of course.' This is our plan. To free our planet from the influence of the Airlia once and for all. I killed the Swarm orb and freed you. If we can destroy this array and kill Artad, we've succeeded. Many people have died so far in this war. We need to end it now. I don't know what your hidden agenda has been and I don't care. Will you do what I tell you to?"

Duncan nodded. "My—our goal—was the same."

"All right. Here's the plan."

CHAPTER 20: The Present

TRIPLER ARMY MEDICAL CENTER, OAHU, HAWAII

Kelly Reynolds opened her eyes and immediately shut them, finding the bright glint of sunlight coming through her room's windows unbearable. She heard someone shutting the blinds and tried to open her eyes once more.

"Take it slowly," a woman's voice said in a whisper.

Kelly opened her mouth to say something, but only a hoarse croak would come out.

Someone used a spoon to put some crushed ice in her mouth and Kelly allowed the chips to melt. The water felt wonderful sliding down her throat. She could see now. A nurse hovered over her, another spoonful of ice ready. Kelly gave a slight nod and the nurse put it in her mouth. She savored the coolness. Then she tried to speak again.

"Mike?"

"Who?"

"Mike Turcotte. I need to talk to him."

"You mean the fellow on the news? The one on board that spaceship going to Mars?"

Kelly weakly nodded. "I've got to talk to him. I know the truth. And he needs to know it too."

" 'The truth'?" Cummings asked.

"Who we are."

MARS

The cruise missiles were lined up along the edge of the cargo bay, pointing forward. Kincaid had done the calculations and was now standing next to Yakov in the control room, giving him slight adjustments to their course as they closed on Mars.

Turcotte and half the Space Command team were crowded inside Duncan's ship, which was still inside the bay. They had their TASC suits on, weapons ready. The armorer had done a quick patch job on Turcotte's suit. Good enough for a seal. They'd off-loaded the two tubes in order to make room. Duncan was at the controls, programming in their course.

"Ready to put the brakes on," Yakov announced over their tactical net.

Duncan stood up.

"What are you doing?" Turcotte asked.

"You don't need me here," Duncan said. "I've programmed the ship—it's called the *Fynbar*, by the way, after one of the leaders on my planet in the revolt against the Airlia—to do what you want. I'm more useful on the mothership."

"That's not the plan," Turcotte argued, as she headed for the hatch.

"Trust me on this," Duncan said. She paused looking up at him. "This is the end. I am sorry about what I did to you, but it was necessary. I hope you'll understand that one day." She reached up and touched the front of the black helmet, as if she could reach through and touch his face. "Good luck."

Then she was out of the ship, the hatch shutting behind her and sealing.

"We've got the Talon on screen," Yakov announced, startling Turcotte. "It's closing on us fast."

"Do it," Turcotte ordered.

Outside the ship, Duncan went into the main corridor, shutting the door behind her. As soon as it was shut, the outer cargo bay door opened. The ship lifted and exited.

In the control room, Yakov saw the ship depart, then hit the controls. The mothership slowed abruptly and halted. Maintaining the momentum, and no longer attached to their cradles, the cruise missiles kept going, exiting the bay and spreading out in the pattern that Kincaid had programmed.

Inside the Talon, Artad watched his tactical display. The mothership had halted and ten objects were still coming forward from it. A craft also had exited the mothership and was descending toward the planet.

He issued orders to his crew quickly.

Once the cargo door sealed behind her ship and pressure was restored, Duncan reentered the bay. She ran over to the empty tube and hit the keys on the side as she slid her *ka* into its slot. The top swung up and she climbed in, lying down. She put a thin metal band around her head. Her right arm had regenerated to the wrist so far. The top closed and the metal band sent microfilaments into her brain.

The machine powered up and removed the memory blocks she had installed.

It took all of twenty seconds. The machine shut down, the lid opened, and Duncan exited. She stood still in the cargo bay for several moments, absorbing the impact of the complete truth. It did not surprise her, given what she had allowed herself to know. It all made sense.

This was the end for her, the end of a millennia-old mission. A mission her partner had given his life for over a thousand years earlier. She went to his tube, leaned over, and kissed the clear covering. She was glad she had buried the real body on Earth.

Then she left the cargo bay and headed for the control room.

"Everyone sealed?" Turcotte asked.

He received positive responses from the other commandos as he stared at the display monitor. They were descending quickly toward Mons Olympus, the *Fynbar*'s engines supplemented by the gravitational pull of the planet.

"Open the hatch," Turcotte ordered.

The Airlia in the control center for the array had the incoming spacecraft locked in. The leader of the survivors hit the hexagonal buttons in front of him, building up power in the array.

Turcotte saw the glow intensify in the center of the array. "Go!" he screamed. They were moving too fast but there was no time to wait.

Instead of a message, the first thing projected outward by the array was a broad pulse of power toward the *Fynbar*.

Turcotte had done several hundred parachute drops during his time in Special Operations. From almost every type of aircraft the military owned from Blackhawk helicopters through massive C-5 cargo planes. But shooting out of the open hatch of the *Fynbar* as it descended toward Mars was a new experience. He was the last one out of the hatch and as he cleared it, he kicked in the jets attached at the base of each leg, keeping himself oriented head down toward the planet at a slight angle from straight descent.

It almost wasn't enough as the pulse of power shot up from the array. It caught one of the commandos as it passed.

The blast ripped open his suit and pulverized the body inside. He didn't even have a chance to scream.

It hit the spacecraft, knocking it off its trajectory and sending it tumbling toward the planet below.

On his display, Artad saw the spacecraft knocked aside. Then he turned his attention to the incoming warheads, which were getting very close. A puny attempt by the humans to attack, but one that had to be dealt with immediately nevertheless. They were on a fixed trajectory with apparently no maneuvering capability.

A golden beam shot out from the tip of the Talon, hitting one missile after another.

The damaged, unmanned *Fynbar* tumbled toward Mars. It hit the edge of Mons Olympus about two kilometers from the array, producing a large puff of red dirt. It bounced, flipped, and skidded along the edge, then down the side, gouging out a three-meter-deep trench in the soft soil until coming to a halt a kilometer from the summit.

Turcotte cursed as he tried to reorient himself. He was coming in very fast. Too fast in his estimation. He got legs down and burned the solid fuel rockets attached to the ends, trying to slow. A small number displayed on the screen in front of him indicated altitude and it was clicking down at an alarming rate. He was slowing, but would it be enough before impact?

"There's an escape pod through there." Duncan was pointing to the left, where a door slid open at her command.

Yakov, Leahy, Quinn, and Kincaid looked at her dumbly for a few seconds. The screen was filled with the sight of warheads exploding just short of the Talon.

"What do—" Yakov began, but Duncan shoved him in the shoulder.

"Go now! It is better to get down to the surface and have half a chance, than stay here, where you will have no chance at all."

Yakov stared at her, the shove moving him not in the slightest. He looked into her eyes for several seconds. Then he nodded. "Let's go."

As they rushed through the hatch, Duncan sat down in the command seat.

The first commando who'd exited the spaceship hit the array, smashed through a panel, and hit the surface of Mars at such velocity that the suit, with man inside, went four feet into the ground. Blood and oxygen poured out of the resulting tears.

The second and third fared little better, their screams just before impact echoing to those still descending. Turcotte realized there was no way he would be able to decelerate quickly enough and he would share their fate.

The fourth man slammed in and died.

Turcotte used a small side jet to change his trajectory slightly.

The fifth jumper, Captain Manning, hit the array, passed through, and died.

Turcotte hit the top of one of the pylons at an angle, the impact jarring him hard inside the suit. He slid along the curving outer edge at high speed. With his free hand he jabbed the tip of Excalibur at the metal. It cut in and was almost wrenched from his grip. Only the power multipliers built into the arm allowed him to hold on to the handle.

The sixth jumper died.

Turcotte's jets were still firing as he continued downward, with Excalibur tearing a gouge along the side of the pylon.

TRIPLER ARMY MEDICAL CENTER,
OAHU, HAWAII

The communications specialist from Fort Shafter seemed uncertain about why exactly he was here. Kelly Reynolds didn't find that surprising. She'd had Nurse Cummings hold up a mirror so she could see herself, and she knew she looked like hell. Breathing took a major effort.

"Move the microphone closer," Reynolds whispered, unable to make her withered vocal cords produce anything louder.

The specialist slid the mike nearer to her.

"Are you sure they'll get this?" Reynolds asked.

"It's on the guard frequency they were monitoring, relayed through their site outside Fort Bragg," the man replied. "There is, however, the issue of time lag."

"What?"

"It takes over two and a half minutes for a radio wave to go from Earth to Mars. The same for return. So it will take five minutes before we find out if anyone hears you."

Reynolds weakly nodded. "Turn it on."

The specialist flipped a switch.

"Mike. Mike Turcotte. This is Kelly Reynolds. Acknowledge if you can hear me. I know the truth now. I know it all. I know who we are. Who humans are."

She let her head fall back on the pillow and waited.

SPACE

Duncan hit one of the hexagonal buttons, and the escape pod was shot out of the side of the mothership, arcing toward the planet below.

She looked forward. The Talon was coming in fast. She knew the shields and weapons had been deactivated on the mothership, which left her essentially defenseless against the incoming ship. She also knew Artad was coming to recapture the mothership, not destroy it.

Which was just fine with her.

Turcotte had the wind knocked out of him as he hit at the base of the pylon, and for that he was grateful, given the fate of the other seven men. Excalibur had left a three-inch-deep gouge down the entire length of the pylon, but it had slowed him enough for him to survive.

He hefted the arm holding the MK-98. He put Excalibur back into its sheath, then reached to the large pack on his back and made sure the tactical nuclear warhead they'd cannibalized from the Tomahawks was still in place. When he'd been in Special Forces Turcotte had served briefly on a SADM—Strategic Atomic Demolitions Munitions—team. He'd supervised the removal of seven of the ten warheads and their preparation.

Unfortunately, once removed from the missile casing, there had been no way to rig them for detonation on impact, only manual activation. Catching his breath, Turcotte looked about. The base of the pylon was about fifty meters from the top edge of the bowl that held the array. He saw no sign of the Airlia.

He moved toward the dish.

Duncan heard the thud as the Talon bumped into the side of the mothership next to the airlocks. She checked the exterior view as the lean ship came into place, exactly where it had left. She hit the control panel and more thuds reverberated through the ship as the clamps locked onto the Talon. Then she sealed the locks with a password so that the Talon couldn't escape.

She tapped a few more commands into the panel. Satisfied, she turned around and waited, facing the entryway.

How close was close enough? Turcotte roughly knew the blast radius of the bomb he was carrying—at least on Earth. He wasn't sure if the effects would be any different here on Mars. It had been a large issue of contention when he'd been on the SADM team because while half the team were the bomb handlers, the other half were snipers whose job was to keep the bomb under what the army termed "positive control with firepower" until detonation. Baby-sitting a nuclear weapon was not anyone's idea of a fun time. Team members had pretty much agreed that despite the assurances of the experts about blast effects, the protective snipers were dead men. In fact, they had assumed that the delay that they were told was built into the bomb to give those placing it time to escape didn't exist.

Turcotte had accepted the same fate when he'd come up with his plan.

He'd also decided that the green glowing component held by the wires had to be the critical node for the array. That was what he needed to destroy in order to ensure that any Airlia survivors could not rebuild the system.

Close enough would be right below the center, Turcotte decided.

The escape pod automatically slowed as it neared the surface of Mars. It still hit at a high rate of speed and rolled for over a mile before coming to a halt. Those inside were strapped in tight to oversize seats, but as the craft rolled, they were spun about in a dizzying fashion.

The interior became a mixture of strapped-in, bruised people and vomit. When the pod finally came to a halt, the four occupants looked at each other. Leahy, the newest member of the Area 51 team, was the first to break the silence.

"What do we do now?"

Yakov unbuckled from the seat and wiped off the front of his shirt. He shrugged. "We wait. There is nothing else to do."

"Wait for who?" Leahy demanded. "For what?"

"Those are both very good questions," Yakov acknowledged. "Most likely we are waiting to die."

"Mike."

Turcotte paused on the lip of the array as he heard Duncan's voice. "Yes?"

"The Talon is here. I've locked it to the mothership so it can't get away. I can see them boarding through the airlock on the display. Artad is with them."

"He's there?" Turcotte had hoped that Artad would try to regain the mothership before sending a message. That's what most generals would do—improve their situation before reporting back to higher command.

"Yes. I recognize him."

"Are you pulling him out of orbit and away?"

"No."

Turcotte frowned. The plan was for Duncan to get Artad away while the drop team—now down to just him—destroyed the array. Turcotte could see several large-tracked vehicles off to his right along with some prefab structures, which he assumed currently contained the Airlia who had finished the array. Along with the controls for the transmitter.

"What are you going to do?" Turcotte checked the upward view. He couldn't see the mothership against the dark sky, although he knew it had to be getting closer.

"Where are you?" Duncan asked instead of answering.

"On the lip of the array."

"Move away. Fast."

"Why? I'm supposed—"

"Do it."

Then it came to him. What she planned to do. He choked back the words of protest because as soon as he understood her plan, he also knew it was the best course of action. Turcotte turned away from the array and activated the jets, leaning forward and moving away quickly.

"Mike?"

"Yes?"

"The others are on the surface. In an escape pod. About five kilometers from the array." She rattled off some grid co-ordinates.

"I've got it. But—"

"The *Fynbar* was shot down by Artad's Talon. It's damaged but I think it will still fly." She quickly gave him some instructions as he bounded away from the array.

When she was done there was a moment of silence. "Lisa."

"Yes?" She sounded distracted.

"I'm sorry it had to go this way."

"It's for the best."

"I know."

"What I did to you was wrong. But I was so lonely after so many years. And I needed help."

Turcotte was heading down Mons Olympus, although the grade was so gentle there was very little angle of descent. "It's all right."

"I have to go now. They're cutting into the control room door."

Turcotte paused, checking the upward view. "What is the truth behind all this, Lisa?"

"Kelly Reynolds is transmitting from Hawaii," Duncan said. "She knows. She'll tell you. Then you need to decide what to do with that knowledge. Good luck." There was the sound of an explosion and the link went dead.

A piece of shrapnel from the breached door hit Lisa Duncan in the shoulder and ripped through her body and the seat she was in, smacking the wall behind her. She hardly noticed the pain after all she had been through recently.

A seven-foot-tall Airlia strode through the hole. He paused when he saw her sitting in the command seat. She knew he was searching his memory and she saw the expression cross his face as he recognized her.

Duncan smiled and hit a red hexagonal button in the arm of the chair. Everyone staggered as the mothership abruptly accelerated.

Artad dashed forward, ignoring her and running his six-fingered hands over the control console.

To no avail.

Lisa Duncan closed her eyes and thought of her husband and son. Of her planet. Of her people.

Turcotte saw the mothership—a black form flashing through the sky. Coming straight down and accelerating so fast he almost lost sight of it as it went into the array.

The concussion from the impact hit him with a tidal wave of red dirt, rock, and Martian air. Turcotte was lifted from the ground and "rode" the front of the wave over two kilometers, before being unceremoniously deposited on the surface.

He scrambled to his feet and looked up. Where the mothership had crashed into the array there was nothing but a huge gaping hole in the side of Mons Olympus.

CHAPTER 21: THE PRESENT

TRIPLER ARMY MEDICAL CENTER, OAHU, HAWAII

"Mike? Are you there? Is anyone there?"

"There's nothing," the radio specialist said. "If they were listening, they'd have heard you by now." He reached forward to turn off the microphone.

"Don't you touch that," Reynolds rasped.

"Ma'am—" the specialist began, but Nurse Cummings reached across her patient, pinched the young man's ear between thumb and forefinger, and gave a slight twist.

"Listen to the lady," Cummings said.

The specialist carefully removed Cummings's fingers from his ear, stood, and left the room. The radio stayed.

"Mike Turcotte?" Kelly Reynolds whispered. "Anyone?"

MARS

Turcotte was on the edge of where the array had been. The mothership had punched a hole in the side of the mountain over twenty times the size of that created by the work of the mech-machines. He could see pieces of debris far below, most appearing to be pieces of the mothership. He could see nothing of the array, the pylons, or the Airlia vehicles. All destroyed.

They'd won the final victory.

Turcotte found it hard to believe after all that had occurred the past several months since he had arrived at Area 51. Aspasia's Shadow. Artad. The Swarm. All dead. Both motherships destroyed.

Mankind was free.

Turcotte checked the TASC suit oxygen level. He had two hours of air left. He'd come this far, he'd give it two more hours of effort. He headed toward the location Duncan had given him for the *Fynbar*.

Yakov reached into a pocket and pulled out a flask. He unscrewed the lid and offered it to the others. Quinn and Kincaid shook their heads, but Leahy grabbed it and took a deep swig.

"Ah, a woman after my own heart," Yakov said as he took the flask back from her and had a drink.

"This wasn't a very good plan," Leahy said.

Yakov chuckled. "You should have seen some of the plans we've implemented in the last few months fighting these aliens."

"How much air do we have?" Quinn interjected.

Yakov looked at the small display panel. "I have no idea. I don't know the Airlia word for oxygen so I don't know which of these indicators is the one to read. However"—he flicked a finger against the panel—"this one looks very low, and given our luck I would guess it is the one."

Turcotte was circling Mons Olympus, staying at the same altitude. He saw a trench in the soil ahead a couple of meters deep and cutting laterally across his path. He looked up and saw an impact point five hundred meters up, near the lip of the volcano. Looking to the right he found Duncan's spaceship a kilometer downslope.

Turcotte turned in that direction. His walk changed into a full-out charge downhill, as he took large bounds in the lesser gravity. His last bound carried him on top of the *Fynbar.* He did a quick exterior inspection. It was dented and battered, but the most critical damage was on the upper, right-front deck, where plating had been ripped open by the Talon's blast.

He went to the rear of the deck and opened a compartment as Duncan had instructed. A large cylinder with a hose and nozzle was inside. He removed it, went forward to the hole in the hull, and turned it on. A red spray spewed out of the nozzle and began filling in the hole. As it hit, it hardened. It took the entire cylinder, but after a few minutes Turcotte felt satisfied he'd sealed the breach.

He went to the hatch and entered the ship. The instrument panel was still aglow, which meant there was power. He continued to follow the succinct instructions Duncan had given him. Preparing to take her own life along with the Airlia's, she had given him the way to save his and the others'. Whatever she had done to him, Turcotte knew they were more than even now.

A light went green—the one Duncan had told him to watch for. Turcotte unsealed the suit and took a cautious breath. The air was breathable. He sat in the pilot's seat and took hold of the controls.

The ship lifted.

Everyone inside the escape pod jumped as there was a loud bang.

Yakov stood. "It is about time."

"What the hell is that?" Leahy demanded.

"I believe it would be Mr. Turcotte."

"But—" Leahy was confused, as were Kincaid and Quinn.

Yakov shrugged. "Who else could it be?" He went to the small porthole in the hatch and peered out. "The ship is here. The hatch is open. I say we hold our breath and make a dash for it."

"Are you crazy?" Quinn asked.

"You want to stay here?"

"How do you know it's Turcotte?" Quinn demanded.

"If it was an enemy, they would not be, how do you say, knocking. They would just blow us up. I think Ms. Duncan had something more in mind when she told us to get in this pod, then jettisoned us." Yakov looked at the other three. "We have no airlock on this thing. Once I open this door, we lose our air. And we all must go together."

Leahy nodded. "Just give me a countdown."

Kincaid edged closer. "All right."

Quinn was shaking his head, but Yakov ignored him. "Three. Two. Exhale hard. One."

Yakov threw the lever and the hatch blew out.

Inside the *Fynbar*, Turcotte saw the four dash across the short space between the ships. He heard the clang of the outer airlock door shutting and watched the gauge on the console as it quickly pressurized.

There was a light flashing on the high-frequency radio the Space Command team had placed on board. He'd seen it as soon as he'd taken the seat. He knew who it was. And while he wanted to know what Kelly had learned while merged with the guardian, he did not want to hear it alone. He felt a tremendous sense of foreboding.

The pressure equalized, and Turcotte hit the button to open the inner airlock, then stood and faced the door. Yakov, Kincaid, Quinn, and Leahy entered the ship.

"My friend!" Yakov threw his arms wide and wrapped Turcotte in them, lifting him off the floor and spinning him about once. "We heard and felt a large explosion." He put Turcotte down and peered at him. "Since you are here, I assume it was not nuclear."

"Lisa Duncan crashed the mothership into the array."

Yakov let out a deep breath. "You were right about her ultimately. That was most brave." He took out his flask and held it up.

Turcotte accepted it and drank deeply.

"And Artad?" Yakov asked.

"He boarded the mothership just before she did it. She locked the Talon down and took him with her."

"Ahhhh." Yakov nodded. "It is done then."

Turcotte knew it wasn't a question. Yakov, even more than he, had fought the aliens and their minions for decades. The Russian sat down in one of the seats. Turcotte greeted the other survivors of Area 51. So few left. He sat back in the pilot's chair, next to Yakov. The green light flashed, beckoning.

Yakov saw it also. "A message?"

"Kelly Reynolds."

Yakov's bushy eyebrows arched. "She can speak?"

"She knows the truth. How all this started."

Turcotte waited. Yakov was the first to nod. "We need to know."

"Why?" Turcotte asked.

"In order to decide what to do next," Yakov said simply.

Turcotte glanced at the others. Leahy seemed a bit confused. Quinn and Kincaid both looked back and he could tell that they would let him make the decision for them.

Turcotte picked up the mike and transmitted. "Kelly. This is Mike Turcotte."

TRIPLER ARMY MEDICAL CENTER, OAHU, HAWAII

Kelly Reynolds was just about to call for the thirtieth time when Turcotte's voice sounded from the speaker.

Kelly Reynolds looked at Cummings. "I think you had best leave for now."

Cummings reached down, made sure the pillows were

stacked correctly behind Reynolds, filled her cup of water, and left the room.

"Mike. This is Kelly. It takes two and a half minutes for my transmission to reach you and the same amount of time for me to hear back from you. I'm going to pause. Let me know if you, and whoever is with you, want to hear what I have to say. Because once I start talking, I'm not going to stop."

Reynolds halted and glance at the clock. The second hand slowly made its way around the outer circle.

MARS

Turcotte had used the time waiting for a response to lift the spaceship up and do a flyby over Mons Olympus to check one last time that nothing had survived Duncan's last mission.

The hole in the side of Mons Olympus where the array had been was huge, the devastation complete.

Then he looked at Yakov. "Home?"

"Home," Yakov concurred.

Turcotte turned the front of the ship away from Mars as Kincaid began plotting the trajectory to return them to Earth.

When Reynolds's message came over the speaker, Turcotte replied immediately. "We're ready. Go ahead."

By the time they heard Kelly's voice again, they were clear of Mars orbit and heading inward toward the sun. The words from the small speaker sounded tinny and distant.

"It all makes sense if you think about what we've learned recently," Reynolds said. "You know now that Lisa Duncan came from another planet. And she is human."

Turcotte glanced at Yakov, realizing that Reynolds was us- ing the present tense because she didn't know what had just happened. "Which brings up the issue of how humans could have developed on two worlds."

Turcotte tensed, sensing what was coming next. Knowing that Kelly was right, that it had been there in front of them all along.

"When I accessed the guardian underneath Easter Island," Kelly continued, "I found traces of the past. Before Atlantis. When the Airlia first came to Earth.

"Mike, they brought us with them. We were planted here by them."

Turcotte leaned back in the seat. He didn't have time to feel the full impact of those last two sentences as Kelly continued.

"Just as Duncan and her people were planted on their world. We were not put on this world to colonize it, although in effect that is what we have done. We are a genetic cousin to the Airlia, which explains why we both breathe oxygen and subsist essentially in the same manner and look roughly the same. We're similar to them because they developed us. They made us. And in the process of doing that they placed specific inhibitors on us as a species. We're mortal with short life spans, while the Airlia live hundreds of times longer than we do. The Airlia made us mortal by blocking the growth of telomeres among our cells which causes us to age and die.

"And we cannot consciously use our minds to their full capabilities. The Airlia placed blocks on how well our two hemispheres could work together and how much of our brains we can access.

"The Grail, as you know, is the key for removing both those blocks. Accessing one side of it not only allows our telomeres to regenerate, it also infects our blood with a virus that can grow cells and heal illnesses and wounds. The other side, the one Duncan did not access, allows the human mind to function to the full extent of its capabilities.

"Why? That's the question you're probably asking now and the one I immediately asked myself when I discovered this.

"We're an experiment. Designed to be cannon fodder. For the Airlia in their war against the Swarm. The Airlia developed us to be soldiers, then seeded planets around the perimeter of their empire with us. On each planet they put a contingent—here led by Aspasia—in charge of maintaining order and controlling the Grail. If we were needed to fight, we would be given access to the Grail and sent off to war to die for the Airlia and their empire.

"From what I could gather we were a relatively new experiment for the Airlia. They seeded about a dozen worlds with humans in a remote part of their empire. Duncan's world was one. Ours was another.

"It didn't work quite the way they thought it would. Aspasia grew fearful of being involved in the war, which was nowhere near Earth. He cut off communication with the Empire and began to rule from Atlantis like a God. He set up a cadre of humans as priests.

"Eventually, Artad arrived with the Kortad, who were Airlia police. They were under orders to bring the planet back into the empire. However, something else occurred that neither side had counted on—the arrival of Lisa Duncan and her companion.

"Their world had been like ours, a vassal of the Airlia. It was the first to be seeded. They revolted and after a bloody war, managed to defeat the Airlia caretakers on their planet. In the process they essentially destroyed their own world. They sent out a captured mothership with teams like Duncan and her partner to find the other seed worlds and help them to overthrow the Airlia.

"Duncan and her partner manipulated both sides when Artad arrived, causing civil war that ended in stalemate, the best any of them could achieve. They gained us time. For us to develop enough to be able to finally fight the Airlia."

There was a pause. "That's pretty much it," Reynolds finally said, an understatement if ever there was one. She paused. "Did we win?"

Turcotte reached forward and picked up the mike. He pressed the transmit button. "Kelly. We've won. We'll be home soon." He released the button.

Silence reigned in the spaceship as each digested the import of what Kelly Reynolds had just told them. All four were so deep in thought they were startled when her voice came out of the speaker.

"Where's home, Mike?"

The answer came without thought. "Area 51."

EPILOGUE: THE PRESENT

AREA 51, NEVADA

The *Fynbar* floated above the seven-mile-long runway that marked the edge of Groom Lake. Turcotte brought it down to the tarmac in front of the massive doors for Hangar One. Both were wrecked, smashed by the attacking forces that had kidnapped Duncan. For Turcotte it seemed years ago, while in reality it had been only a few days.

Once the ship was stopped, he opened the hatch and exited, followed by Yakov, Quinn, Kincaid, and Leahy.

The survivors stood on the seven-mile-long runway dwarfed not only by it, but the mountain which the nearby massive hangar was built into. Mike Turcotte, Yakov the Russian, Major Quinn, Larry Kincaid, and Professor Leahy. The roll call of the living. Other names rang in Turcotte's thoughts. Peter Nabinger. Che Lu. Lisa Duncan. All of whom had given their lives. And the millions more who had died in the battle to defeat the aliens.

He realized the others were looking at him, waiting. He faced them. "We don't have a mothership so we can't help other worlds. We don't have the Grail or Master Guardian either. Both went down with Lisa Duncan on Mars when she destroyed the alien array.

"We are free of the aliens, though. That was her goal. And ours. And it must remain our goal. We know there are Airlia artifacts still here on Earth, hidden away. Some discovered by governments and kept secret, some not yet found. And we know for certain there is life out among the stars. The Airlia. The Swarm. Neither of which wishes us well. And undoubtedly other life-forms." He paused, trying to articulate thoughts which had assailed him over the past year ever since arriving here at Area 51 and being confronted with the reality that we were not alone among the stars and that the world had been occupied by aliens since before the beginning of recorded time.

"What about telling the world the truth?" Yakov asked, cutting to the core as usual.

"Could the world handle it?" Turcotte asked in turn. "If you had asked me that question yesterday, I would have said the truth must be told. But that was before I knew what the truth was. Now—" He shook his head. "What good would it do? The world knows there are aliens. That they threaten us. Telling people that we were 'grown' to serve as soldiers for the Airlia in their war against the Swarm will destroy all the faiths. Beyond that, people will also know we destroyed their chance at immortality with the destruction of the Grail.

"Duncan's people developed enough to overthrow the Airlia on their planet without the aid of the Grail. We did the same here. And beat the Swarm. Who knows what the future holds for mankind if we are uncorrupted by alien influences?" He looked at Leahy. "Tesla invented his weapon on his own. Our future is ours to make.

"The original charter of Area 51 was a wise one. It worked until Majestic was corrupted by the Temiltepec guardian. I say we pick up that charter. We join it with that of the Watchers."

Turcotte held out his hand, palm up. "Are you with me?" The others reached forward and placed their hands on top of his. "We know the aliens were here," he said. "We know they changed human history. Their presence and their technology almost destroyed the human race many times in the past and will in the future if we do not prevent it. We must guard the truth and the planet. We will watch from here. From Area 51. And we will act when we need to."

Robert Doherty is a pseudonym for a best-selling writer of military suspense novels. He is a West Point graduate and served as a Special Forces A-Team leader before writing full-time. He is also the author of *The Rock, Area 51, Area 51: The Reply, Area 51: The Mission, Area 51: The Sphinx, Area 51: The Grail, Area 51: Excalibur, Psychic Warrior* and *Psychic Warrior: Project Aura*. For more information go to www.BobMayer.org

READ ON
FOR A PREVIEW OF
ROBERT DOHERTY'S
NEXT BOOK . . .

THE PAST

EGYPT
8000 B.C.

Before the Third Age of Egypt, which was the rule of the Pharaohs, there was the Second Age when the Shadows of the Gods made by Horus ruled, and before that, beyond the borders of what man knew as recorded history, there was the First Age when those creatures who called themselves Gods ruled the humans who lived along the lush banks of the Nile.

For the people it was the time of the rule of the Gods who came to Egypt from the legendary land of Atlantis beyond the Middle Sea after the great Civil War among the Gods. It was fifty-five hundred years before the Great Pyramid would be built by the Pharaoh Khufu according to the plans of the Gods handed down in secrecy. For now the Giza Plateau was graced only by the alien beauty of a magnificent Black Sphinx, over three hundred feet long with red eyes that glowed as if lit from within. The Black Sphinx, set deep in a depression carved into the plateau, guarded the main entrance to the Roads of Rostau, the warren of tunnels and chambers under the Plateau where the Gods lived, and from which they ruled through the high priests and occasionally came forth to look out upon their subjects, an event that was becoming rarer and rarer. There were rumors that the Gods were growing older, but how could that be, if they were indeed Gods?

Deep under the plateau, along one of the minor branches of the Roads, was a dead-end corridor with three cells along one side. In the first cell were what appeared to be a pair of black metal coffins seven feet in length by three wide and high. They were not coffins however, but special prisons, each holding a body. At the head of each was a small glowing panel with a series of hexagonal sections on which were etched runic marking in the language of the Gods.

Inside the tube closest to the cell door was a half-man, half-God, whose existence was one of unending exhaustion and pain. His name was Nosferatu and he had vague memories of sunlight and playing in the sand while a woman—his mother?—stood nearby, keeping a watchful eye on him. Even then, though, he'd been kept separate from the others, the true humans, children of the High Priests who could look forward to serving the Gods as their parents did while Nosferatu's fate was to be one of service also, but in a much different way. It was so long ago, he wondered sometimes if the vague memories were not memories at all but instead a dream, but he held on to the concept that he could not dream something he had never seen. He must have been above ground in the sunlight sometime. He remembered palm trees and the sun reflecting off a sand dune and even the blue water of the mighty Nile flowing by.

Three hundred years he'd been trapped in this tube in this cell underground. Not as a punishment, for he had done nothing to deserve this fate other than to be born who and what he was, but to serve the purpose for which he had been conceived: to be sustenance for the Gods.

And although he had been the first, Nosferatu was not alone. There were four others in tubes in the two adjoining cells that he could reach with hoarse whispers. And in the tube across from him in this cell was Nekhbet. His love. Bastard spawn of the God Osiris and a human High Concubine, brought here over a hundred years ago, when Nosferatu was beginning to believe the world existed only of the mute priests who opened the lid and fed him every day and the Gods who came every full moon to drain his blood. Now, once every twenty-four hours he got to sit, chains around his waist keeping him in the tube, and see his love while the mute priest held the silver flask containing the blood that had been collected from supplicants to his lips. Even in the dim light and the grave circumstances, every day during that brief interlude Nosferatu always marveled in her beauty. Alabaster skin, high cheekbones, black-red eyes, she was tall and willowy with blazing red hair flowing over her shoulders like a fiery waterfall. He always believed she represented the best of human and God.

Nosferatu's skin was also pale white, his hair bright red. In the flicker of the single torch that lit the corridor outside and reflected in through the bars of the cell, his eyes had a reddish tint to them and the suggestion of an elongation of the pupil. He was tall, well over six feet in height, and slender. His skin was stretched tight over his bones, giving him a skeletal appearance. He was indeed half-man, half-God, as were his prisoner comrades. Although he had been alive over three hundred years he appeared to be in his mid-thirties, the mixed blood of the Gods and constant feeding of human blood allowing him a longer life span.

In the beginning he had tried to count days, a most difficult task since no sunlight penetrated this far under the Giza Plateau along the Roads of Rostau into the realm of the Gods. He'd worked off of the opening of the tube and the blood he was fed once a day, keeping track. But after the number went into the thousands, he gave up. What did it matter? Even with the half-blood of the Gods and the constant feeding, he knew he was very slowly getting older and that he would spend all of his very long life here.

He heard the latch holding the top down slide and closed his eyes, prepared for the invasion of torch light that came with each feeding. He felt the shift in the air as the lid was swung up.

"The Gods must die or you will soon."

The words echoed off the stone walls of the chamber and the shocked face of Nosferatu as he opened his eyes and blinked. Leaning over him was a woman—a human, not a God—dressed in a long black cloak with silver fringes standing behind the bars that blocked the doorway to the cell. She did not wear the signs of the priests and only men whose tongues had been cut out and ears punctured had been down here to feed him all these long years. She had short black hair, dark eyes and pale skin. She was the first human other than the priests who fed him that Nosferatu had seen in over two hundred years.

She looked deep into his eyes, then reached up and placed a finger on his throat, feeling his faint pulse. She then looked at the shunt in his neck from which he was drained once a month and lightly touched it. "You've been used for a very long time, haven't you?"

Nosferatu slowly sat up, the belt around his waist chained to the bottom of the tube, keeping the lower half of his body in place. Around each arm and leg were straps with leads going into the side of the tube. Each evening before he went to sleep, sharp pain came through those leads, causing his muscles to quiver and work themselves in tiny movements. And each morning he came awake to the same pain. There was a headpiece, shaped like a crown, in the tube, set in a small recess near the top, but Nosferatu had never had it put on his head by the priests of Gods so he didn't know its purpose.

He looked over at the other tube. The woman caught his gaze and went to it, opening the top by tapping the appropriate hexagon on the panel. Nekhbet sat up, blinking. He could see that Nekhbet was also wondering who this stranger was and what she knew of their situation. The woman came back over to him, waiting for an answer. He didn't reply, waiting to see if she would tell him more. He had patience—if there was one thing three hundred years of imprisonment taught, it was that trait.

"You won't last much longer," the woman finally continued. "You have no choice. If you do not act, you will be dead soon. Each time they drain you, the percentage of their blood in you is reduced. Soon you will no longer be effective. Then they will take another human female and make your replacement. They may already have a child, like you were once, growing up, guarded closely on the surface, ready to come here and be placed in this tube and drained as needed. They are very good at planning for their own needs."

Nosferatu finally spoke. "How do you know this?"

"It is their way. They are not Gods, but creatures from—" the woman pointed up. "From among the stars. They use us—humans—and they use you, half of their blood, half human. It is hard for me to determine which is the worse of their sins. At least what they are doing to you is obvious. Their rule of the humans is more devious, pretending to be that which they aren't." The woman shrugged. "There is also the possibility the Gods may go into the long sleep as their brethren have done in other places in which case they must kill you and the others they keep down here as you will longer be needed."

Nosferatu tried to grasp the concept but it had been so long since he'd been on the surface he could barely remember the sun, never mind the stars. And how could one be from them? If they weren't Gods, then what exactly were they? And what did that make him? And what was this long sleep she spoke of?

"Why do you want to help us?" Nekhbet asked. "You are human. We aren't. We're half like them."

"Because you must hate them as much as I do and more than those above," the woman replied. "The humans—" she shook her head—"they are like sheep. Simply happy their harvest comes in and the Gods make all the decisions for them."

Nekhbet's lovely voice floated from across the chamber. "Even if we kill the Gods the priests will then slay us, won't they?"

The woman glanced over her shoulder at Nekhbet. "Not if you are immortal."

Nosferatu was the first to grasp the significance. "The Grail?"

The woman nodded. "You kill the Gods. You go to the lowest level of the Roads of Rostau and recover the Grail and then partake as has been promised by the Gods since before the beginning of time. You become immortal."

Nosferatu frowned. "Why haven't the Gods partaken of the Grail then instead of doing this to us?"

"It is against their law to do so," the woman said. "They have very, very long lives. The Grail is only for—" She shook her head. "You would not understand. It is beyond this world."

"Who are you?"

"My name is Donnchadh. I have fought the Gods in other places," the woman said. "That should be enough for you. Your enemy is my enemy."

"Your enemy is our parents."

"One of your parents," Donnchadh corrected, looking him in the eyes. "Your other parent was human, taken by an Airlia—the Gods—for their pleasure and to produce you so they can use you. The Gods deserve neither your homage nor your respect. They will drain you and kill you without a second thought once they have a replacement ready."

"How can we do this which you propose?" Nosferatu demanded, rattling the chains that held the belt at his waist.

Donnchadh pulled aside her robe, revealing six daggers tucked into her belt and a three-foot-long piece of black metal. "Tonight. After the ceremony of the Solstice. You can follow them from the Ceremony to their hidden places along the Roads." She pulled the metal rod out of her belt and placed the tip inside one of the links of chain that bound him. She raised an eyebrow. "Do you want your freedom?"

Nosferatu looked across the way at Nekhbet. Even if the woman lied, even if this was a trap, he didn't care. If he could simply hold Nekhbet in his arms after three hundred years of yearning, it would be worth it. "Yes."

Donnchadh twisted the rod and the link slowly gave, and then popped open. She went to work on the other chains and within five minutes Nosferatu was free. He removed the straps around his arms and a red light flickered on the console but he ignored it. Grabbing the lid, he pulled himself out of the tube.

When his feet reached the ground, he took a tentative step and his legs buckled, tumbling him to the floor. Donnchadh was already at work on Nekhbet's chains as Nosferatu struggled to his feet. The tube had worked his muscles twice a day, but his body was so unused to moving, that he had to put a hand against the wall to steady himself. Driven by a force stronger than gravity he took a step. And then another. By this time, Nekhbet was free, the woman helping her out of the tube. He staggered across to Nekhbet and took her in his arms.

With the touch of her flesh against his, Nosferatu was transported from the stone chamber that had been his prison for centuries. He wrapped his arms tight around her slight frame as if their flesh and bones and blood would meld together and they would become one.

"Are you tired?" she whispered.

"Not anymore."

"You are weak, though." He blinked as she offered her neck to him, the blood pulsing in the vein, the short tip of the shunt drawing him in. He knew he needed the energy, but from Nekhbet?

Her voice was a seductive whisper. "Take as they take, my

love. You are the eldest and must lead. You need the strength. I am younger. I can afford to give it to you. I want to give it to you. It will make us one as nothing else can. And you must lead us."

He couldn't stop. His lips curled around the shunt, the one-way valve opening at the touch of moist flesh on the outside. The first taste of blood was electrifying, a charge throughout his body that brought every nerve screaming alive as it coursed through his veins. Decades of exhaustion faded. Her blood, with its alien component, was so much more than the human blood he was fed each day.

The strange woman's voice was an irritating buzz, trying to bring Nosferatu back to reality. "The ceremony has started above. You do not have much time to free the others and be ready."

Nosferatu did not let go of Nekhbet. Minutes of touch could not compare to the centuries of longing from across the prison chamber. And the blood, the power he felt pouring into his body from Nekhbet. Is this what he gave to the Gods? He forced his eyes open. He could see her neck so close, the skin white, the beat of the artery so slow now, her eyes closed. Startled, he released his lips and stepped back. Nekhbet staggered and would have fallen had he not caught her.

"I am sorry," he whispered. "I took too much."

Nekhbet shook her head, slowly opening her eyes, but the dark pupils had difficulty focusing. "It is all right. You need the strength."

"If you do not act now, you will die," Donnchadh pressed.

Nekhbet let go first, running a hand across Nosferatu's face. "My love, we must do as she says. It is our only chance. We must free the others."

Reluctantly, Nosferatu let go of Nekhbet. He followed Donnchadh out into the corridor where she opened the door to the next cell. Shabeka and Salihah were held here. Twins, man and woman, who had been brought into the darkness nearly seventy years ago, as best Nosferatu could determine. Nosferatu watched as the woman opened their tubes, noting which of the hexagonals she pressed. He shushed their questions, working swiftly to free them from their chains, and they moved to the third cell and released Mosegi and Chatha, the youngest of the six, another male-female pair, chained up and entombed for only about twenty years. There were six half-breeds, because there were six Gods who needed sustenance.

As soon as the last were free of their tubes, the strange woman, Donnchadh, turned toward the exit to the last cell. "I will leave you to do what you must."

Nosferatu put a hand out, stopping her. "Tell me more of the Gods. Why do they need to do this—" He lightly touched the shunt in his neck.

"Their alien blood has—" she seemed to search for the right word—"something in it that keeps them alive, but it requires food—your blood. Since you are half-breeds your blood has some of this in it also, which is why you have lived longer than a human would."

"I am immortal?" Nosferatu had shied away from that possibility because it meant he would spend an eternity chained to the wall.

Donnchadh shook her head. "No. But if you drink human blood to feed the alien part of your blood—and don't get drained of any more of what you have—you can live a very, very long time." She pointed to the end of the short corridor. "You can go to the right and get out a secret door near the Nile. The ceremony will start shortly in the Sphinx pit. Wait until the Gods appear, then follow them down the main Road of Rostau."

"But—" Nosferatu wanted to know more but Donnchadh was moving away and then was gone to the left.

The other five looked at him, waiting. "Follow me."

Prostrated before the massive paws of the Black Sphinx were fifty priests, chanting in an alien tongue the same prayers their ancestors on Atlantis had sung: *"We serve for the promise of eternal life. We serve for the promise of the great truth. We serve as our fathers have served, our fathers' fathers, and through the ages from the first days of the rule of the God who brought us up out of the darkness. We serve because in serving there is the greater good for all."*

The chanting echoed off smoothly cut stone walls that completely surrounded the Black Sphinx. It was over two hundred feet below the surface of the plateau, reachable only via a set of stairs cut in the stone wall. Just below the chest of the beast, a dark opening was cut into the rock beneath the paws, one of the entranceways to the sacred Roads where only the select high priests were allowed to go and from which the Gods rarely ventured forth anymore.

Hidden in the shadows along the edge of the depression, among a pile of discarded building stone, watching the chanting priests, were a half-dozen figures wrapped in black cloaks—Nosferatu and the other five half-breeds. They had the sharp daggers given to them by the strange human woman clutched in sweaty hands. It was the ceremony of the summer solstice and the priests were thanking the Gods for a bountiful crop produced by the rich soil along the banks of the Nile and for keeping away the floods that ravaged the land every so often.

The six waited, hunched over among the stones, for the ceremony to be over. They were patient because their goal was the ultimate prize, that which generations of priests such as these had prayed for but which they had decided to seize this night: eternal life. They had escaped from the Roads via an entrance on the bank of the Nile, and then made their way back here under the cover of darkness. For Nosferatu the night air filled his lungs with freshness after centuries underground. After so much time of pitch black in his tube, he could see in the starlight as if it were daylight.

"Will the Gods come?" Nosferatu asked.

"Isis and Osiris have come to give the final blessing every

year as long as any can remember," Mosegi whispered in reply. "I saw them myself at this ceremony before I was brought below."

Isis and Osiris were the two lead Gods. There were four others, but they were spotted even more rarely. It had been many years since all six had been seen together on the surface. Nosferatu did not know which of the three male Gods his father was. For all he knew, it might have been Osiris himself.

The chanting paused as two figures appeared in the dark entryway. They were tall, thin, and unnaturally proportioned. From the forms it was obvious they were male and female but as they pulled back their hoods it was also obvious they were not human. Catlike red eyes peered down at the priests. White alabaster skin glistened in the glow of the torches. Elongated ears drooped on either side of their narrow heads. And when the male of the pair raised his right hand in acknowledgment of the priests' prayers, six long fingers, festooned with jewels, waved their blessings.

Nosferatu recognized them from the thousands of times they had come to his cell and fed from him. They were Isis and Osiris, the Goddess and High Protector of Egypt. Who had ruled from beneath the ground for over two thousand years. Egypt had prospered under their reign, the borders expanding down the green belt of the Nile and west and east to the edges of the desert. It was the cradle of civilization, the place where the majority of the survivors of the fall of Atlantis had been brought by the Gods. Beyond the borders of the God's reign, there were humans, but they lived like animals.

Unseen by Nosferatu's group, the priests and the Gods, there was a fourth party in the depression, not far from them. A man covered with a gray cloak that blended with the stone named Kaji. He was tucked into a slight crack in the rock wall. He saw the priests, the Gods Isis and Osiris, and the group of six hiding on the opposite side. He was as still as the rock that surrounded him and as patient. He was a Watcher, the fifty-second of his line, sworn to observe the Giza Plateau and the Gods. His line had watched from the very beginning, when the Gods had first arrived with the survivors of Atlantis.

When the priests got stiffly to their feet and shuffled off away from the Black Sphinx toward their stone temple near the Nile, the Watcher remained still, eyes on the small group across the way. Only one man remained in the open, the High Priest, standing in the entranceway to the Roads of Rostau between the Black Sphinx's paws. As the High Priest turned to follow Isis and Osiris into the depths, the group sprung into action, Nosferatu in the lead.

The High Priest was reaching to use an emblem around his neck to shut the stone door to the entranceway when Nosferatu leapt at him, dagger point in the lead. The tip of the blade punctured the side of the High Priest's throat and Nosferatu pulled the handle hard to the side, severing the man's jugular and throat, preventing him from crying out a warning to the Gods who were ahead of him. The blood from the High Priest's still beating heart sprayed over Nosferatu, drenching his face and chest. Nosferatu's tongue snaked out, tasting the blood. He blinked, staggered, and felt a new surge of power. He leaned forward, mouth wide open and drank in the weakening surges of arterial blood until the High Priest died and there was no more. With his free hand Nosferatu removed the emblem from the High Priest's neck. Etched on it was an image of an eye within a triangle.

Nosferatu moved into the tunnel, Nekhbet right behind him, the other four carefully stepping over the body of the High Priest.

And behind them, like a shadow, the Watcher followed, keeping low to the ground and moving silently.

Nosferatu ran on the balls of his feet, his silk slippers making no sound on the smooth stone. He felt powerful, stronger than he could ever remember feeling, all from simply the taste of the High Priest's blood on top of what Nekhbet had given him. He caught a glimpse of the tall figures of Isis and Osiris as he came around a bend in the tunnel and he skidded to a halt, trying to control his breathing, sure the Gods would hear him in pursuit, but they continued around another bend, out of sight. He glanced over his shoulder. Nekhbet was right behind, her hand reaching up and touching his shoulder lightly. He felt a wave of confidence from her touch. After all, she was the daughter of the High Protector. And in whispered words over the years she had pledged herself to him—if they succeeded tonight she would be at his side for eternity.

When the other four caught up, Nosferatu continued the pursuit, blood-soaked dagger at the ready. He heard the rumble of a large stone moving and he picked up the pace, knowing the Gods had secret passageways that even the High Priests knew nothing of. Doors that appeared out of solid rock and disappeared just as quickly.

He dashed around the bend in the tunnel. A stone was beginning to slide down at the end of the corridor twenty feet away. Nosferatu was prepared for this. He dove forward, sliding along the smooth stone, the piece of black metal the strange woman had carried in his off-dagger hand. He stuck it in the way of the descending door, one end on the floor, the other up. The bottom edge hit the metal and the door shuddered for a moment, pressing hard on the metal, and then halted, leaving a gap.

Nosferatu let out a sigh of relief. Peering ahead under the door he could see two flickering shadows on the left side of the wall, and then they disappeared. He glanced back. Nekhbet was next to his legs, the others crowded behind her, daggers grasped tight in their hands.

He knew now was not the time to hesitate. He slid forward, underneath the door, into the lair of the Gods. Nosferatu got to his feet, peering about. There was light ahead, around a curve to the right, which explained the shadows he had seen.

The only sound was the scrape of cloth on stone as Nekhbet slid through, then the others. He waited a minute, letting his eyes adjust as much as possible, but the light hurt, and he kept his eyelids closed to slits to protect his sensitive pupils.

Nosferatu nodded forward and began moving down the corridor, dagger held out in front. He pressed his back against the left side wall and edged along the corridor, trying to peer around the bend. The stone walls were cut perfectly smooth, the work of the Gods, not human hands.

The priests said the Gods had built the Roads of Rostau in the very beginning after arriving from beyond the Middle Sea. And that there were six duats (chambers) down here where the Gods lived and kept their secret sources of power. The Grail was said to be secreted in one of the duats along with other wondrous things of which there were only whispers and vague memories of an earlier time when the Gods walked the Earth openly and flew about in the sky in golden round chariots. Now the Gods hid down here, ruling through the priests, rarely seen, as if they were hiding from something, but what could Gods be hiding from? Nosferatu often wondered. There was only one answer—other, more powerful Gods. As a child, he had heard the stories of the Great Civil War, when God had battled God and Atlantis had been destroyed. To him that meant one thing—they were vulnerable.

None of the six noted the figure that silently followed them. The Watcher slid under the door, and then froze as a hatch on the top of the tunnel slide open. Kaji froze, covering himself with the gray cloak, and watched with wide eyes what came out of the small space and headed down the corridor in pursuit of the intruders.

Nosferatu came around a corner and bumped into Osiris. It was hard to say who was more startled, but Nosferatu was the quicker to react. He jabbed with the knife, the point puncturing Osiris's chest. Nosferatu continued his momentum, throwing all his weight behind the shaft of metal.

Osiris grabbed Nosferatu's throat with his six-fingered hands, squeezing. Nosferatu twisted the blade in the God's chest, ripping through flesh, piercing the heart. Red eyes went wide in shock, and then life faded from them. Isis finally reacted, jumping to her partner's defense but she was swarmed under by the other five half-breeds, their daggers rising and falling with the deadly blows they rained down on her body. Decades, centuries of imprisonment, vented forth and over fifty blows punctured her skin. Blood spattered over all and tongues snaked out, tasting the God's blood.

They couldn't help themselves. Their plan disintegrated into a feast of blood as all six lay on top of the two bodies, licking, tasting, and tearing at exposed flesh to get to veins. They even suckled at Osiris's corpse, drawing the still blood from him.

And that was when the strange beast came upon them from behind.

Only Nosferatu had enough awareness. He spun about from Osiris's body in time to see the thing come around the curve. A glowing gold orb, about two feet in diameter with black, hard legs all around, scuttling along the floor. Mosegi was the last in the party and the first to die as the strange creature reached him. Two metal legs, pointed at the tip, struck, punching into Mosegi's chest and coming out the front.

Blood upon blood. Death upon death. Chatha died next. Nosferatu sprung to his feet, dagger at the ready, knowing it would not stop the beast.

But something did. It poised, two arms up, sharp ends pointed at Nekhbet, but not striking.

A bolt of gold hit Shabeka in the chest, knocking her back unconscious. The other four Gods appeared in the corridor behind the beast, long spears in their hands. Another bolt came from the tip of one of the spears and hit Salihah with the same result.

"Come." Nosferatu reached for Nekhbet. Too late as she

was struck and knocked into him. He pulled her body back along the corridor, away from the site of the murders. Two of the Gods halted there, checking the bodies, while the other two pursued. A door rumbled open in the floor in front of Nosferatu and he almost fell into the black hole. A hand beckoned.

"Come," a man's voice called.

Nosferatu paused, something he would regret for thousands of years. The two Gods arrived, spears ready. He dove into the hole, pulling Nekhbet with him as one of them struck. The blade sliced cleanly through Nekhbet's wrist.

Nosferatu fell with her severed hand clutched in his, slamming into the side wall of the tunnel, tumbling, sliding, the reality of what had just happened not sinking in until he hit the bottom of a cross tunnel.

"Come." The same figure was urging him to move.

Nosferatu remained, still feeling the rapidly cooling flesh clutched in his hand, his mind replaying what had happened. He scrambled to his feet, looking up the passageway down which he had slid, reaching up with his free hand to grab hold of the lip and pull himself in.

"No," the voice hissed.

Then he heard the clatter of metal on stone and knew the beast was coming down after them.

"This way," the man urged, pulling at his arm. Nosferatu followed.